IT'S COMPLICATED

FINDING PROVIDENCE PREQUEL

JILL BURRELL

First edition: May 2021
Library of Congress Control Number: 2021908045

ISBN: 978-1-955507-00-4 (eBook)
ISBN: 978-1-955507-01-1 (pbk)

To my mother,
who taught me the joy of getting lost
in a story—both in reading and writing.

CHAPTER 1

*G*rant Foster splashed cold water on his face and grabbed a handful of paper towels. *I can't afford to lose my job. Not now. Not with Reagan and Josh depending on me.*

Blotting his face dry, he checked his chin in the mirror. The nick where he'd cut himself shaving this morning was barely noticeable.

He dampened his hands and ran his fingers through his hair to tame the unruly waves, wishing he had a comb with him. How many times had he raked his hands through it already today?

Why does the big boss want to meet with me?

Mr. Davenport, the CEO of 3D Media—the Portland-based, full-service marketing and advertising company—did not invite employees to his office for social visits. In social settings, Alexander Davenport was a jovial man. At least, he had been on the few occasions Grant had interacted with him at company parties—but in his office, he was a shrewd businessman.

Grant dampened a paper towel and rubbed at a speck on his suit coat, remembering the last time he was called into Mr. Davenport's office. Almost nine years ago—about a year after he'd started working at 3D—he'd made a major mistake and mixed up multiple clients' accounts, breaching the company's privacy policy. He'd recognized his mistake early and owned up to it, but that visit to Mr. Davenport's office had not been pleasant.

His boss, Aaron Hardman, had been by his side on that visit to the CEO's office, and he'd stuck his neck out for Grant. Thanks to Mr. Hardman and many hours of overtime, Grant had saved his job and had built a satisfying career at 3D Media.

Is that about to change today?

He racked his brain for anything he might have done that would preempt this meeting. Last time, the email was of the get-in-my-office-now urgency. This time, the email from Mr. Davenport's secretary came as an invitation for Grant to meet with the President and CEO to discuss an important matter. He'd had a full twenty-four hours to worry about what the important matter might be.

A full twenty-four hours filled with anxiety tying him in knots. A twinge of guilt tightened his chest for the way he'd taken his frustration out on Reagan this morning when she almost made him late for work. Such chaos had become par for the course since his organized, predictable life got turned upside down a year ago.

Noting that his sleepless night had only left minor shadows under his eyes, he straightened his tie, took a deep breath, and let it out slowly. *It's going to be okay.*

It has to be.

Forcing determination and confidence into his step, he turned away from the mirror and pulled open the bathroom door. "It's going—"

An "Oomph" cut off his words.

Unsure if the grunt came from him or the woman he'd plowed into, he jerked to a stop. Her eyes widened, and she let out an additional cry as she teetered backward. His hands shot out and grabbed her shoulders, preventing her from falling.

He kept hold of her, studying her face for signs of pain. Had he hurt her? He was certain he'd stepped on her foot.

Wide brown eyes with long dark lashes stared back at him. Beautiful eyes.

His gaze roamed over her face. Besides an olive complexion and thick black hair, she had high cheekbones, a delicate nose, and full lips. She was striking in an eye-catching red blouse that complimented her coloring.

He struggled to remember the woman's name. Celine? Celia? They'd collaborated on a few ad campaigns, but she worked in a different department, so they'd never worked closely together. But that hadn't stopped him from noticing her. At roughly five foot six, she was too curvy to be considered slender, but few would consider her overweight. She was simply soft curves in all the right places.

Grant didn't date coworkers, though. He preferred to keep his private life separate from his work. Getting involved with a coworker made things messy if the relationship didn't work out. But the woman he held was one he'd often thought he'd like to get to know better.

"Um... you can let go of me now." A hint of chocolate and mint tickled his cheek.

An insane urge to taste her lips filled him. Shocked, he shoved her away, releasing her so fast she teetered backward again.

And once again, he grabbed her arms and pulled her close. "Sorry."

She scowled at him, a deep V forming between her brows.

He released her again, this time slowly. He took a step back as he pulled his hands away. His fingers caught on her purse strap and flung it from her shoulder. The small red purse dropped to the floor, scattering its contents.

"Oh no." Gasping, she sank to the floor. He joined her, but she held up a hand. "Please, don't. You've done enough already."

She was right. He couldn't see how he could do anything but make this situation worse.

Feeling like a bumbling idiot, he stood and watched her scramble to gather the contents of her purse. A couple crumpled receipts, a wallet, pen, tube of lipstick, a small bottle of lotion, cell phone, and sunglasses. *How did she fit it all in there?* The purse didn't look that big.

"I don't need this kind of added stress today," she mumbled under her breath.

Guilt swept over Grant. His own stress ratcheted up, and the bass drum at the bottom of his skull picked up its pace. *Me either.*

A slender, brightly colored, wrapped object beside his shoe caught his attention. Heat filled his face, no doubt making the ruddy spots on his cheeks stand out, as he recognized the unmistakable feminine hygiene product. He shifted his foot away from it as much as he could, which wasn't much since he was already pinned against the bathroom door. He waited for her to notice it. When she made no move to grab it, he nudged it forward with his shoe.

Her hand hesitated for a moment before snatching up the item and shoving it into her purse. After a last look around to make sure she had everything, she moved to stand up but fell forward, hindered by the snug fit of her pencil skirt.

Suppressing a groan and wishing he'd walked away already, he took her elbow. With slow, deliberate movements, intent on not causing more problems, he lifted her to her feet. "Sorry about all that. I'm afraid I'm a little distracted this afternoon."

Oh, brother. Would she think there was a double entendre in his words? Because she was definitely distracting. Frowning at himself, he shoved his hands into his pockets and pressed his back against the restroom door again.

Her breathy, "Thanks," sent a zing of warmth coursing through his veins. "I'm a little scattered myself." She gave a tight, self-deprecating chuckle as she waved at the floor where the contents of her purse had been scattered.

Recalling that he didn't have time for this, he gave her a brief smile. "I have an... um, appointment. Sorry again about all that."

"Me too," she said. "I mean, I have one too... an appointment, that is. But I need to pee... first."

Grant's eyebrows inched toward his hairline as heat filled his cheeks. *I did not need to know that.* Side-stepping to keep from running into her again, he walked to the nearby elevator.

He pushed the button then looked back over his shoulder in time to see her shapely backside disappear into the restroom.

No. He definitely didn't need this kind distraction right now.

~

CELESTE HIGHTOWER LEANED against the bathroom door after it closed behind her and groaned. "I need to pee first?"

Did I really just say that? To Grant Foster, of all people?

Grant was the epitome of tall, dark, and handsome. Okay, so most men were taller than her five foot six inches, but that didn't make him any less handsome. Nor did it make his steel-gray eyes any less striking. He was the one all the single—and a few of the non-single—women daydreamed about around the water cooler. Celeste typically avoided gossip, but that didn't keep her from silently agreeing with all the women who had a crush on Grant Foster.

The last thing she needed today was the humiliation of dumping her purse in front to the hottest guy at the agency. Heat filled her face again as she remembered his shiny black dress shoe nudging her tampon toward her.

How embarrassing!

Pushing off the door, she used the facilities before studying her reflection in the mirror. *Is this the last time I'll use this restroom?*

No. If things didn't go well in Mr. Davenport's office today, she'd be back here crying her eyes out. She needed this job—especially now that she didn't have a roommate anymore to share the rent. She couldn't afford to fail.

Celeste had worked long and hard to prove herself. Failing now would be the ultimate disgrace. If she lost her job, her father would hear about it in no time, and he would never let her forget she'd failed.

But why does Mr. Davenport want to meet with me?

She asked her boss, Stacy, this morning, but she only got a shrug in response. Stacy's mind was already elsewhere since she was due to have her first baby any day now and start twelve weeks of maternity leave. Stan Patterson had already been slotted to fill in during Stacy's absence, so what did Mr. Davenport want with Celeste?

Taking a deep breath, she fluffed her hair and applied her favorite red lipstick—a shade that matched her blouse and always earned her compliments. She needed the confidence boost, today more than ever. Especially after that disastrous run-in with Grant. The man was even more handsome up close. And he smelled great—a perfect combination of cologne and fabric softener, mingled with a natural male scent.

Though she had something of a crush on Grant, Celeste was glad she didn't work in the same department as him. The few times they had worked together, it had been almost impossible for her to concentrate.

Each time she'd worked with him, she'd gotten her assignment and returned to her office to work. Besides being an introvert, she simply found it easier to not have to work in the same room as Grant Foster.

CHAPTER 2

*G*rant looked at his watch as he stepped off the elevator on the third floor. *Only three minutes to spare.*

He knew he could be a little obsessive and compulsive sometimes, but there was nothing wrong with being early to appointments and wanting things a certain way. He worked hard to keep his life orderly because order brought stability and contentment. Those were things he'd had little of this past year.

Sharon, Mr. Davenport's secretary, looked up and smiled. "Hi, Grant. Mr. Davenport is on a call right now, but he'll be with you in a few minutes."

He sucked in a deep breath and took a seat. He couldn't believe he'd had the urge to kiss Carla or Cecelia or whatever her name was.

Who has the desire to kiss someone whose name they don't even remember?

Not him. Grant didn't do things like that. He was never rash and impulsive. That's probably why his sister, Reagan, called him uptight and neurotic.

The boss's door opened, and Mr. Davenport stuck his head out. "Grant, come on in."

Grant pasted on a smile as he stood and buttoned his suit coat. He fought to keep his breathing steady despite the earthquake happening in his stomach.

At six foot three, Alexander Davenport was an imposing figure, who answered only to the board of directors now that his partners had retired. He smiled as he shook Grant's hand.

The smile is a good thing, right? Mr. Davenport didn't smile the last time Grant was ordered to come to his office. Not once.

Mr. Davenport invited Grant to sit in an armchair that looked much more comfortable than it felt. In front of him sat a coffee table with two file folders and three bottles of chilled water.

Who's the third bottle for?

Taking the casual setting as a good sign, Grant tried to relax.

"Aaron Hardman has good things to say about you."

Relief filled Grant, and he curbed the smile that threatened to split his face. This was a let's-talk-about-your-future meeting, not a pack-up-your-things meeting. Unsure how to respond, he dipped his chin and murmured, "Thank you."

"You've been with 3D for ten years now. Is that right?"

"Yes, sir."

"You've done some amazing work over the past few years. I'm especially pleased with the work you did on the Bowman Sporting Goods and Sutherland Restaurants' accounts."

Grant was relieved Mr. Davenport remembered those things and not his major goof-up when he'd been relatively new here.

"Thank you, sir, but it was a team effort. I only did my part."

He'd played a big role in those ad campaigns, but advertising took teamwork. If he remembered right, the team member from the Creative Services Department on both projects had been the black-haired beauty with gorgeous brown eyes.

"Good answer, son. Everybody likes a team player."

Did he just call me son?

"And all successful teams need excellent coaches. Strong leaders who can take charge and shape and mold their players all while ensuring the ball stays in play."

Mr. Davenport was an avid sportsman, both on and off the field.

He always threw out sports analogies at their monthly personnel meetings. Grant filed this latest analogy away with all the others, still trying to get beyond the fact the big boss had called him son.

Did he call everyone younger than him son? Even though Mr. Hardman was like a father figure to him, he'd never called Grant son.

"There's no point in beating around the bush here." Mr. Davenport's voice pulled him from his musings. "I'm sure you're aware Aaron Hardman will be retiring at the end of the year?"

Grant nodded. The end of the year was ten months away, but when he'd heard the news last month, he'd hoped to get a promotion. But Randy Evans, who'd been here two years longer than Grant, was assigned to fill in for Mr. Hardman while he was on a three-week cruise celebrating his forty-fifth wedding anniversary. So Grant figured his chances of getting the VP position were slim.

"It's time for conditioning."

"Excuse me?"

"Before the sports season starts, even before tryouts, athletes are expected to show up for conditioning." Grant's confusion must have shown on his face because Mr. Davenport kept talking. "You show up every day and you give it one hundred percent. You play your hardest because the coaches are watching. We see you fall and watch to see if you'll get back up. We see your grit and determination."

Something stirred in Grant's chest at Mr. Davenport's words. He'd always given one hundred percent to everything he did, and as long as he worked here, he'd continue to give his best to 3D. He leaned forward with his breath trapped in his chest. Was Mr. Davenport saying what Grant thought he was saying? Did he have a shot at filling Mr. Hardman's position as Vice President of Marketing?

"So, how about it? You ready for conditioning, son?"

This time his use of the word *son* sounded less like an endearment and more like a challenge. A challenge Grant was ready to accept. "Absolutely, sir."

"That's my boy."

The CEO was a lot more personable than Grant had ever realized. He decided not to put much stock in his use of *my boy* and *son*. Not that he couldn't use another father figure in his life now that Mr. Hardman was retiring. Especially now that he played the role of father figure himself. A role he wasn't well suited for.

Mr. Davenport picked up one of the file folders from the coffee table. "Here's your conditioning, try-outs, and your first touch down all rolled into one. I'm putting you in charge of this project. If you succeed, you'll be awarded *MVP.*"

Sucking in a sharp breath, Grant held Mr. Davenport's gaze, hoping he hadn't imagined the emphasis the older man had placed on MVP. Marketing Vice President. Excitement shot through his veins like a surge of electricity when Mr. Davenport nodded and smiled.

He reached for the folder, hoping his boss—the coach—didn't notice the tremor in his hand.

"I'm sure you're aware of all the negative publicity surrounding the Livingston Hotel Empire."

Grant nodded. His skin crawled as snippets of last year's news reports filled his mind. *Palmer Livingston, head of the international hotel chain, has been arrested on allegations of a prostitution ring associated with his hotels in most major cities. Evidence of sex trafficking has been linked to many of his international hotels.* Such allegations concerning the five-star hotels had shocked the nation. Livingston Hotels were high-class establishments and catered to the rich and famous and fortune-five-hundred-level businessmen.

It had pleased him to hear the hotel mogul got sentenced to thirty-five years in prison, and not a minimum-security prison that resembled a resort. No, they had sentenced him to a maximum-security prison with all the other hardened criminals. As far as Grant was concerned, Palmer Livingston was right where he belonged.

"It's no surprise their hotels have suffered, and stock prices have plummeted," said Mr. Davenport. "The Livingston Hotel Empire is headed for bankruptcy. Palmer's son, Miles Armstrong Livingston, has vowed not to let that happen." He pointed at the file Grant held. "Miles is demanding a complete revamping of the Livingston Empire. His mother and the Livingston board of directors are supporting him."

When Miles had been questioned concerning his involvement in the scandal surrounding the Livingston hotels, Grant had been doubtful of the son's innocence. But the courts had determined he was not involved with the prostitution or sex trafficking. Miles' recent press conference disavowing himself from his father's actions, during which he also disowned his father, had gone a long way toward proving his innocence. He'd even taken action to change his name. He now went by Miles Armstrong, keeping his mother's maiden name.

Grant opened the file and scanned the pages comprising financial reports, business plans, and hotel remodel sketches as Mr. Davenport talked. The face of each hotel would undergo significant architectural changes.

Revamping? Total makeover was more like it.

Miles planned to change everything: the hotels' name, logo, slogan, website—although that would be done in-house. And he wanted the focus of the new ad campaign to be all-inclusive, appealing to families as well as the corporate business class.

This was a big deal. Probably the largest project 3D had ever landed. Overwhelmed, Grant reached for his water bottle and twisted off the cap. It slipped from his trembling hand. He caught it, barely managing to keep from spilling it on the folder covering his lap.

That was a close one. I just got handed the ball, and I almost fumbled it already.

He scoffed at himself as he guzzled half the bottle. *Now I'm thinking in sports analogies.*

"Here's the game plan. For the next six months, this is your sole responsibility. I'm assigning you an assistant coach. The two of you will have the conference room on the second floor at your disposal. You'll work together to decide which players you want on your team." He raised a finger. "You'll have to share some of those players with other teams while they fulfill their responsibilities on other contracts. But I'm counting on you to call the shots."

Assistant coach? Did Mr. Davenport ever talk normally? Without referencing sports?

There were a handful of people here at the agency Grant hoped he wouldn't have to work that closely with. *Hmm... maybe I should request the raven-haired beauty from Creative Services for my team.* No, that was a bad idea. She was extremely talented, but she'd be too distracting, and he couldn't afford to be distracted on this project.

He smiled at Mr. Davenport, trying to look enthusiastic instead of overwhelmed, like he felt. "Great. Who's my assistant coach?"

"An incredibly talented woman from Creative Services, Celeste Hightower." Mr. Davenport looked at his watch. "I'll have you send her in on your way out."

Celeste. That was her name. Not Celine or Celia.

He reached for his water bottle again as the blood drained from his face, and an uncomfortable feeling settled in his gut. Was it the attraction he felt for her that made him nauseous? Or was it the thought of trying to maintain control and succeed while dealing with the daily distraction?

He wasn't too sure at the moment. He hadn't even stepped onto the field, and already he wanted to call a timeout.

CELESTE'S HEAD shot up at the knock on her apartment door. Laying down her pencil and sketchbook, she stood and stretched. She glanced at the clock on the stove on her way to the door.

How is it one o'clock already?

She opened the door to find her best friend holding takeout from their favorite Chinese restaurant. She pulled Amy into her apartment and into a hug. Unable to ignore the press of Amy's swollen belly, she held on an extra few seconds. Everything was changing, and Celeste hated change. Especially when she wasn't sure it was for the better.

"I know I just saw you a few days ago, but I've missed you," Celeste said when she finally released her friend.

"I miss you too, C."

They had shared an apartment for the past seven years—since they were both eighteen. But four months ago, Celeste had moved out after

Amy's boyfriend, Lance, insisted on moving in. Amy had tried to convince her to stay—it was a two-bedroom apartment after all, but Celeste had no desire to be the third wheel. Besides, Amy would need the extra bedroom in a couple months for a nursery.

Celeste's stomach growled as the aroma of the Chinese food filled her small apartment.

"Judging by the sound of your stomach and the artwork littering the table, you haven't eaten today, have you?" Amy said as she advanced into the apartment.

Giving Amy a sheepish grin, Celeste bent over the coffee table— the only table she had at the moment—and gathered up the sketches strewn across it. She'd left most of the furniture she and Amy had bought together behind when she moved out, arguing that she could afford to replace the necessary furniture. A proper table hadn't been deemed necessary yet, especially since a used coffee table was so much cheaper than a dinette set.

Not that she had much room for one in this tiny apartment. Once she got her student loans paid off, then she would make things like a larger apartment, a kitchen table, and a nicer sofa a priority. Of course then she wanted to work on her master's degree. She earned good money at 3D, but now that she no longer shared the rent, it would be a while before she'd have the luxury of expanding her budget. Besides, she rarely entertained.

Since Celeste had moved out of the apartment she'd shared with Amy, they'd made it a point to get together for lunch on Saturdays. It was one of the few times their conflicting schedules allowed.

She wasn't about to let her relationship with Amy dwindle. They were too good of friends. Celeste had been there for Amy when her mother kicked her out at seventeen, and Amy had returned the favor six months later when Celeste's father gave her an ultimatum that resulted in her leaving home. And six months ago when Amy discovered she was pregnant, Celeste vowed to be there for her through that too.

"Those sketches aren't for your stories," Amy said as she set the carry-out bags down on the table Celeste had cleared.

"No, they're for work. A new, high-profile project." Celeste tucked the sketches into a folder.

"Cool. How are your stories coming?"

Celeste grabbed two plates from the kitchen and plopped down on the couch. "Slow. The artwork's a piece of cake, but the words haven't been flowing lately. I'm having a hard time trying to figure out what conflicts to throw at my characters and the lessons they need to learn."

Amy started opening food cartons, eliciting another rumble from Celeste's stomach. "And you're still planning on finishing the complete series before you submit it to the publisher?"

"Not necessarily the entire series, but I want to get five or six books done."

If the next book took as long as the last one to write and illustrate, it would be another year before Celeste was ready to query her children's picture book series about a clumsy fairy trying to find her place in the world.

She hoped that since she already did some freelance illustrations for Hi-Lo Publishing—a company that published children's and adult books plus everything in between—she wouldn't have to spend months querying. Hopefully, when Celeste finally found the courage to reach out to Penny Halstrom, editor of the children's line at Hi-Lo, her relationship with the woman would work in her favor.

Conversation lagged while they dished their food. Celeste piled her plate high with sweet and sour chicken, beef broccoli, fried rice, and egg rolls. When she got caught up in her work, she forgot about mundane tasks like eating. And she'd been caught up with sketching ideas for the new project from the moment she got up this morning. A project she'd be working on with Grant Foster.

"Guess who I ran into at work yesterday," she said around a bite of egg roll.

Amy pretended to put serious thought into her answer even though they played this game all the time. She always asked the same questions in the same order.

"Someone famous?"

Celeste shook her head as she stuffed her mouth with sweet and sour chicken.

"Male or female?"

"Male," she mumbled around the chicken.

"Do I know him?"

"You know *of* him."

"Let me guess, you ran into the boss and made a fool of yourself."

Celeste swallowed. How did Amy always do that? As usual, she was wrong but oh so close. Would it have been less embarrassing to spill her purse in front of Mr. Davenport? Would she have told him she needed to pee too? After her embarrassing run-in with Grant, she'd been plenty rattled by the time she entered the big boss's office. Especially since Grant's pleasant masculine scent hung in the air, and warmth clung to the chair Mr. Davenport had shown her to. A chair she was certain Grant had just vacated.

"I saw Mr. Davenport yesterday, but he's not the one I *ran* into."

Amy's hand froze with her egg roll halfway to her mouth. "Are you saying you literally ran into some man?"

Trying to ignore the heat filling her cheeks, Celeste finished chewing another bite before answering. "Not *just* some man. And I didn't just bump into him. I dumped my entire purse at his feet, although that was kind of his fault."

Amy's eyes widened, and she dropped her egg roll on her plate. "You ran into Grant Foster and dumped your purse at his feet? That's who it was, wasn't it?"

Celeste and Amy shared everything with each other, including their secret feelings for unattainable people and relationships. Because crushes were safe. Relationships were scary. It was too easy to let people down or get your heart broken when you opened it to someone. They'd both had a crush on the same good-looking dentist for years. And they each had a celebrity crush as well as an at-work crush.

Lance Hayes had been Amy's at-work crush. His band played every Friday and Saturday night at the bar and grill where Amy waitressed. And now, Amy was pregnant with Lance's child. Celeste still had mixed feelings about that. In her mind, the playboy singer wasn't good enough for her friend.

Turning her thoughts back to Grant, she affirmed Amy's guess. "His eyes are so much prettier up close, Aim. And he smelled nice." Then she told her best friend about the whole ordeal, including the errant tampon and her inability to stand up by herself, thanks to her pencil skirt.

Amy laughed so hard tears filled her eyes.

"It gets worse," Celeste said. "I was so flustered by the time he stepped away that I told him I needed to pee." The words came out as a groan.

Amy howled with laughter. Setting her plate on the table, she pressed her hands to her bulging stomach. "Sounds like you've been hanging around me too long. I'm usually the one who speaks without thinking." Amy dissolved into another fit of giggles. "Now *I* need to pee."

Celeste waited patiently, face flaming, while Amy went to the bathroom. A single giggle escaped when she returned.

"I'm never going to be able to face him again," Celeste groaned.

"It's not like you work with him that often. I'm sure he will forget all about it by the time you work another project together."

"By Monday? I doubt it." Celeste set her plate on her lap and covered her face with both hands. "Aim, Mr. Davenport assigned me to work closely with him on a big project."

"How close?"

"Close, close. As in, he and I are heading up one of the biggest contracts 3D has ever landed. Actually, he's heading it up, but I'll be working with him every step of the way. For six whole months."

"Will this be a good thing or a bad thing?"

The question reminded Celeste that Amy knew her so well. As much as she'd like Grant Foster to notice her, she preferred not to be noticed by anyone. Even though she wasn't particularly shy—she had no problem speaking her mind—she was still an introvert. She could work well with a group, but she preferred to work alone. And she could get up and speak or present in front of a group if she was prepared—she didn't do extemporaneous—but she'd much rather let someone else do the talking.

"I don't know," she moaned. "I'm excited by the challenge the project poses, and Mr. Davenport let me know there would be a sizable bonus if all goes well. So, that's good, but I don't know if I can bear to work with that gorgeous man all day every day."

Amy picked up her egg roll again. She wiggled her eyebrows. "Who knows, maybe something will happen between the two of you, and you'll be following me into motherhood soon."

Celeste thought about Ian and Olivia from the Client Services Department. They were the cutest couple. After they had dated for eighteen months, everyone laid bets on how much longer it would be before they got married. Then one day, Olivia asked to be transferred to a different department. She got her transfer but ended up quitting anyway four months later. Nobody understood what happened. Both Ian and Olivia remained tight-lipped about what tore them apart, but there had been whispers in the cafeteria that Ian had a child from a previous relationship, and Olivia couldn't handle that. Ian had eventually found another job too. Many of Olivia's friends continued to blame the break-up on him.

"No way," Celeste said. She wasn't opposed to settling down, but she was only twenty-five. She had plenty of time to think about marriage and children. She didn't want to offend Amy, but she was glad she wasn't in her friend's place.

"Speaking of motherhood..."

Celeste's food stuck in her throat at the tone of Amy's voice. She took a quick drink of water, her eyes never leaving her friend.

Amy's eyes dropped to her plate.

"Hey." Celeste reached over and took Amy's hand. "What's wrong?"

"Lance's band has the chance for a gig in Seattle."

A chill shot through Celeste. It was one thing to feel like a third wheel because your best friend was in a relationship and about to become a mother, but to have Amy move away... Celeste couldn't handle that much change.

"What do you mean? Are you going with him?"

"No, it's a temporary gig."

Relief filled Celeste. She wasn't losing her best friend, yet. "Meaning?"

"They'll be playing at a nightclub in Seattle Monday through Thursday, then they'll come home every weekend to play Fridays and Saturdays at Charlie's."

"That's good, isn't it? More exposure for the band." Except Amy didn't act like it was good news as she pushed her broccoli around her plate.

"The gig is supposed to last two, maybe even three months."

Understanding dawned on Celeste. Amy was due in two months. Lance might miss the baby's birth.

This didn't surprise Celeste. It was good Lance's band was getting more exposure, but it figured that he would only think about himself. Any man worth his weight would consider how this would affect his pregnant girlfriend.

A decent man would have married his girlfriend after getting her pregnant.

Hiding her distaste for Lance, she squeezed Amy's hand. "Whatever you need, I'm here for you, Aim."

Amy gave her a watery smile. "I knew I could count on you, C. Will you go to the childbirth and Lamaze classes with me?"

CHAPTER 3

*G*rant shoved the file folder Mr. Davenport had given him on Friday into his computer bag, along with the three legal pads he'd filled this weekend with notes. One filled with slogans and ad campaign ideas, another filled with data and demographics and nearby attractions for each hotel, and the third contained step-by-step planning for how the ad campaign would play out, including a detailed marketing plan.

He stepped to the bottom of the stairs. "Reagan and Josh, it's time to go. I'm leaving in ten minutes."

A groan from Josh, who had probably just rolled out of bed, floated down the stairs, followed by a, "Hold your horses. We'll be down when we're ready," from Reagan.

Grant stifled a groan and went to the kitchen to pack his lunch. Reagan and Josh were uncooperative enough on a good day, but today... he swore they were conspiring against him.

Ever since he walked through the door Friday evening, feeling overwhelmed, his mind racing with ideas, it had been one thing after another. From needing to help Josh complete four late math assign-ments, to having Reagan break curfew not once but twice this weekend. He'd had to drag her out of bed at noon on both Saturday and Sunday.

The late nights gave him plenty of time to brainstorm concerning the Armstrong account, but they also raised his stress level. He was fed up with Reagan's behavior. It had been almost a year since his parents died, and Reagan was still testing the limits.

This morning, he'd gotten up an hour earlier than usual so he wouldn't feel rushed. He'd already given himself the mental pep talk he needed to lead with confidence. He planned to get to the office early and get settled in the conference room before Miss Hightower arrived. He'd be the perfect picture of calm, collected, and in control.

If Reagan and Josh don't make me late, that is.

From now on, he'd think of her as Miss Hightower. No more thinking of her as the striking, raven-haired beauty. He'd keep it professional, no matter how attractive he found her.

"Five minutes, guys!"

Shouldering his laptop bag, he grabbed the muffins and protein drinks that would be Reagan and Josh's breakfast before heading out to the garage. His sister and brother never wanted to get up early enough to eat a proper breakfast, but they always got ornery with him for rushing them out of the house without giving them time to eat, especially Reagan.

She was always angry about something. He'd tried to be understanding and give her the space and time she needed to grieve the loss of her parents. At times, he'd blamed her moodiness on hormones—he'd had a girlfriend who was always less pleasant to be around during that time of the month. Then one day, Reagan started biting everybody's head off, slamming doors, and crying over everything and nothing.

His face flamed just thinking about the difficult, uncomfortable conversation he had with her. Once he'd understood the problem, he'd offered to take her to go buy tampons, even though it was the last thing he wanted to do. Not that he thought himself too manly to do that—he'd done it once for his girlfriend, Laney, in an emergency—

but to have to buy them for his little sister was a different story. Especially when she refused to go to the store with him.

"I can't go looking like this. What if I see someone I know?" she'd cried.

So Grant had gone alone. He'd bought a dozen items they didn't need so he wouldn't feel so conspicuous buying the tampons. But he'd bought the wrong brand. Reagan insisting that he take them back and get the right ones still angered him. He'd argued with her about them all being the same until she graphically described why she didn't like that brand.

Grant had grabbed the box and stormed out of the house. No way would he go to the service desk to return a box of tampons. He'd thrown them in the trash before buying the *right* ones, along with more stuff they didn't need. That was a mistake he'd never make again. And now, not only did he buy the right tampons regularly for her, they had a year's supply of shampoo, deodorant, and toothpaste.

He climbed in his Dodge Charger and honked the horn. The kids knew they had sixty seconds to get in the car, or he would leave them. They were on their own at that point to find a ride to school. And missing school resulted in the loss of their cell phones.

Grant could be a little obsessive—okay, maybe more than a little, but the upheaval in all their lives this past year had been a nightmare. He'd sold his two-bedroom condo and moved into his dad's house so Reagan and Josh wouldn't have to leave their home. But learning to parent two teenagers had been almost more than he could bear.

Most days, he felt like he barely kept his head above water when it came to parenting. It might be different if he wasn't doing it alone, but his girlfriend, whom he'd been on the verge of proposing to, had dumped him the moment he became Reagan and Josh's guardian.

"I don't want to be a mother, especially not to a couple of teenage brats," she'd declared. When Grant had excused Reagan and Josh's difficult behavior due to their grief, Laney accused him of choosing them over her. "You don't love me. You've never fully let me in. You keep all your emotions so close I swear you're emotionally stunted."

The accusation had stung like a slap to the face, and Grant had to wonder if she was right, especially considering his history.

As difficult as the breakup had been on top of everything else, he was grateful for the eye-opener. He was glad he'd seen Laney for the self-absorbed, immature woman she really was. She'd only told him she wanted kids because that's what she thought he wanted to hear. At thirty years old, he'd been ready to settle down and thought he was ready to start a family, but he hadn't been ready to be a parent. Not to teenagers, anyway. He wasn't about to let his siblings be placed into foster care, though.

It had been a rocky ride ever since. Their home life had been chaos, and his work had suffered. Thank goodness he had an understanding boss. Mr. Hardman had been the one to tell Grant he needed to set limits and stick to them.

That's what he'd done. The rules hadn't been well received and weren't always followed—Reagan breaking curfew being a prime example—but they brought him a measure of peace.

Relief filled him when the garage door opened, and Josh stumbled out, followed moments later by Reagan. Grant checked the clock on his dash.

Good. If traffic wasn't too bad, he'd get to the office twenty minutes early.

Thirty minutes later, after dropping Reagan and Josh off at the intersection shared by the middle school and high school—with a reminder for Josh to turn in his math assignments—Grant pulled into the parking lot of 3D Media. He grabbed his computer bag and pasted a smile on his face.

After a brief elevator ride to the second floor, he walked with long strides to the conference room, hoping he looked more confident than he felt. He stepped in and froze.

Celeste Hightower, looking gorgeous in a royal blue blouse, already sat at the conference table.

GRANT STOOD for a full three seconds staring at Celeste. He hadn't expected her to be here this early. He'd counted on having a few extra minutes to get settled and mentally prepared to take charge.

He'd been Director of Content and Development for the past two years, so leadership wasn't new to him. But this was the chance to become a vice president. He couldn't foul this up.

Feeling like an idiot, he gave Celeste a smile and slid his computer bag onto a chair. He extended his hand.

"Good morning, Miss Hightower. I'm Grant Foster."

Her left eyebrow rose in a delicate arch as she smiled and shook his hand. "I know who you are, Grant. Please, call me Celeste."

"Right."

He sucked in a deep breath. Of course she knew who he was. They'd worked together on several projects. And she wanted him to call her *Celeste*. It was such a graceful and pretty name. Like her. Using her first name would make working together in this small conference room feel... intimate.

"Celeste, sorry. I guess I'm a little surprised to see you here already. Do you always arrive this early?"

If she did, he would be hard pressed to get here before her. He doubted he could get Reagan and Josh out of the house any earlier. They already complained about having to sit at school for twenty minutes. He kept reminding them they could walk instead.

A hint of pink tinged her cheeks as she smiled this time, her nose scrunching a little. "No, I hoped getting here early would help me look competent. Especially after what I said the last time we... ran into each other."

Grant bit back a smile as he remembered the fiasco last Friday outside the restrooms.

Was that the only reason she arrived early? Or did she feel as overwhelmed by this project as he did? Did she have as much riding on it as he did? He knew Stacy, the VP of the Creative Services Department, was having a baby, but he hadn't heard she was quitting.

He chuckled. "I felt the need to arrive early for the same reason. The competent part, not the... other." Feeling warmth creep up his neck, he shoved his hands into his pockets. "Looks like we have something in common already. I'll make you a deal. I won't get here earlier than seven fifty-five tomorrow if you won't."

She laughed—a light musical sound—and something warmed inside him.

"Deal. Sounds like we're both overachievers, aren't we?" A V formed between her eyebrows as she tilted her head. "That means we will either work well together or drive each other crazy."

Judging by his reaction to her laugh, Grant had a feeling it would be the latter, but he wasn't so sure it would be in a bad way. Except, those kinds of distractions didn't belong in the workplace.

Keep it professional.

Shrugging, he pulled the folder Mr. Davenport had given him from his bag, followed by the three legal pads he'd filled with notes.

"I guess that's why Mr. Davenport selected us for this job," he said in his best "take charge" voice. "I assume you're aware that Livingston —now Armstrong Hotels—needs help with their rebranding and the full extent of marketing services requested?"

She nodded, and Grant picked up the first notepad.

"We have six weeks to come up with three soft campaign launches before we pitch to Armstrong's people. The pitch will include three of each of the following: new slogans, new logos, and commercial sketches." He paced a tight line beside the table as he flipped through his notepad.

"First, we'll do a data analysis on the company's previous marketing tactics and the success of each. We need to carefully weigh public opinion concerning Palmer Livingston's sentencing along with the media's reaction to Miles Armstrong's promise to transform the hotels inside and out. Then, we need to look at the best way to ensure the re-branding maintains the corporate business clientele while subtly shifting its demographics to be more family friendly."

He took a deep breath and pressed onward. "We'll consider promos and arrange for test groups. A seamless streamline from old to new may be difficult to achieve considering the recent negative publicity surrounding the Livingston Hotels. Although with the architectural changes Armstrong is making, innovative and engaging might be the best way to approach this."

Celeste pulled a file from her bag and a stack of what looked like a variety of sketches while he talked.

"Are you always this intense?" She broke in when he took a breath. Her left eyebrow arched again as she regarded him.

"Intense? What do you mean?"

"Will I need to put up with this domineering, I'm-in-charge attitude for the next six months?" She made air quotes with her fingers as she said I'm in charge.

Had he been that bad? He'd meant to sound assertive and let her know he took this project seriously and was competent to lead it, but he didn't mean to come across as bossy.

"There's a lot at stake," he said, defending himself.

"Like what?"

When he didn't respond, she tilted her head and studied him. "What's at stake for you?" She waited a moment before continuing. "When Mr. Davenport asked me to collaborate on this project with you, he told me to meet you here this morning so we could get to know one another and determine whether we could work well together."

What happens if she decides she can't work with me?

He didn't look forward to working closely with Celeste, because of his attraction to her, but he couldn't do this without her. She was the best artist and graphic designer in her department. He needed her on this team.

Grant took a seat across from her and cleared his throat. "You're right. We should get to know one another. I'll go first. I've been with 3D Media for ten years. I have a Master of Fine Arts from Multnomah University. I started working here during my junior year of college as an intern, and I've been here ever since. I've worked mainly in the Marketing Services Department, in about every position possible. I'm currently the Director of Content and Development." He listed a few of the prominent ad campaigns he'd worked on, belatedly remembering Celeste had worked on each of them as well.

He stopped talking and looked at her expectantly, letting her know it was her turn.

"That's it?" When he nodded, she shook her head. "I thought you'd at least tell me one thing that doesn't appear in your bio on the website."

She read my bio.

Of course she had. He'd read hers first thing after Mr. Davenport informed him he'd be working with her.

Celeste shrugged. "Well, if we're only bothering to get to know each other on a professional level, then I guess all you need to know about me is that I've been with 3D for four years. I started as an intern here as well. I work in the Creative Services Department. I have my BA, and I'd like to get MFA at some point. I'm a skilled artist." She said the words with conviction. "I can produce any kind of art you want."

"Great. So, I'm the writer and you're the artist. I'm sure we'll make a great team."

Her left eyebrow rose again.

"What? Why do you keep doing that thing with your eyebrow?"

Her brow inched a little higher as she pointed at it. "This thing?" When he nodded, she said, "This is me calling you on your BS."

"My BS?"

"Are you always going to repeat and question everything I say?"

He could tell by the quirk at the corners of her mouth she was trying not to smile.

Grant leaned forward. "I'm in charge of this project. Of course, I'm going to question you, especially when you say you're calling me on my bull—"

"Profanity isn't allowed in the workplace," Celeste hissed as she pitched forward in her seat.

He swallowed the rest of the word and ground his teeth together. This woman was infuriating. Six months of working with her would be the longest of his life.

No, that wasn't true. Nothing could top the difficulty of the first six months after his dad and Catherine died.

"Mr. Davenport warned me that you took your work seriously and could be uptight, but I had no idea you were this overzealous."

Biting his tongue to keep from saying something he might regret about her sassy attitude—something that might get back to Mr. Davenport—Grant dropped back in his seat, folded his arms, and took a deep breath. "Fine. You think we need to get to know each other on a more personal level? How about you go first? Tell me all about your-self—your hopes, dreams, and fears."

Celeste leaned back in her chair, her olive complexion turning a delightful shade of pink.

Grant crossed his arms over his chest and waited.

CELESTE SQUARED HER SHOULDERS, pressing back into her chair. Put like that, the idea of getting to know each other on a personal level didn't sound so appealing after all. Although, she was dying to know more about him. She was especially curious to know if he was single. The girlfriend he'd brought to company parties multiple times over the past few years hadn't been by his side during the last two parties.

Celeste was not about to bare her soul to find out more about him. She wouldn't share her dreams of becoming a children's author with him. Amy was the only one who knew she'd been writing and illus-trating children's books, and she wanted it to stay that way. For now.

Grant gave her a smug smile. "Nothing to say?"

"Okay, fine. We don't need to share our hopes and dreams with each other." *And certainly not our fears.* "But would it hurt for us to get to know each other a little? To help us learn each other's artistic styles and creative processes?"

He looked perplexed. "Like what?"

"You know what? Never mind. I thought maybe it would help us get on the same page when it comes to coaching this team."

Grant smiled and his posture relaxed. "He used the sports analo-gies on you too?"

"I'm not sure that man knows how to communicate without talking about sports. I feel sorry for his wife."

"Could you imagine living with that day after day?" Grant shoved his fingers into his hair, making it stand on end. "I was only with him for twenty minutes, and I started thinking in sports analogies. And I'm not that into sports."

She laughed, and Grant joined her.

"There's another thing we have in common," she said, pointing a finger at him. "His analogies drive us crazy."

He nodded. "Look, Celeste, I'm confident we can work well together. We've done it in the past, not this closely, but we've done it. If building a friendly, *working* relationship is important to you, then I'm game. But like any good friendship, we shouldn't have to force it."

She didn't miss the emphasis he put on *working*. Was he telling her he was okay being friends as long as they kept it work appropriate? That was the smart thing to do, she knew that, but it didn't change the fact that she wanted to know more about him.

"You're right, but people usually become better friends in social settings. Since there won't be much opportunity to socialize while we work, how about we make a deal to answer one question for each other every day?"

He studied her for a long moment before asking, "What kind of question? You don't strike me as the type that would be content knowing my favorite color."

She shrugged and gave him her sweetest smile. "Favorite food, color, music... the possibilities are endless. If we work together the full six months, that's twenty-four weeks, at five days per week... eventually you'll have to answer some harder questions. But so will I."

Why did I say that? Do I really want this handsome man to know my deepest, darkest secrets?

Okay, so she didn't really have any deep dark secrets, other than she'd had a crush on Grant for most of the four years she'd worked here.

Could they answer the hard questions and keep their relationship strictly professional?

She studied Grant as he weighed her proposal, the muscle in his jaw repeatedly flexing showed his indecision. Was he coming to the same conclusion she had about the difficulty of maintaining a professional relationship if they shared personal information with each other?

As usual, he looked impeccable in his dark suit and tie, although his hair hadn't quite settled back into place after he ran his fingers through it. The disarray added to his attractiveness. His gray irises—ringed by dark blue—made his eyes striking and hypnotic. Her gaze followed the line of his face down to his mouth.

What would it feel like to be kissed by those lips?

Pulling her thoughts away from that dangerous path, she opened her mouth to tell him to forget the whole thing, when he spoke.

"Okay, but we start with simple questions."

Celeste had no control over the smile that split her face. She shouldn't be so excited about this, but she was. She clapped her hands. "Agreed, but today... I want you to answer the question I already asked you."

Grant's brows furrowed. "What question?"

"What's at stake for you with this project?"

He tugged at his collar. "Um... I'm not sure I can answer that... yet."

"It's the VP position, isn't it?" When he didn't readily volunteer information, she pressed forward. "Everybody knows Hardman is retiring, and either you or Randy Evans will take his spot."

Grant cleared his throat. "Randy is filling in for him now... while he's on vacation."

Celeste laughed. "That's such a noncommittal comment."

The corners of Grant's mouth turned up, but he said nothing.

Her eyes narrowed on his face as she nodded her head. "You're going to be the next VP of Marketing. Everyone knows Randy doesn't have the personality for it." She lowered her voice. "He barely has any personality at all."

Grant burst into laughter. The sound, rich and deep, was contagious, and she joined him.

"That was so rude," he whisper-hissed while fighting the laughter.

"It's true, though. You know it is."

He nodded and chuckled again.

Celeste suspected Randy was a borderline genius, but he didn't have the people skills to be a VP. He rarely made eye contact and spoke in mumbles.

Their laughter died down, and she said, "For what it's worth, I think you'll make a great VP."

"Really?"

The uncertainty in his voice made her think Grant questioned his ability to fulfill the role he'd soon assume.

"Really. You'll see." She waved her hand at the table. "By the time we're done with this project, you'll have full confidence in your ability to lead an entire department."

He smiled and gave her a nod. "Thanks."

Trying not to get caught up in his gorgeous smile, she said, "Speaking of which, if we don't get at it, this project won't get done."

"Not so fast." Grant leaned forward in his seat. "I get to ask you a question now."

"But you didn't even answer my question. I had to answer it myself."

"You got your answer, didn't you?"

Celeste rolled her eyes. "That's not fair. If I have to answer a question for you, then I should get to ask one you actually answer."

He contemplated that for a long moment. "Okay."

"Good," she said with a smile. "Ask away."

"I know we agreed to start with the easy questions, but I'd also like to know the *real* answer to the question I already asked *you*." When Celeste gave him a blank look, he asked, "Why do you do that thing with your eyebrow? And don't tell me it's you calling me on my BS. I want a genuine answer."

All humor faded as a band tightened around her chest. No, this was not a simple question. In fact, it bordered on downright hard and *way* too personal.

It was Grant's turn to study her face as she debated how to answer without telling her entire life story that would clearly expose her biggest fear. The fear of failure.

She dropped her gaze to her fingernails as she tapped them on the table, feeling her father's full condescension as though she were still a teenager. No matter what she did, she'd never been good enough. In his eyes, she would never measure up.

"Celeste?" The concern in Grant's voice pulled her back to the present.

Pasting on a smile he would surely recognize as fake, she said, "It's something I do when... I find a man overbearing and condescending."

His brows furrowed. "Meaning you find me overbearing and condescending." It was a statement, not a question.

She gave a half shrug. "Sorry."

He shook his head. "No, I'm sorry. I didn't mean to come across like that. I'd hoped to look competent." He put his elbows on the table and leaned forward. His eyes were full of such tenderness it sucked the breath from her lungs. "And Celeste, I'm sorry for the way you were treated by whoever taught you to do that." He pointed to her left eyebrow.

She lowered her gaze and sucked in a deep breath. When Grant had walked into the conference room a few minutes ago spouting how things were going to be, she'd thought him as arrogant and authoritarian as her father. But her father had never apologized to her for anything. Ever.

She forced a laugh that sounded as tight as her chest felt. "So much for not asking the hard questions, huh?"

"I didn't mean to tear open old wounds."

She waved a hand. "Until today, I thought those wounds had healed." She sucked in a sharp breath and forced another smile. "But I guess not."

"Maybe someday, you'll trust me enough to tell me about it." When Celeste gave him a doubtful look, he continued. "Turnabout is fair play. You have my permission to ask me a hard question."

"And you promise to answer truthfully?"

Grant nodded, but he looked like he'd rather walk across hot coals.

31

Celeste thought for a moment of what she really wanted to know about him. Her eyes fell to the stack of legal pads in front of him. He'd been as busy this weekend as she had. Why?

"Okay, tell me why the VP position is so important." She held up a finger before he could answer. "And you can't say money or prestige."

A look of regret crossed his face. "Wow, you don't pull any punches, do you?"

Celeste said nothing. She would not let him out of answering this question by answering it for him. She met and held his gaze, letting him know this was a safe zone. No matter what he said, she wouldn't judge him for it. Like he hadn't judged her.

He took a deep breath, gave a slight nod, and said, "Because I have people at home depending on me."

For the second time in only a few minutes, all the air whooshed from her lungs. She wasn't sure what she'd expected him to say, but it wasn't that. Did this mean he was married with a kid at home? Had his wife not come to the company parties because she'd been at home with the baby?

A pang of disappointment pierced her heart. She'd never consider dating a coworker. Those relationships always turned out messy. But a part of her had hoped Grant would be as interested in her as she was in him. Never mind that nothing could come of it.

CHAPTER 4

"I think we should go with this one for number three." Grant picked up one of the full-color renderings Celeste had created from her original sketches for the Armstrong Hotels' new logo. It was similar to several others, fitting Armstrong's requirements, but unique in its own way.

Celeste was an incredible artist. Last weekend, she'd sketched a dozen different sample logos. Some with similar colors and lines and others that were drastically different. But each of them contained amazing detail, design, and depth. It was difficult to narrow it down to three to present to Armstrong.

"Are you sure?" She picked up another design and stepped toward him. "You don't think Miles Armstrong will like the bold colors of this one?"

He resisted the urge to take a step back. He could barely concentrate as it was. They had only worked together three days now, but the subtle scent of her perfume did crazy things to him every time he got close to her. She reminded him of a tropical island.

Today, she wore a coral blouse with turquoise jewelry, and she smelled as fresh and alluring as she looked. The scent of coconut and fruit wafted his way every time she moved her head. The piña colada scent mixed nicely with the subtle scent of her perfume that made him imagine sunshine, sand, and flowers. The closer she got, the stronger the scent became, along with the desire to pull her into his arms.

A crazy urge to skip out of work and go to the beach swept over him. Not a beach on the Oregon coast though—they were too rocky and cold, especially this early in the spring. No, he wanted to go to a tropical island with white sand and blue waters. And he wanted to take Celeste with him. He didn't typically ogle women—they deserved to be respected—but he couldn't help wondering what her curves would look like in a swimsuit.

His internal temperature skyrocketed, and he had to put some distance between him and Celeste. He walked to the other end of the table and shoved his hand into his trouser pockets.

"I like the lines and color scheme of the other one. It speaks of adventure in an understated way." Grant sure hoped what he said made sense because his mind felt muddled.

They'd been debating the logo designs for nearly an hour now. He wanted to put his foot down and insist he had the final say since he was the senior employee here—or as Mr. Davenport would put it: the head coach. But he didn't want her to think he was being domineering.

She tilted her head and studied the third design he'd selected. "Adventure, huh? Maybe we could use that in the slogan."

"So, are we agreed?" Keeping the table between him and Celeste, he lined up his three favorite designs.

She folded her arms over her chest and scrutinized the designs before shifting her gaze to him. Her lips turned up, and twin dimples winked at him.

"Those are my favorites too. But I wanted to make sure we didn't discount the others too easily."

These were her favorite? Yet she'd made him argue the merit of each design before giving in? Grant scowled at her.

Her eyebrow rose in response, and he resisted the urge to grin.

Now that he understood why she did that with her eyebrow, he found it kind of cute. It was her way of being sassy without being disrespectful and causing contention. He was tempted to argue with her just to see how high it could really go.

He gave himself a mental shake. They had important work to do. He couldn't let himself get sidetracked by a shapely eyebrow and a pretty face.

"Great. Let's move on to slogans for the rebranding campaign." He grabbed one of the legal pads he'd filled up last weekend. "Keeping in mind some of Livingston's past campaigns, I've made a list of slogans."

"I thought Miles wanted the rebranding of the hotels to take an entirely different direction than what they were under his father." Her eyebrow only inched up a margin.

How disappointing.

"He does. That's why I've also made a list of entirely new slogans for the Armstrong Hotels." He grabbed another legal pad. "But I don't think we should discount previous ad campaigns that were successful."

This time when her eyebrow rose, a nod accompanied it. Celeste might say she used that little quirk only when someone—meaning a man—was being domineering and condescending, but she was impressed right now.

Grant was sure of it. He was equally sure they would spend hours arguing about the slogans, because Celeste would want to thoroughly discuss each and every one before deciding to keep or discard it.

A surge of adrenalin shot through him, expanding his chest. Today was going to be another extremely stimulating day. The last time he'd enjoyed his job this much was when he'd been an intern. He loved his job, and he was good at it, but he hadn't realized how invigorating it could be to work with someone so incredibly talented and outspoken.

Working with Celeste Hightower for the next six months was bound to be the sweetest form of torture. Because as much as she aggravated him, she also made him feel so alive.

~

CELESTE WIPED the grease from her chin with a napkin then tossed it into the tray that had held the best street tacos she'd ever tasted.

"Finally, you're finished. I ate two more tacos than you, and I finished five minutes ago." Grant slurped the last of his soda then rotated his chair and tossed his cup into the wastebasket behind him.

"I like to enjoy my food, not inhale it."

He chuckled. "If you think I inhaled my food, you should see my brother, Josh, eat."

Grant has a brother. She savored this tidbit of information. The man took his work seriously, which was good, but it had made it hard to get to know him. She looked forward to lunchtime each day.

When Celeste had returned to the conference room with her lunch Monday afternoon, Grant had come looking for her. She'd told him she was used to eating at her desk and didn't mind eating alone, but the look on his face said he felt sorry for her.

She didn't stop him when he'd joined her.

They'd eaten lunch together every day this week, either bringing lunch from home or going to the cafeteria on the first floor. Today, Friday, to celebrate the progress they'd made this first week, they'd visited the taco truck at the park across the street.

They had nailed down their three soft proposals for the big pitch. They would spend the next three weeks developing each proposal, complete with advertising strategies and commercial sketches.

"Is it question time?" Celeste asked after a long drink of water. She probably shouldn't enjoy this part of the day as much as she did, but she liked learning more about him and what made him tick.

After their rocky start on Monday, they'd gotten down to business and worked together to develop a plan of action. Grant was well prepared and organized, but he'd asked for her input every step of the way and acted like he valued her opinion. He hadn't turned out nearly as demanding and condescending as she'd first thought. Unfortunately, it strengthened her attraction toward him.

She felt like the worst person ever for being attracted to a married man, especially since he'd done nothing to encourage her attraction. Except for their casual conversation at lunchtime, Grant was all business.

He even sat at the opposite end of the eight-foot conference table to work. At first, Celeste had been offended, thinking he didn't enjoy working with her. But every time he bent over her to study one of her designs, she got a whiff of his cologne and it wreaked havoc on her senses. It's a good thing he kept his distance.

She couldn't help herself, though. She argued with him on almost everything they discussed, making him question his choices until he was certain it was the right decision. Not that he made poor choices. On the contrary, he was usually right, but Celeste figured if he became confident in defending his choices and his leadership ability, he'd make a stronger leader. Especially if he was willing to consider his peers opinions.

"It's my turn to go first today, isn't it?" Grant's deep voice pulled her from her musings.

She nodded, curious about what he'd ask today.

As if by unspoken rule, they had both stuck to the easy questions the past few days. Easy, but not at all boring. Their questions usually sparked entertaining conversation that lasted the remainder of their lunch break.

She'd learned they shared a love of eighties music. It was Grant's music of choice when he worked out, and her favorite for cleaning —which was the closest she came to working out. She'd also learned he had multiple pet peeves—people leaving their stuff everywhere, especially in common spaces shared by others. He hated when people didn't follow the rules, and people who were perpetually late drove him crazy. She'd made a mental note to always be on time and to keep her creative chaos to a minimum in the conference room. She'd also discovered that what he considered his greatest strengths—organization and neatness—his sister called his biggest weakness.

It had excited her to learn he had a sister. When she'd asked more about her, he'd said she was much younger than him, and they weren't that close. Then he looked at the clock and promptly brought their lunch break to an end.

"Okay, I've got a two-part question today."

"Two-part? As in two questions?" Celeste couldn't keep her left eyebrow from rising. Mostly because Grant hated it when she did that.

"Come on, it's not like you haven't asked multiple questions some days."

"They were follow-up questions," she defended.

"Fine, my second question will be a follow-up question."

Celeste bit back a smile. She liked arguing with Grant because she could see it drove him crazy. Especially when she questioned his leadership—which she did regularly to keep him humble, but not so often she truly aggravated him.

She gave a dramatic sigh. "Fine, ask away."

He sat up straighter in his seat and looked at her. "Who is your hero? And my follow-up question is why? In case you want to consider that as you think about your answer."

Celeste tried to ignore the hitch in her pulse as Grant stared at her with his piercing gray eyes. *Why did the man have to be so handsome? And married?*

Focusing on his question, she debated her answer. "I'd have to say someone like Joan of Arc or Amelia Earhart."

His eyes widened, and he gave an appreciative nod. "Hmm... I guess I don't need to ask why."

"You could, but it would make you look ignorant."

He laughed. "Yeah, it would. But doesn't it bother you that their noble acts of heroism ended up getting them killed?"

She shrugged. "That didn't make them any less courageous and heroic." When he responded with another nod, she continued. "I'll add Rosa Parks to the list. Her courage didn't end up getting her killed."

Another look of admiration filled Grant's face. "No, but it sure didn't make life easy for her."

"Life wasn't easy for her before she refused to give up her seat on the bus," Celeste pointed out.

"True. So, you admire courageous women." It was more a statement than a question.

"Doesn't everybody? I mean, you probably admire courageous men instead of women, but isn't that typical of most people?"

"I suppose so, but not everybody thinks like we do. My ex-girlfriend, for example, idolized the Kardashians."

Ex-girlfriend? Did he mean the blond who had come to the company parties with him? If he hadn't married her, who was he married to?

She rolled her eyes at the Kardashian comment as her mind raced.

They discussed for a few minutes how so few young people had truly heroic idols anymore. Courageous people who stood for something and fought to make the world a better place.

When the conversation died down, Grant looked at his watch. "We have ten minutes before we need to get back to work. What's my question?"

Are you married? Celeste's mind screamed.

She really wanted to know the answer, but she was not about to ask that question. Then he would know she was interested in him. She mulled it over for a moment, wondering if there was a less obvious way of finding out the same information. Then an idea struck her.

"What one chore around the house would your wife like you to take over permanently?"

Grant frowned. "I'm not married."

"You're not?" Did her voice sound a little too excited?

He shook his head.

"But on Monday you said you had people at home depending on you. I assumed..."

He propped his elbows on the table and shoved his fingers into his hair. "You assumed I had a wife and children at home. I wish that was the case. The wife part anyway."

The last of his words came out a mumble, and Celeste wondered if she'd heard him correctly. She opened her mouth to speak, but no words came out. She honestly didn't know what to make of his comment. He's not married, but he wanted to be? But he had children at home?

"If I had a wife, maybe things wouldn't be so hard." The words came out a combination of a moan and a growl.

His head hung, and again Celeste wondered if she'd heard him correctly. "Grant? Are you okay?" She fought the urge to walk around the table and sit beside him.

He shook his head a few times before raising it. A mask of professionalism quickly replaced the vulnerability she'd glimpsed on his face. "Sorry about that." He didn't meet her gaze. Instead, he looked at the clock. "We'd better get back to work." He pulled his laptop toward him.

He was upset about something going on at home. Something that would be easier if he had a wife. A strange sensation swept through her, simultaneously setting her stomach aflutter and tightening her chest. Grant needed help.

Confused, Celeste stared at him, willing him to look at her. She cleared her throat.

He finally glanced at her, and she could tell the moment he spotted her raised eyebrow, because he scowled. She hadn't meant to raise it. Sometimes it had a mind of its own.

She pointed at her eye. "This means I'm confused, not that you're being overbearing."

His brow relaxed, but he remained hunched over his computer.

"Please clarify something for me. You're not married?" At the shake of his head she asked, "But you have children at home?"

How did she not know Grant was a single father? The company parties were family events, yet he'd never brought little ones to the parties.

He let out a short laugh akin to a snort. "At fifteen and thirteen years old, Reagan and Josh would balk at being called children, but they are still kids." Her confusion must have shown on her face, because he said, "My younger half-sister and brother live with me."

Stunned, Celeste stared at him. *Grant is raising teenagers.* Facing such a task alone must be incredibly daunting. No wonder he wished he had a wife.

He turned back to his computer. "It's time we get back to work."

Celeste had a million more questions, but his face said he was done talking unless it pertained to work.

CHAPTER 5

here are you? Do you realize what time it is? Grant hit send on his text to Reagan and checked the clock for the hundredth time.

Eleven thirty.

Reagan was supposed to have come home an hour ago. He'd reminded her of her ten thirty curfew before agreeing to let her hang out with her friend, Shelby, tonight. And Reagan had promised she'd be home on time. He should have grounded her after she came home late last weekend, but he'd tried to be nice and cut her some slack, hoping she would see him as less of a dictating older brother and more as a friend.

And where did that get me?

Right here, waiting for her to come home, wondering where she was, and what she was doing. No matter what he did, how hard he tried, he hadn't been able to earn Reagan's trust and respect. She was defiant and constantly balked at the rules, picking which ones she wanted to follow. Because following all of them was simply too much to ask.

He thought about how Celeste raised her left eyebrow when she found someone overbearing and domineering. If Reagan had a similar tell, it would be the eye roll. She constantly rolled her eyes when Grant laid out or reviewed the rules. Even a simple rundown of upcoming weekly activities earned him an eye roll.

He looked at the clock again. Eleven forty. He would have driven the three blocks to Shelby's house thirty minutes ago, but Reagan had texted around seven to say they were going to the mall, and Shelby's mom would bring her home.

Why weren't they back yet? What time did the mall even close? What on earth did girls do at the mall for four hours? It's not like Reagan had much money to spend.

At least Josh didn't give him the same headache Reagan did. But as he contemplated Josh's solitary evenings at home, concern filled Grant on his brother's behalf. Josh didn't always spend every weekend at home—sometimes he hung out with his friend, Brad. But if Brad was busy or out of town, like tonight, Josh spent all evening alone in his room.

He'd tried to get Josh to watch a movie with him, but Josh's typical response of, "No thanks," left Grant floundering. He saw so much of his lonely teenage self in his brother that he wanted to fix it, but he didn't know how.

The one thing he'd craved after his mother died when he was thirteen was his father's attention. But his dad had shut down emotionally, and Grant had lost both of his parents. He wanted to meet Reagan and Josh's need for a loving family, but he didn't know how. How did he show them he cared? He had no idea what that looked like.

Car lights flashed through the front room window, and Grant bolted from his chair. He stepped to the window and pulled back the curtain in time to see Reagan lean over the center console of a blue Mazda and lock lips with the blond boy behind the wheel.

Grant's blood turned hot, and the weight of a massive boulder settled in his gut. *Great!* It was bad enough Reagan insisted on breaking all the rules, but she was doing it with a guy. He was not ready to deal with that issue yet. His moment of weakness today when

43

Celeste asked about his wife came flooding back to him. He hated dealing with these conflicts alone.

The kiss was brief—thank goodness—and before he knew it, Reagan climbed from the car.

He dropped back into the recliner, reminding himself to be calm.

Reagan came through the front door and closed it softly behind her. She froze when she saw him sitting there.

He made a show of looking at the clock. He kept his voice as even as he could, despite his inner turmoil. "Have a seat."

Reagan gave her signature eye roll. "I'm tired. Can't we talk tomorrow?"

"You should be tired, because it's almost an hour past your curfew." Pleased with how even he'd kept his tone, he gave her a smile. Hopefully, she wouldn't think him the enemy.

Another eye roll. "I know. Don't worry, I'll go straight to bed." She stepped toward the hallway.

"*Don't worry?* You say that like I can turn it off if I want to."

Reagan spun around. "It's not like you really care about me or Josh. We both know you only moved in here so we wouldn't end up in foster care."

Grant's hands curled into fists as heat coursed through his body. How many times had they had this argument? Was Reagan trying to pick a fight? If he lost his patience and started shouting—like he usually did—she'd feel justified in rebelling even more. Tonight, he was determined not to lose his cool.

"Reagan, please sit down. We need to have a talk." He kept his voice firm, yet gentle.

Reagan dropped onto the sofa with a dramatic sigh. Instead of looking at him, she held her chin high and stared straight ahead at the family picture on the wall. He recognized her attempt at defiance—he'd seen it often enough—but he also saw a glimpse of the lost little girl in the way she wrapped her arms around herself.

He leaned forward in his seat. "I know I'm not good at expressing my feelings, but I do care about you and Josh. And when people care about you, you should be considerate of their feelings."

"I'm sorry. I didn't mean to come home late." The words sounded more like a platitude than an apology.

Was she saying what she thought he wanted to hear, hoping he'd let her off the hook? He may have done that in the past, but not this time. Tonight, he would hold his ground. He had a feeling if he didn't, the issues they discussed tonight would become much more serious.

"Shelby and I ran into some friends at the mall, and then we went over to one of their houses to hang out."

Grant tamped down the fury building inside him. "I appreciate you informing me you were going to the mall. But I'd like to know; was meeting up with friends at the mall planned?"

Reagan's eyes narrowed at the same moment her shoulders and chin rose. If she were an animal, her hackles would definitely be up with that posture.

Silence filled the room, and the boulder lodged in his midsection twisted. "Reagan, I'm trying to trust you and give you some freedom. I'm asking you to have enough respect for me to tell me the truth. Whose house did you go to?"

She dropped her eyes and picked at her fingernail polish. "Jace and Liam picked us up at the mall shortly after Shelby's mom dropped us off. They took us to their friend Aiden's house."

Grant pressed. "Was there a party at Aiden's house or just friends hanging out?" Not that one was better than the other. When she didn't answer, he asked, "Was there adult supervision there?"

"Aiden is eighteen."

The acid in his gut intensified. "That's not the kind of adult supervision I meant, and you know it. Were Aiden's parents there?"

Reagan shook her head.

He pinched the bridge of his nose, trying to stave off the headache that always hit when he and Reagan butted heads. He sucked in a deep breath, partially to calm himself and partially to see if he could detect the odor of alcohol on Reagan who sat a few feet away. He couldn't smell any, but that meant nothing.

"Was there alcohol there?"

Reagan rolled her eyes, then glared at him. He held her gaze, letting her know he expected an answer. He waited her out.

"A few of the guys were drinking beer, but I didn't have any, I swear. And I never plan to. I think it smells disgusting."

Her response pleased Grant. He hoped her attitude stayed that way.

"Is Jace the guy who brought you home?" When she gave a quick nod, he asked. "Did he have anything to drink?"

"Only one beer, but it was hours ago."

Grant didn't know whether to pummel the kid for taking his sister to a party with underage drinking or respect the fact that even though Jace was underage, he'd limited himself to one beer and had had nothing to drink for some time before driving Reagan home. Grant ground his teeth together, compounding his headache.

"How old is Jace?"

Silence filled the room as Reagan again picked at her nails. When she didn't immediately answer his question, the muscles between Grant's shoulder blades knotted, sending tension up his neck.

"Seventeen." It was said so quietly he wondered if he'd heard her right.

Two years didn't sound like a big deal, but Reagan was only fifteen. She was too young to have a boyfriend. He fought to keep his voice even when he spoke again. "Where did you meet him?"

"I met him a couple weeks ago when Shelby and I went to the football game with Mason."

"Is he a friend of Mason's?" If that was the case, Grant wouldn't worry so much. As far as he knew, Shelby's older brother, Mason, was a good kid.

"Not really."

"What's that supposed to mean?"

Reagan sighed, but her shoulders hitched up. "Mason knows Jace, but they don't hang out together."

Too bad. He shouldn't judge Jace by whether he was friends with Mason, but Grant couldn't help thinking about the guys he'd known in high school who'd dated younger girls. They only had one thing on their minds, and the thought that Jace had targeted Reagan for that reason made Grant want to vomit.

He rubbed his tired eyes. "I saw you kiss Jace in the car. Have you... Have you done more—"

Reagan sprang to her feet. "No. But even if I had, it's none of your business!"

Grant got to his feet too, his patience reaching the breaking point. "It's my responsibility to keep you safe, Reagan. You're too young to be hanging out with seniors. Guys like Jace only have one thing on their mind. They keep pressuring young girls until they wear them down enough to get what they want." He didn't mean to raise his voice, but his concern for Reagan had him practically shouting.

"Jace isn't like that. He cares about me. He would never pressure me to do something I didn't want to do."

Grant hoped she was right, especially the part about her not wanting... A shudder rippled through him—he couldn't even think about that word and his little sister in the same sentence. Desperate to protect her, he lashed out. "You've broken curfew three times now. You're grounded."

"What? I told you the truth! I'm showing you respect!" Reagan's voice was every bit as loud as his, if not louder.

They'd probably end up waking up Josh. It wouldn't be the first time.

"If you respected me, you would have come home on time, and you would have answered my texts. And you never would have gone to a party without my permission."

"If I had asked for permission, you never would have given it."

"Da—" Grant bit off the swear word. "Darn right I wouldn't have. You shouldn't be hanging out with older boys who are drinking. Period."

"It doesn't matter one bit to you that they offered me a beer and I chose not to take it, does it? All you care about is everything I've done wrong. I'm so sick of your rules. You're not my dad, so stop trying to act like it." Reagan stormed out of the room and headed to the stairs.

"Reagan." He followed her.

She stopped on the fourth step and turned and glared at him.

"I mean it; you're grounded. For two weeks. And I need your cell phone. You can have it back in a day or two. I'm going to download an app that allows me to track your location and monitor your communications."

"You're going to spy on me with my own phone?" she screamed.

If Josh wasn't awake before, he definitely was now.

"Yes, until you learn to respect and follow the rules. If you can't make better choices, then I'm going to help you." He paused for a moment before adding, "I could take your phone away altogether, if you'd rather." He held out his hand, letting her know he was serious.

"Ugh. I hate you! And I hate it here! I can't wait until I'm eighteen." She pulled her phone from her back pocket and threw it at him.

It sailed over his head, but he caught it before it hit the wall behind him. The impact stung his hand.

Reagan stomped the rest of the way up the stairs and slammed her door, punctuating the drama with a scream.

Groaning, Grant turned and dropped onto the second step and set Reagan's cell phone beside him. He propped his elbows on his knees and buried his face in his hands.

So much for staying in control and not shouting.

CHAPTER 6

*G*rant pushed away his empty salad container and looked down the table at Celeste, who stared at him with a mischievous smile. Her sandwich was only half gone, but she seemed to have lost interest in her food.

"It's question time, isn't it?" He made a show of grimacing, but it was fake. He'd enjoyed getting to know her a little more each day over the past two weeks.

Not just the artistic genius, who had amazing ideas and no limit to her creativity, but the beautiful woman who loved old musicals and yoga pants. Not that she wore them to work—that just happened to be her favorite piece of clothing. She always dressed professionally for work in a fitted skirt or slacks—usually in black, charcoal, or navy—and a pretty blouse in jewel-tone colors that complimented her complexion and dark hair. She always looked amazing, but he'd love to see her in yoga pants.

She nodded. "Do you want to go first or should I?" Before he could answer, she rushed on. "I should warn you that I want to ask a more personal question today."

A personal question?

He'd made it clear on Monday, after the sudden feelings of being overwhelmed had assaulted him last Friday and his resulting moment of weakness, that there would be no more personal questions. Because when he'd told Celeste he wished he had a wife at home, he found it all too easy to imagine her as his wife.

He'd been half tempted to eat lunch somewhere else this week, but he didn't want to offend her. Besides, that would have meant he would have to eat with some of his male colleagues who enjoyed making inappropriate comments concerning his and Celeste's working relationship. Eating here alone with her added fuel to their fire, but he'd rather be with her than with them.

For that reason alone, he really should eat lunch anywhere else but here. With her.

He worked hard to maintain a level of professionalism between them. It wasn't easy, especially after that first day when he'd wanted to hold her in his arms to comfort her and promise to never let another man hurt her again. Anyone looking through the glass wall that separated the conference room from the offices on this floor could never fault him or Celeste. They were rarely within touching distance of each other and never for longer than necessary.

They took their work seriously and made a great team. They'd accomplished a lot in the two short weeks they'd been working together. She complimented him perfectly, always thinking of the things he overlooked. Once he'd seen that her talents extended beyond the visual arts, he'd felt bad for saying she was the artist, and he was the writer that first day. She was every bit as skilled with words as he was.

The problem was, anytime he leaned over her shoulder to examine her sketches or something on her computer, he'd notice things—like the fact that her hair was actually dark brown, not black, or the way her perfume sent all thoughts of professionalism racing from his mind. The scent made him want to whisk her away to the beach where they could forget they needed to maintain a professional relationship.

His temperature had skyrocketed that first day as he pictured Celeste in a swimsuit. So, he'd promptly moved his laptop to the other end of the table and had worked from there ever since, communicating with her from eight feet away.

Would a more personal question disrupt their successful working relationship? Because Grant had enough difficulty keeping things professional. He didn't want to feel anything more for her than the attraction he already fought.

Knowing she wouldn't let it go, and hoping he wouldn't regret it, he said, "You ask your question first." He raised a finger as she opened her mouth to speak. "But I reserve the right to pass if it's too personal."

Celeste's brow creased as she frowned. "Fine. Then I reserve the same right." When he nodded, she asked, "Why do you always sit at the other end of the table?"

Yep. Too personal.

Refusing to answer might look like an admission of guilt. She'd probably guess he couldn't bear being close to her. At the very least, his refusal to answer would only make her more curious. But he couldn't tell her the smell of her perfume filled his mind with very unprofessional thoughts and being close to her made him want to pull her into his arms and kiss her.

"Admit it. You're avoiding me." There was a challenge in her eyes.

His first instinct was to deny it, but yesterday when she'd arrived before him and set up her laptop near the end where he usually worked, he'd gone to the opposite end of the table. He'd felt bad when a look of hurt had crossed her face, but he hadn't relented.

Grant scrambled for an answer that wasn't the truth and wouldn't sound stupid. He'd already tried to make it sound like he didn't want to cramp her creative space, and he'd also said he was claustrophobic and needed plenty of elbow room. Both times, her left eyebrow had risen, calling him on his lies.

Dang, he loved it when she did that.

Focus.

He bolted to his feet and walked to the window, shoving his hands into his pockets. It was a lame question to refuse to answer, but he couldn't think of a single answer that either wouldn't hurt her feelings or give away his attraction to her.

When the silence stretched between them, he looked at her over his shoulder. Her eyes were downcast, but that didn't hide the disappointment and hurt on her face.

"Let me guess, you're going to pass?"

Grant felt like a jerk. Would she accept a half-truth and let it go? *It's worth a try.*

He turned and smiled. Working hard to inject the right amount of joviality into his words, he said, "I'd like to refuse because the question is much too personal and more than a little embarrassing." He paused as though dreading having to divulge a secret. "If you must know, Miss Hightower, it's your perfume. It reminds me of a tropical island and every time I smell it, I want to be somewhere other than work." He bit his tongue before admitting, *I find it, and you, very distracting.* "I can't believe you're forcing me to admit that I daydream about the beach while I'm at work."

He watched to see if her left eyebrow would shoot up. It only rose a fraction. She didn't totally buy it, but she accepted his explanation. He let out the breath he hadn't realized he'd been holding, only to suck it back in again when she spoke.

"What a relief. I thought you hated working with me."

He stepped closer to her, bringing himself within arm's reach. "Celeste, that's not it at all. I love working with you. You're intelligent, talented, and witty. I..." He raked his fingers through his hair as he bit back the words he wanted to say. Words that weren't appropriate for a working relationship. "We need to keep this..." He waved his hand back and forth between them. "This friendship strictly professional."

A look of disappointment crossed her face before she nodded. "You're right. Maybe we should do away with the questions."

"No." Then, because he felt like his hasty response might give away how he felt, he said, "I mean, it's good to get to know each other, right? On a professional level, anyway." He shouldn't, but he really wanted to know more about Celeste Hightower.

I must be a glutton for punishment.

Her lips turned up in that mischievous smile again, and his heart skipped a beat. "I hoped you'd say that, because I have a list of questions a mile long I can't wait to ask you."

～

"I WALKED RIGHT INTO THAT, didn't I?" Grant groaned.

"Yep." Celeste tried to tone down the smile that came unbidden. Grant admitting her perfume made him think of tropical islands meant he'd noticed her perfume. If he'd noticed the subtle scent, maybe, just maybe, he'd noticed more than her perfume.

It was horrible to think like that since they needed to keep their relationship professional. He was right of course. He was right about most things. It made sense for him to sit as far away from a female coworker as possible, for propriety's sake. Especially with the wall of glass that gave everyone on the other side a view of them.

She appreciated hearing that he thought her brilliant and witty, though. And knowing he liked her perfume gave her ego a massive boost.

"So, I guess it's my turn to ask you a question." Grant's words wiped the smile off her face. He sat two chairs away and faced her, his gaze boring into hers. He often did this—looked like he was giving something serious thought—when he was obviously trying to rile her.

It usually worked.

"What's in it for you?" he said.

"Excuse me?"

"Our first day working together, you showed up with a notepad full of notes and dozens of sketches that must have taken you all weekend to draw. So, what were you trying to prove? What's at stake for you?"

Celeste felt the blood drain from her face. Grant had no idea how weighted that question was to her. And how personal a truthful answer would be.

She leaned back in her chair, feigning a carefree posture. "Would you believe I have no social life and had nothing better to do?" Unfortunately, that was the truth.

"Nope. Try again."

She shrugged. "It must be the overachiever in me."

His gaze narrowed on her face. "I believe you're an overachiever, but I also believe there's a reason for it. Why do you feel the need to prove yourself so spectacularly?"

She folded her arms and chewed on the inside of her cheek. If she told him the truth, she'd be sharing with him a lot more than her need to prove herself. Could she go there with a coworker? A coworker determined to keep their relationship professional.

Looking him square in the eye, she said, "Because failure isn't an option."

Grant's eyes widened.

Had she said the words with too much vehemence?

"Why?" he asked.

"Why what?"

"Being an overachiever myself, I hate to fail as much as the next person. But you have a stronger conviction concerning failure than anyone I know. I'd like to understand why you fear failure."

I'd like to understand.

The sincerity in his words brought tears to Celeste's eyes, and she looked away. How many times had her father *demanded* to know what she was thinking or why she'd done the things she had? And when she'd explained, he never understood. Because it wasn't what he wanted to hear. It wasn't what he wanted for her.

"Hey. Are you okay?" Grant pushed the chair separating them back and closed the distance between them.

She swiped at the single tear that had escaped onto her cheek and gave him a weak smile. "Is it too late for me to pass on the question?"

"Hey, I won't force you to answer, because I have a feeling someone has forced you to do too many things you didn't want to do. But like you said last week, maybe these wounds haven't healed. Maybe you need to talk about them."

Celeste looked at the glass wall that separated them from the cubicles. Most of their coworkers had returned to their desks. "Maybe, but this isn't the time or the place."

His gaze followed hers, then he looked at his watch. "We have ten minutes left on our lunch break. Take a walk with me." He stood and held out his hand.

Her left eyebrow arched as she regarded his long, strong fingers. She found his bossiness attractive because she realized he was nothing like her father. Grant's bossiness was him being decisive, not controlling. That he was willing to push professional boundaries to help her work through her issues was sweet, but it wasn't a good idea.

He dropped his hand. "Sorry, I didn't mean to be demanding."

"It's not that. Ten minutes is not near long enough to... to discuss... my problems."

"So, we'll take an extra-long lunch break today."

Celeste gave him a weak grin. "Since when do you break the rules?"

"Since my *friend* needs someone to talk to."

The emphasis he placed on friend warmed her heart, and she heard herself say, "Okay."

Celeste tugged her jacket tighter around herself as she strolled along the path that circled the park across the street from 3D Media, wondering why she'd come out here.

She'd tried to change her mind about coming out here, but Grant had worn her down. He'd determined if they left the conference room at different times, and they both went to the restroom before going outside, no one would be any wiser. But that didn't change the fact that they should maintain a professional relationship.

She sucked in a deep breath. The air smelled clean for a change. The early spring sunshine carried just enough warmth to be pleasant. The birds must agree, because their songs filled the park as they flitted from bush to tree and back again.

Rapid footsteps approached from behind, and a smile tugged at her lips. In the few minutes she'd waited for Grant to catch up to her, she'd decided she had only agreed to come out here because she wanted to see how long she could make serious, strait-laced, obsessive, Grant stay away from the office.

If she wanted to keep him out here very long, she'd have to tell him the entire story, but she wasn't sure she wanted to do that.

"Hey," he said, slightly breathless, as he slowed his pace to match hers.

Celeste chuckled. "Did you run to catch up to me?"

"No, but I'm so out of shape even walking fast gets my heart rate up. I'm afraid I've let myself go this past year since chaos took over my life."

Did chaos taking over his life have something to do with his brother and sister moving in with him? Or something else entirely? Ever since last Friday, she'd wished she could talk with him about whatever he was dealing with at home, but he'd made it clear personal stuff was off limits.

"So..." he said when she didn't speak. "Are we going to talk?"

She rolled her eyes and said in a mocking tone, "I'm breaking the rules here, Celeste, so hurry and bare your soul so I can get back to work before anyone notices how long I've been gone."

Grant stopped walking.

Celeste stopped too and turned to look at him. The hurt on his face tightened her chest.

"Just because I take my job seriously, doesn't mean I don't know how to be a friend."

"You're right. I'm sorry. I didn't realize how hard it would be to talk about this."

He motioned to a bench tucked away in the trees twenty feet ahead of them. "Let's sit, and you can take your time deciding what you want to tell me."

She let him lead her to the bench. Like a gentleman, he waited for her to sit first before sitting beside her. What surprised her was how close he sat. She could feel the warmth emanating off him. And the smell of his cologne warmed her in a different way.

I shouldn't feel this attraction for my coworker.

Focusing on the things she wanted to say, she tried to block out how distracting his nearness was. She cleared her throat. "My mom and dad were both successful attorneys. They planned to have three or four kids, but she could never get pregnant again after I was born. So my dad hung all his hopes on me. He planned my life out for me. Valedictorian, law school, an internship in his office, and eventually, I'd become a partner. We'd rule the courtroom together."

"I've heard of Burkhart, Hightower, and Aldridge. So that's your father?"

Nodding, she plucked a leaf off a nearby bush and broke it into small pieces, letting them fall at her feet. She kept her eyes glued to the decimated leaf when she spoke again. "My mom was a good buffer, telling me I could be anything I wanted." Her throat tightened, and she swallowed the tears that always accompanied thoughts of her mom. "But when I was thirteen, she was killed in a car accident."

Grant's sharp intake of breath brought her head up. "I'm so sorry, Celeste. I know how painful that must have been."

Her left eyebrow inched up of its own accord. His words sounded so sincere, but no one really understood what she'd gone through. Then she saw the sheen of tears in his eyes. And with the tears, she saw all the pain she'd experienced when she lost her mother.

He cleared his throat. "I lost my mother to cancer when I was twelve."

Celeste's throat clogged again, preventing her from speaking. Instead, she reached over and clasped his hand. He turned his palm up and sandwiched her hand between both of his. The tightness of their grip expressed all the things they couldn't say. They remained silent for several long moments, sharing their grief and comforting each other.

Grant found his voice first. "I didn't realize we had so much in common." She nodded, and he continued. "I take it with your mom no longer there to act as a buffer, your dad became more demanding and abusive."

"He wasn't abusive per se, but he was very strict and overprotective. Almost to the point of smothering me. I wasn't allowed to go to any ball games or after school activities. Parties were out of the question. He expected certain behavior, and if I didn't obey, there were always sharp consequences. Most of the time, it was easier to go along with his demands than deal with the consequences." She smiled. "Other times... my rebellious streak came out, and I did what I wanted despite the ramifications."

He chuckled. "Was it worth it?"

She looked down at their joined hands. His warm, strong fingers still laced with hers felt so good, but this was wrong.

She laughed and pulled her hand from his on the pretext of tucking her hair behind her ear.

"It was definitely worth it. The biggest conflict came when I refused to fill out applications for law school. Naturally, he wanted me to go to Yale, his alma mater, but he was willing to make a concession if I really wanted to go to Harvard. He refused to listen when I told him I didn't want to go to law school, period. He called my desires to pursue a career in art foolish." The familiar tightening in her chest and the churning she got in her stomach any time she'd argued with her father settled in. If talking about her father could still make her feel like this, then she hadn't dealt with that baggage.

Because nothing had changed. He still saw her as an incompetent child destined to fail, no matter what she did.

"My father always expected perfection. Perfect attendance, perfect grades, a spotless house. Almost daily, I heard him say, *Failure isn't an option.* The day I went to apply for the art program at the Portland Community College..." She swallowed hard at the lump that filled her throat again. "He told me if I walked out that door, not to bother ever coming back."

Grant put a comforting hand on her shoulder. "I'm sorry, Celeste."

She poured every ounce of her pride into her posture and gave him a tight smile. "I moved in with my friend Amy—into her dinky studio apartment—and started school. *Failure isn't an option* is now my mantra because I refuse to prove him right. He's convinced that because I didn't do things his way and chose a career in art instead of law that I'll always be a failure."

"Have you seen him since the day you left?"

"In the last seven years? Twice. The first time, about three months after I left home, he came to the copy center where I worked and told me I could come back home if I would admit I was wrong. He said he could probably pull some strings and get me into Stanford so I could stay on the west coast."

Grant snorted. "Wow. Now I see where you get your stubbornness from."

"Hey!" She punched his shoulder. A smile covered her face when he rubbed the muscle.

"What about the second time?"

"I didn't actually talk to him that time, but I'm certain I saw him at my college graduation. My friend, Amy, swears she saw him too, so I know it wasn't a figment of my imagination."

"It goes to show he cares about you, even if he has no idea how to show it."

"Maybe, but it feels like he's lurking around the corner waiting for me to fail so he can swoop in and say *I told you so*."

They lapsed into silence for a long moment, then Grant said, "And I thought I had it bad after my mom died."

"What happened with you?"

He took a deep breath. "The opposite. I was an only child also, and after my mom died, my dad checked out emotionally. He buried himself in his work." He gave a heavy shrug. "He made sure all my physical needs were met. Kept up with my schooling enough to make sure I wasn't failing. However, I think that can be attributed more to effort on my teachers' part than his. Sometimes, we'd go weeks without speaking more than a handful of words to each other."

"Yeah, I'm not sure which is worse—being smothered or ignored," Celeste said, and Grant nodded agreement. "It's amazing you turned out so good." When he looked at her with raised eyebrows, she clarified. "Most teenagers in situations like yours turn to drugs and gangs. But you didn't."

"Well, I didn't get perfect grades by any means, but the day before my mom... died, she made me promise to keep going to church. And I did, even when my father was too deep in his grief to accompany me."

"Wish I could say the same. Church attendance was one of those things my father was adamant about. So, after I moved out, I stopped going. I've thought about going again the past few years, but I didn't want to go alone, and my friend Amy often works on Sundays."

"I promised my mom I would make her proud, and I think my church attendance helped me do that."

Celeste leaned over and bumped his shoulder with hers. "You're about to become a VP. I think she'd be very proud."

"I'd like to think so." He leaned toward her, and his shoulders continued to press against hers.

The warmth seeping through her jacket compounded her attraction for this man she had so many things in common with.

Life isn't fair!

Why was it when she finally found a man she could be herself with —a man that made her feel whole—he was off limits?

"What about your dad? Did he ever come around?"

Grant tensed. The action pulled his shoulder away from hers, filling her with both relief and disappointment.

CHAPTER 7

*T*ension coiled in Grant's body at Celeste's question. He
shifted, pulling his shoulder away from hers. Instantly, he
regretted the action.

The warmth and softness of her touch calmed something inside
him—an unrest that had been a part of him for a long time. So long he
couldn't remember ever living without it. Except maybe before his
mom got sick.

He didn't want to talk about his dad. About how Evan Foster had
learned to love again, but he still hadn't cared about his son.

He looked at Celeste. Her beautiful brown eyes stared at him full
of patience and trust. She'd trusted him with her painful past. Could
he trust her with his?

Yes. The answer whispered through the breeze that stirred her
hair, blowing a strand across her face. Without thinking, he reached
up and smoothed the strand back, tucking it behind her ear.

He shouldn't touch her like this. It made it that much harder to
maintain his professionalism. But her proximity and the things she'd
shared with him had already nearly crumbled his resolve to keep her
at arm's length.

Because he desperately wanted to pull her into his arms and hold her until she believed in herself and realized she didn't need to prove anything to anyone.

He stretched out his legs and rubbed his hands on his thighs. "My dad..." the words croaked out. Heat filled his face. He hadn't squeaked that badly since he'd passed up puberty. He cleared his throat and tried again. "Two years after my mom passed away, one of my dad's coworkers convinced him to go to counseling to help him with his grief. It only took four months for him to get over my mom after he started seeing the counselor and another three to propose to her. They got married one week before my birthday. He was on his honeymoon in Hawaii when I turned fifteen. They brought me home a couple souvenirs, but he never told me Happy Birthday. Never apologized for missing it."

Celeste's hand found his again, and he hung on as pain pierced his chest—as razor-sharp and barbed as he'd felt on his fifteenth birthday. He sucked in a sharp breath. Apparently, he and Celeste had one more thing in common: he obviously hadn't dealt with his Daddy issues either.

"He seemed happy, so I tried to be happy for him. Things improved a little, but I think it was because Catharine encouraged him to make the effort. But not much changed between us. He simply wasn't there during the most difficult time of my life, and what little effort he put out wasn't enough to form a real relationship."

"I'm so sorry, Grant."

"My sister, Reagan, was born two days before I turned sixteen. My birthday got overlooked with the excitement of bringing a new baby home from the hospital. Then two years later—one month after I turned eighteen—my little brother, Joshua, was born. That was the day I moved out. Not because I didn't want to be around my family anymore, but I'd heard my dad and stepmom talking, wishing they had another bedroom for the baby. So they wouldn't have to put both of the little ones together." He shrugged. "Besides, it was time for me to be on my own."

"Did you ever go back home?"

"To visit, yes. Funny thing was, they ended up moving to a new, bigger house a year after I moved out. Catharine, my stepmother, really was nice, and I wanted to have a relationship with my little sister and brother, but they were so much younger than me. We never got very close." He shoved a hand into his hair as regret swamped him.

"This is the brother and sister who are living with you?"

He read the hesitation in Celeste's face as she asked the question. With the way he'd shut her down so quickly last week when he'd been overwhelmed by his responsibilities, he didn't blame her. He stroked the back of her hand to let her know it was okay. Since the first time he touched her a few minutes ago, he couldn't bear to stop. He loved the contact with her.

I'm in so much trouble. He was falling hard for this dark-haired beauty.

He sucked in a deep breath. "Yes. My dad and Catharine died in a car accident almost a year ago. Reagan and Josh didn't have any other relatives except a great-aunt who lives in a nursing home. If I hadn't agreed to be their guardian, they would have been put into foster care."

"I can't imagine how difficult that must have been for all three of you."

Grant tried to infuse some humor into his voice. "It's been rough, but no one's killed anybody yet, so I guess that's a good thing."

Judging by the creases in Celeste's forehead, he'd failed. At the humor thing. *Who am I kidding? I've failed at being a parent too. Miserably.*

"How have Reagan and Josh handled the death of their parents?"

"About like you'd expect. I made sure they got some counseling, but..." He raked his right hand through his hair again while keeping hold of Celeste's hand in his left. He wasn't ready to release it yet. "Dealing with the grief is only a small part of the challenges they face. I sold my condo and moved into my dad's house, so they wouldn't lose that too, but..."

"But what?" When he didn't answer right away, she squeezed his hand. "You can tell me, Grant. I've been there, remember?"

"Reagan is so angry all the time. She's always shouting and slamming doors. I can't do anything right by her. And she ignores all the rules—taking off without permission and breaking curfew. And then there's Josh..." The frustration in his voice turned to desperation. "He hardly talks to me, or anyone for that matter. He stays shut up in his room most of the time. Doesn't do his homework. Maybe if I'd really gotten to know them before Dad and Catharine died, things wouldn't be so hard now." He swallowed the emotion tightening his throat. "But I have no idea how to be a parent. I don't know how to reach them. I don't know how to show them I care. I'm not sure what that even looks like."

Celeste pulled her hand from his, and he missed her touch immediately.

She angled her body toward him and put her hands on his shoulders, forcing him to face her.

He welcomed the contact.

"Yes, you do. Do you know why I got emotional back at the office?"

He shook his head.

"You told me you wanted to understand why I was afraid to fail. My overbearing, domineering father never once wanted to understand how I was feeling or what I wanted."

"It's different with you," he whispered.

"Why?"

His mouth went dry. He couldn't tell her she was easy to read because he was so attracted to her.

She put her palm on his cheek and a sense of warmth and comfort swept through him, ramping up the attraction that consumed him.

"Can we be friends?"

He frowned. "We are."

"No, I mean real friends. Outside of work."

There was nothing Grant wanted more. He needed a friend. He'd let most of his close friendships lapse over the past year. And now, with Mr. Hardman on vacation, Grant needed someone to talk to. Someone to tell him he wasn't completely screwing up.

But if he spent time with Celeste outside of work, it would only be a matter of time until he ruined their professional relationship. Because even though he'd always prided himself on his self-control, he felt it slip every time he was near Celeste. Like a rubber band stretched beyond its limit. At some point, he would snap. And he couldn't afford to ruin their working relationship.

He stood up and stepped away, but she was right beside him, her shoulder pressed to his arm. "I want to help you, Grant. I want you to be able to pick up the phone and call me when you're having a rough day. I'll be there for you, day or night. And I want to meet Reagan and Josh. I'm not some kind of grief expert, but I know what they are going through, and I know they need a friend as much as you do."

"I can't let you—" He cut his words off because he was afraid of letting her come to mean any more to him than she already did.

She must have misinterpreted his words because a look of hurt crossed her face again. "You can't let me be a part of your personal life, because I might mess it up, is that it?"

He bit back the swear word that came to his lips. He wasn't at work, so it shouldn't matter, but as a rule, he tried not to swear in front of women. He took her by the shoulders this time.

"No, that's not it at all. I don't doubt you'd be an amazing friend. But I can't be around you all the time because I'm so da—" he bit back another cuss word. This woman brought out such powerful emotions in him. "I'm so dang attracted to you. And I can't afford to screw up our working relationship by getting emotionally involved with you."

Celeste's eyes widened, and he wished the ground would open and swallow him. Then she smiled. A full, gorgeous smile that pulled his gaze to her mouth.

"Are you saying you find more than my perfume distracting?"

Grant groaned and stifled the urge to kiss that smile off her face by dropping his hands and stepping away.

"Does it help to know I'm attracted to you too?"

He looked back at her as warmth swelled in him. Her smile still taunted him.

"No," he growled.

"Listen, we have an excellent system at work for keeping things professional. Couldn't we find a way to be friends outside of work? Maybe set rules to keep things platonic?"

He let out a deep sigh. "I need a friend, Celeste. I'd love to have someone to talk to, but when I look at you, friendship is the farthest thing from my mind." Then, because he wasn't nearly as strong a man as he would like to think, he turned back to her and cupped her face in his hands. His voice came out a husky whisper when he spoke again. "All I can think about is doing this." He lowered his lips to hers.

He knew kissing her beautiful lips would feel amazing, but he was completely unprepared for the intensity of the spark that ignited in him. Warmth shot through his veins. A warmth so comforting and calming to the unrest deep inside him that he never wanted to stop kissing Celeste.

Her arms snaked around his waist, and her lips parted, begging him to deepen the kiss. He slid his hands into her hair and obliged. He needed her to push him away, maybe even slap him, so he'd remember why this wasn't a good idea. Because, at the moment, he couldn't think of a single reason he shouldn't kiss Celeste for the rest of his life.

He continued to caress her lips with his for another long, spectacular moment before wrenching his mouth from hers with a groan. Loathe to let her go, knowing he would miss the connection to her, he held her tight and pressed his cheek to her temple.

"I shouldn't have done that." His words were husky and breathless.

"No, you shouldn't have." Her voice was as breathless as his. "And I shouldn't tell you how glad I am you did or how much I enjoyed it."

A smile pushed its way past his guilt. "No, you shouldn't." He let out a heavy sigh. "A workplace romance is a bad idea."

"I know. They rarely work out. I mean, look at what happened between Ian and Olivia last year."

"Right. When it doesn't work out people talk, things become uncomfortable, and everyone is miserable." He pulled away enough to look into her eyes. "Please tell me I haven't ruined everything. I still need you." And then, because he saw in her eyes the same desire that burned in him, he added, "On the team, I mean. And I need you as a friend, but I'm afraid I've screwed that up too."

She shook her head as she pulled away.

He grabbed her hands to keep from losing the connection he felt with her.

She smiled. "We can admit we're attracted to one another—"

"And there is an undeniable spark between us," he added.

She nodded. "But we can return to work and keep it strictly professional, like we've done for the past two weeks."

He nodded his agreement. They could do this. They both knew a work-place romance wasn't a good idea, especially with how important this project was. "It won't be easy, but we can do this. Strictly professional."

"We can do this," she echoed. "What happens when this project ends?"

He traced the curve of her jaw with his finger. "This is probably the wrong answer, but I'd like to see where this leads."

"Me too," came her breathy whisper. "It's going to be a long six months."

It took every ounce of his self-control to keep from kissing her again. "Yep."

"Can we be friends, though?"

He should say no, but he couldn't. Knowing she wanted a relationship with him, even if it wasn't the relationship they both desired, meant a lot to Grant. It meant that she cared about him as much as he cared about her. For someone who'd spent most of his life feeling unloved, it meant the world to him.

He turned and tugged her down the path, still gripping her right hand. "We need to keep it platonic. As I demonstrated today, I'm not strong enough to withstand temptation if we aren't both working to avoid it."

"Right. I'll be the strong one when you're feeling weak, and you can be the strong one when I'm weak."

Grant smiled, but his voice dropped as he said, "I sure hope you can carry your weight."

~

CELESTE FORCED her eyes to remain on her laptop when Grant returned to the conference room. She'd been here for five minutes already, thanks to his insistence they return separately. She'd been fighting a smile ever since.

The memory of his lips on hers and his reluctance to release her hand as they left the park were already cherished memories. His sigh had been as heavy as hers when he gave her hand one last squeeze before letting her fingers slip from his as they left the cover of the trees.

It killed her knowing their attraction was mutual, but they couldn't act on it. She agreed with Grant—an office romance was a terrible idea. But she was realistic enough to know not acting on their feelings wouldn't make them go away. She feared no matter how platonic they kept things, inside and outside the office, she was falling for Grant Foster. Hard.

Would they finally be able to admit their feelings when this project was complete? Hope filled her chest, only to be dashed by the realization that six months was a long time to deny the attraction that had developed in the past two weeks.

An invitation from Grant to a shared document popped up in her email. She clicked on the link. Two documents opened: the first titled **Rules for Work**, and the second, **Rules for a Platonic Friendship**.

Of course, the man who always followed the rules—until this afternoon—wanted a clear, concise plan. He was right though; if they were going to keep things platonic, they couldn't overstep the bounds, ever.

She smiled, tilting her head enough to peek at him out of the corner of her eye.

"Don't look at me like that," he said, lips barely moving despite his back being to the door.

"Like what?"

"Like you want to take another walk to the park."

She bit back a giggle. She wanted to take another walk alright.

With him. Grant had done a one-eighty during their extra-long lunch break. As much as she loved it, things couldn't stay this way. Not if they were going to maintain the professionalism needed to complete this project.

She typed the first rule on the Rules for Work document: **No Flirting!**

"Right, sorry," came his quiet reply from the other end of the table.

They were quiet for some time, taking turns adding rules to the lists. The Rules for Work page filled up quickly. They both knew the appropriate behavior for the workplace and had no problem writing it down.

Celeste couldn't hide her shock when he added: **No doing that eyebrow thing!**

"What? Why?" Her words came out louder than she'd intended.

"Sh..." He glanced over his shoulder at the open door then typed something on his computer.

A message from Grant popped up on her screen via their inter-office messaging app: *Because it's so stinking cute, it's distracting!*

Biting back a smile, she typed: *Fine!* Then she added: **No being overbearing and domineering!** to the work document.

Grant messaged: *Why?*

Celeste: *Same reason.*

Grant: *Really? I don't remind you of your father when I do it?*

Celeste: *You might if you could actually pull off a stern look. You look kinda sexy when you do it.*

A poorly disguised chuckle rose from the other end of the table before Grant squelched it. He typed again: *Stop flirting!*

Celeste: *Who's flirting? I was simply stating the truth in a non-teasing way.*

Grant let out an audible sigh before typing: *This isn't going to work.*

Celeste: *Sure it will. Let's just finish the lists and get back to work.*

Grant: *Okay, but don't be offended if I suddenly decide to work in my office where there are fewer distractions.*

Celeste: *You took the words right out of my mouth.*

She glanced at him. His eyes, full of longing, were on her. All the emotion and desire she'd felt while in his arms flooded over her, making her want to return to the park. She let him see the longing in her own eyes for a moment before turning back to her computer. Gripping the arms of her chair, she fought the urge to gather up her laptop and return to her regular office.

If she left, people would wonder why. Those who knew her the best wouldn't think much of it, since they knew she liked solidarity, but others would think there was something wrong between her and Grant. People already speculated about them enough; walking out would add fuel to their fire.

Focusing on the task at hand, she clicked on the **Rules for a Platonic Friendship** document and added the first rule: **No holding hands!**

Almost immediately he added: **No Kissing!**

Celeste: **No Touching, Period!**

In the message box from Grant: *Right.*

Celeste had half expected him to point out how redundant the rules were, but his single-word response reminded her that the more specific the rules, the better chance they had of keeping things professional.

GRANT DID his best to stay focused while he and Celeste spent the better part of an hour making an exhaustive list of rules for their platonic friendship. Rules that included specifics such as **No late-night phone calls** (unless it's an emergency) and **No hanging out together** (unless other people are around).

They had also agreed on **No watching movies alone together** (especially not romantic movies) and of course they **Can't sit by each other** while they watched, because that would be too intimate.

She'd added: **We each pay our own way when we go out somewhere**, and he'd amended it with: **No going out alone** (since it would be too much like a date).

He sure hoped he could remember all the rules he insisted they needed.

They gradually stopped adding rules to the list and returned to their work. A task that was much harder than he expected because he couldn't get the memory of their kiss out of his head or the desire to do it again.

Three hours later, Grant groaned and stretched when his cell phone vibrated on the table, breaking his concentration. He groaned a second time when Reagan's face popped up on the screen. He was not in the mood to deal with her right now.

Celeste looked up from her computer. Her eyebrow inching up as she gave him an are-you-going-to-answer-that look.

He pulled his gaze away from her raised eyebrow and snatched up his phone. "Hello."

"Can I hang out with Shelby this afternoon?" Grant could barely hear Regan's voice over the sound of hundreds of excited teenagers in the background eager to start their weekend.

"No, you may not. You're grounded, remember?" Feeling bad for the volume of his voice, he rotated his chair, turning his back to Celeste. He should leave the room, but he wanted his coworkers out in the cubicles to hear his conversation with Reagan even less than he wanted Celeste to hear it.

"Please, Grant. I'm trying to be respectful, like you said." He had to hand it to Reagan. She really did sound contrite. Unfortunately, he knew it was all a facade. His sister could go from sweet to screaming in a heartbeat. "I'll be home by ten, I promise."

He braced himself before answering. "No, Reagan. Grounded is grounded. It doesn't automatically lift so you can hang out with your friends on the weekend."

"But I stayed home every night this week. I did all my chores and homework every day."

Except for Reagan's sullen attitude, this past week had been much easier than most as far as she was concerned, but Grant knew he needed to stick to the rules. If he waffled, Reagan and Josh would take advantage of that and walk all over him. Especially Reagan.

"I'm sorry. I'm not lifting your grounding. You need to walk home with Josh."

"Well, what am I supposed to do all weekend?" And here came the yelling. "I'm not going to just sit around watching movies with you and Josh!"

He held the phone away from his ear. "That's your choice, but you're not hanging out with Shelby this weekend."

An expletive blasted his ear, followed by, "I hate you!" Then the line went dead.

He lowered the phone and let out a heavy sigh. Dropping his head back against his chair, he stared at the three logo designs for Armstrong Hotels that Celeste had drawn on the white board.

"That sounds like one angry, hurting girl." Celeste's quiet voice came from the other end of the table.

He looked at her. Her brown eyes were so full of compassion he was tempted to dump everything on her. He wanted to pound the table and tell her how frustrating it was to parent teenagers. No matter what he did, no matter how hard he tried, he couldn't do anything right in their eyes, especially Reagan's.

"You should have heard the fight we got into Friday night when she missed curfew, again." Grant propped his elbows on the table and rubbed his temples.

Silence filled the room for a long moment, then Celeste cleared her throat. "I know it's not my place to question your parenting methods, but maybe..."

When her voice was replaced by the tapping of her nails on the table, he looked up. She stared at him with her brow furrowed.

"Maybe what?"

"I'd like to meet your brother and sister, and I was going to suggest we all go out and do something, like bowling." She gave a half smile and shrugged. "But since Reagan's grounded... maybe I could come over and hang out. Maybe we could make homemade pizza and play games or something."

Grant wanted to jump at the chance to spend the evening with Celeste, but his mind latched onto the rules they had written, attempting to find a reason why spending time together was not a good idea. But her suggestion didn't break any of the rules. If they didn't touch or sit by each other, it should be fine. He'd make sure they didn't end up alone together.

"I don't profess to be an expert of any kind—with teenagers or with helping others through their grief—but I know what they are going through. Maybe having another adult around, besides their bossy big brother, will diffuse the situation a little."

He liked the idea of having another adult around, especially one as beautiful as Celeste. And that was the reason he should say no, because he couldn't let himself get sidetracked by her beauty. But the thought of having adult backup appealed to him.

More than it should have.

CHAPTER 8

"No!" Grant threw the pile of cards in his hand on the table as soon as the dice Celeste had rolled settled on seven.

Celeste, Reagan, and Josh all laughed.

Celeste clapped her hands. "Yes! Now maybe we can keep him from winning. How many cards do you have, Grant?"

Too many. He'd collected a lot of resource cards on that last round of Settlers of Catan and was planning on upgrading two more villages to cities. It would have given him enough points to win the game, but now he had to put half of his cards back.

"Count them out loud so we know you're not cheating," said Josh.

Surprised by the change in Josh tonight, he picked up his cards and began counting. Reagan too, for that matter. He doubted it would last after Celeste left, but he couldn't deny she had a way with kids. It had taken little effort to get Josh out of his room once he realized Grant had a beautiful guest over and she'd brought dinner.

Sort of, anyway. Celeste had volunteered to make the pizza dough and bring all the toppings. She'd assigned him to provide the soft drinks and dessert. He'd opted for easy, with ice cream sundaes.

Reagan had taken a little more coaxing to get out of her room. It helped that if she wanted to eat, she had to assemble her own pizza. By the time she'd done that, Celeste had gotten her talking about school and her friends. Reagan had surprised Grant by staying in the kitchen while the pizzas baked and stuck around to eat with them. Then Josh had talked her into playing a fast-paced card game with them by convincing her it would be more fun with four people instead of three.

They now played a different game. A game he'd been about to win until Celeste rolled a seven.

"Fourteen, fifteen, sixteen!" Everyone joined in as Grant counted his cards.

"Ouch! You need to put eight cards back," said Celeste. Though her words were probably meant to sound sympathetic, her tone was anything but.

He looked over the top of his cards at her. He'd thought sitting opposite of her at the table would be better than next to her. He figured there would be fewer chances of accidentally touching. He hadn't counted on their feet bumping against each other under the table occasionally. Celeste had finally tucked her legs under her, but every time he looked up, he saw her warm brown eyes smiling at him.

A twinkle filled her eyes now. Like the one that had been there after their kiss this afternoon.

"Come on already. Put eight cards back," said Reagan.

He pulled his gaze from Celeste and his mind away from their kiss. He hoped he didn't look as lovesick as Josh did every time he looked at her.

Keeping the cards he needed to build at least one city, he put eight of his cards back, scowling at each of his opponents in turn. He wasn't sure why, but everyone had ganged up on him. He wanted to be upset, but this was the most pleasant Reagan and Josh had acted in months, maybe even a whole year.

Reagan picked the dice Celeste pushed her way up. "Wait, Celeste, you have to move the robber."

Great. Grant watched Celeste move the robber to his stone quarry.

The one spot that would do the most damage to his chances of winning. He couldn't collect while the robber was there, and if he couldn't collect, he couldn't get the resources to build another city. To make matters worse, she got to take one of his remaining cards.

Celeste reached across the table and wiggled long slender fingers tipped with maroon nail polish. Trying to keep his gaze off her pretty face, he focused on her hand. The hand he'd held this afternoon to comfort her. The hand that had squeezed his to comfort him. The hand he'd hated to release as they walked out of the cover of the trees.

"Let her have a card." Josh smacked Grant's shoulder.

Celeste had been trying to pull a card from his hand, but he'd been gripping them so tightly as he remembered holding her hand that she hadn't been able to pull it free.

"Sorry." He relaxed his hold. The card she pulled was one of the five he needed to build his city. Releasing a groan, he scowled at her.

Her eyebrow rose as she grinned at him.

Why had he thought he could kiss her then go back to a professional, strictly platonic, relationship? Knowing she was equally attracted to him didn't help. At all.

And friendship? He wanted so much more than that.

He pulled his gaze away from her and focused on the game, doing his best to keep his edge. But Josh laid down a road and stole Grant's longest road card, taking two of his points. He put up a fight, but it was all downhill from there, and ten minutes later Josh won.

As they cleaned up the game, he could see indecision in Reagan's eyes. She was having fun, but she'd never admit it. He feared she might slip away. Then she'd hole up in her room for the rest of the night.

"Who wants dessert?" Grant stood and went to the kitchen, leaving the others to follow. He hated not being a gentleman and waiting for Celeste, but he was afraid if he treated her as anything other than a friend, he'd end up touching her and lose his control altogether.

The others joined him by the time he had the ice cream and toppings laid out. He and Celeste did the same dance they'd done while making their pizzas. If Grant stepped close, she stepped away, and when she got too close, he moved back. According to the rules, they each kept their distance from one another. But that didn't stop him from appreciating how sexy she looked in yoga pants and a baggy sweatshirt with her hair pulled up in a messy bun.

He liked how comfortable she was just being herself. Laney had always dressed to impress, even when they stayed in and watched a movie.

Yep. He liked Celeste. A lot.

He wasn't sure that was a good thing.

CELESTE'S PHONE chimed as she put the leftover pizza toppings in the fridge.

Grant: *Can I call you?*

The text caused her pulse to kick up a notch. As much as she would love to hear his voice, they had agreed on no late-night phone calls unless it was an emergency.

And this wasn't an emergency unless something went drastically wrong in the last fifteen minutes since she left his house. She looked at the clock. Ten fifty-five. They had all been having such an enjoyable time, it had been hard to call an end to the evening. She guessed Reagan and Josh were not usually this pleasant and cooperative and knew Grant hated putting an end to the pleasantness.

She'd seen her own feelings mirrored on Grant's face more than once. It made the evening both enjoyable and torturous.

Her phone chimed again as indecision warred within her.

Grant: *I know we agreed on no late-night calls but saying thank you in a text feels so inadequate.*

Celeste's thumb hovered over the keyboard, tempted to send a short, *you're welcome* in response.

Instead, she typed *yes* and hit send before she could change her mind.

Her phone rang before she made it out of the kitchen. Not wanting to appear too eager, she walked over to the couch and sat—

one leg tucked under her, the other hugged to her chest—before answering.

"Hello."

"Hey." A sigh accompanied the single word from Grant as if he thought she might not answer despite her giving him permission to call.

The deep baritone of that single word sent a shiver down her spine. She loved the sound of his voice.

"I had fun tonight."

"Thank you for everything."

They spoke at the same time, and they both chuckled.

Celeste hurried on. "I enjoyed meeting Reagan and Josh. Thank you for letting me come over."

"I'm the one who needs to thank you. I've never seen Reagan act that civil, and I'm pretty sure Josh has a crush on you."

She laughed, but when the silence stretched between them, she imagined Grant shoving his fingers through his hair as he fought the urge to admit he had a crush on her too.

A crush that she reciprocated.

He cleared his throat. "You know, I don't think I've ever seen Josh that animated. Especially not in the past year."

Unsure what to say, she remained quiet.

Grant started talking, hesitantly at first, then with more gusto, about the challenges of trying to step in as a parent of teenagers. He told her how Josh reminded him of himself after his mother died and the difficulty of reaching him.

Her heart broke for both Grant and Josh when he admitted he feared Josh might become so depressed he might try to harm himself. And she heard the words he wasn't saying. That he'd considered such a thing when he was young.

Celeste listened, her heart aching for him. She offered words of encouragement, assuring him he was doing the best he could.

"Don't give up. You'll get through to him eventually. At some point, you'll find something that'll help you click with him. He might need more counseling. At any rate, I'm here for you. I'll help you in any way I can."

"Thank you. I can't tell you what that means to me."

They talked about Josh for a few more minutes before the discussion turned to Reagan and the challenges Grant was dealing with concerning her. He told her about his sister meeting up with much older boys who drank and did who knows what with these younger girls. He shared his fears that Reagan might end up in a situation she couldn't handle. And how terrified he was of the erratic behavior hormones trigger in her.

Celeste laughed. "She probably plays it up because she knows it makes you uncomfortable."

He was quiet for a long moment. "Did you do that to your dad?"

"Absolutely. Besides the fact that I truly had less tolerance for his domineering attitude at that time of the month, I didn't hesitate to let him know I was in no mood to be dictated to. Sometimes I got weepy, but mostly I got ornery and impatient. My dad learned to recognize my moods and learned there were times it was best to leave me alone."

"Huh."

Silence followed Grant's grunt, and she laughed. "I can practically hear your mind working, trying to connect Reagan's behavior to her cycle."

"I don't track her cycle. That's too weird. But... there are certain behaviors that make it obvious when she's..." He cleared his throat, obviously uncomfortable talking about such things. "Honestly, Reagan is difficult all the time."

"She's dealing with a lot." As the clock changed to midnight, Celeste continued to talk, sharing with him the things she'd gone through as a teenage girl without a mother. How difficult it was to approach her dad about certain things, especially with as strict as he was.

"I'm an introvert, so I never rebelled too badly when it came to members of the opposite sex, but you need to be careful. If you push too hard, you may end up pushing Reagan right into this guy's arms. My friend, Amy..."

Celeste thought better about what she'd been about to say and stopped talking.

"What about your friend?"

"Nothing. I shouldn't have brought her up."

"Celeste, please." Grant's voice dropped, sending a shiver of awareness through her. "I want to get to know you better, and I'd like to know more about your friends."

"Friend," she corrected. "I really only have one friend, Amy Lawson." Sucking in a deep breath, she plunged on, hoping Amy would never hear the things she was about to say to Grant. And praying, if she ever did, that Amy would forgive her for the sake of their friendship.

"Amy's mom got pregnant with her when she was seventeen. The father split, and her mother didn't want her. She should have given Amy up for adoption, but she didn't. So Amy grew up in the lousiest of home environments, where she was neglected and ignored. I honestly think her mother was incapable of showing love. Amy moved out when she was seventeen because her mother..." Celeste's heart hurt all over again for her best friend, as she remembered how Diane Lawson had chosen her boyfriend over her daughter.

Celeste cleared her throat and used her shoulder to hold her phone to her ear while she pulled the elastic from her messy bun. She shook her hair out before continuing, "Well, I'll just say Amy was better off for getting out when she did. My point is, Amy never knew what affection felt like, so when some guy..." Celeste had a hard time hiding the disdain she felt every time she thought about Lance. "When Lance turned on the charm and showered her with attention, Amy fell for him. Hard. She doesn't see what a playboy he is."

"Maybe she'll be the reason he settles down," Grant said.

"I doubt it. He's going to Seattle for three months for a part-time gig, leaving a pregnant Amy here alone."

"Oh," Grant's quiet voice came across the line. "Okay, that really didn't make me feel any better. Did you tell me this because you think Reagan might end up like Amy? Do you think if she doesn't get healthy affection here at home, she'll be tempted to seek it elsewhere?

What if I push too hard in my attempt to show I care? Will I drive her into Jace's arms anyway?"

"Grant, I only told you about Amy because I want you to recognize that Reagan might react completely opposite of Josh. His struggle with his loss is causing him to pull away from everyone and every-thing. But Reagan's loss may cause her to go searching for a replace-ment for the relationships she lost."

"But how do I meet both of their needs? I meant it today when I said I'm not sure how to show I care. I didn't exactly get a lot of affec-tion growing up, remember?"

"I know, but you can do this."

"What makes you so sure?"

She took her time answering because her response would lead them into dangerous territory. "Because, I felt the sincerity in the affection you showed me today."

Silence filled the line.

"You mean when I... held your hand and comforted you?"

"I mean all of it. Holding my hand, kissing me, hugging me. I felt how much you cared." Celeste cringed. She hadn't intended to make her voice drop, but by the time she finished talking, her voice had a seductive quality to it.

The sharp hiss of Grant's indrawn breath reached her ear. "And this is why we need this rule of no late-night phone calls. I think we'd better end this call before I tell you how sexy you looked in your yoga pants tonight. Thank you for everything, Celeste. Good night."

When the line went dead, Celeste chuckled. She thought about how tempting it had been all evening to stand close to enough to Grant to touch him, and how challenging it had been not to let her gaze linger on the lips that had kissed hers that afternoon and wonder what the five o'clock shadow on his jaw felt like.

Yep, it was going to be a long six months.

Before hauling herself off to bed, she sent Grant a text: *Sorry I made it awkward. But I meant what I said. You can get through to Reagan and Josh. Don't give up. Don't be afraid to reach out and touch them or tell them how you feel.*

She was halfway through brushing her teeth when her phone dinged.

Grant: *You made it... something, but it wasn't awkward. My last girl-friend accused me of being emotionally stunted, so thank you for that.*

Grant was not emotionally stunted. Celeste only had to think about the things they'd shared with each other today to know that wasn't true. And when she thought about their kiss, well... there was plenty of emotion... and enough chemistry there to start a forest fire. As much as she'd love for him to kiss her again, they couldn't afford to let that happen.

~

THE SERVER HAD BARELY WALKED AWAY after taking their order before Amy turned to Celeste. "Okay, spill it."

"Spill what?" Celeste asked before taking a sip of her water.

"You know what. You smiled and got a dreamy look in your eyes when I asked you how working with Grant was going."

Yes, and Celeste had been saved by the bell—or rather the nurse who taught the childbirth class—and hadn't answered. She'd spent the next hour and a half alternating between being grossed out and worried about what Amy would have to go through to deliver the tiny human growing inside her.

Celeste's thoughts turned to Grant now—the touch of his hand, the husky timber of his voice when he'd told her how sexy she looked in her yoga pants, the feel of his lips on hers. Warmth filled her as a smile stole over her lips.

Amy let out a little squeal. "I knew it. Something happened this week, didn't it?"

Celeste braced her elbows on the table and leaned forward. "He kissed me."

"What? When?"

And then it all came pouring out. Celeste told Amy about her and Grant's walk in the park, about their shared grief concerning their mothers, and their fathers' polar opposite reactions. She told her about his recent loss and how it had left him raising his teenager sister and brother and the challenges he experienced now.

"Man, I feel for the poor guy. But everything you told me gave zero detail about the kiss." Amy snapped her fingers in front of Celeste's face. "Get on with it. Give me the good stuff."

Celeste laughed. This was exactly how she expected Amy to react. She leaned back now and wrapped her arms around herself. "While we were at the park yesterday, I told him I wanted to be his friend outside of work so I could be there for him when he needed someone to talk to. He said he didn't know if he could handle that, because every time he looked at me, all he wanted to do was kiss me. And then he did. Right there in the park. Hidden among the trees. And it was amazing."

Amy's initial reaction of a gasp now slipped out as a sigh, matching Celeste's. "I can't believe serious, by-the-book Grant kissed you in public during an extended lunch break."

"I know, right?" Celeste laughed as she remembered Grant teasing her about returning to the park. "It was so unexpected. He was like a totally different person once he let go a little."

"Does this mean you two are seeing each other now?"

I wish.

Celeste grimaced. "It's complicated." She then launched into a list of the reasons why dating a coworker wasn't a good idea and how they couldn't risk the project they worked on for the sake of a relationship. She told Amy about the lists of rules they had made to keep things professional at work and platonic outside of work.

Amy frowned. "So no more kissing in your future?"

"Nope." Celeste wished she could give a different answer, but this was how it needed to be, for now.

The server brought their food, and they continued to talk while they ate. Celeste told Amy about hanging out with Grant and his siblings last night and their lengthy late-night phone call.

Amy grinned around a bite of burger. "Breaking the rules already, I see."

Celeste froze with a French fry halfway to her mouth. Amy was right. She and Grant had only just established the rules, and already they had justified breaking them. Remembering how abruptly the call had ended after entering dangerous territory proved how necessary the rules were.

She dropped the fry and scowled. "But we can't keep breaking the rules, Aim. It makes it all so much harder, and we absolutely cannot jeopardize this project." She laid her arm across the table and flopped her head onto it with a groan. "This is going to be the longest six months of my life."

Amy rolled her eyes. "Oh, please. Stop being so dramatic. Enjoy the fact that the man cares enough about you to not rush you into a relationship." She rested a hand on her swollen belly, and guilt shot through Celeste.

Amy was right, again. There were worse things than taking a relationship slow and keeping it platonic. It should be sufficient to know Grant cared about her enough to not imperil both of their jobs. And Grant did care about her. She'd felt it in his gentle touch, his soft words, his amazing kiss.

Yep. She was lucky.

Celeste wasn't so sure she could say the same for her friend. Especially since the wistful look that filled Amy's face made Celeste wonder if Amy had ever felt that kind of assurance from Lance. Knowing what she did of Lance, Celeste doubted it. The thought made her heart heavy. Amy was an amazing person who'd had such a tough life. She deserved the love of a good man. Unfortunately, Lance wasn't that man.

"Speaking of caring about you..." The tone of Amy's voice shifted to wary, drawing Celeste's full attention. "Your dad came to Charley's last night."

Amy's words stole the air from Celeste's lungs and sent a chill down her spine. "He did? What did he want?"

"He wants to see you. Wondered if you'd be willing to have lunch with him."

"Why?"

Amy shrugged. "I'm sure he'd never admit it, but I think he misses you. Maybe he regrets driving you away."

"I doubt that. He probably wants to gloat over the fact that I haven't really gone anywhere with my career." Celeste couldn't hide the cynicism from her voice.

"What do you mean? You have a great career."

"I'm only one of many artists at an ad agency. I make decent money, but if I'd gone to law school, I'd be making four times what I'm making now. I'm sure my dad would love to remind me of that."

"Or maybe he simply wants to know what's going on in your life. Maybe he wants the chance to tell you he's proud of you or that he cares about you." Amy's voice dropped as she finished speaking.

Celeste felt like a heel. She knew Amy would give anything to have her mother care enough to reach out to her, even if it was with criticism and judgment. Grant had probably felt the same way before his dad died.

"So... what did you tell him?"

Amy shrugged. "I told him I'd let you know, and I suggested he wait a couple weeks to give you time to get used to the idea."

"Good thinking, but I doubt it'll do any good. I don't plan to subject myself to his domineering, overbearing, judgmental—"

"I think you should at least consider seeing him. Maybe he's changed."

Celeste doubted it, but she could see how sensitive this subject was to Amy, so she dropped it. "I'll think about it. If he contacts you again, tell him I'll call him if I decide to have lunch with him." That way, he wouldn't continue to hound Amy. Hopefully.

Amy nodded. "I'll be honest with you. He didn't look that great."

A band tightened around Celeste's chest. She leaned forward in her seat; all thoughts of eating gone. "Do you think he's sick?"

As much as she hated the thought of her father lurking in the wings, waiting for her to fail, she didn't want anything to happen to him. There was a sense of comfort in knowing he was always there, even if they didn't agree with each other.

"I don't know. He didn't necessarily look sick, but he has definitely aged since I saw him last."

Seven years was a long time, but was it long enough for her and her father to overcome their differences?

Had he changed?

Celeste had definitely grown and changed, but she wasn't sure it was enough to help her see eye to eye with her father.

CHAPTER 9

$\mathcal{G}$rant looked up when someone strode through the open door of the conference room. Every muscle in his body tensed at the sight of Mr. Davenport. The man rarely left his office unless it was to attend a meeting in one of the conference rooms.

But they didn't have an appointment scheduled with the boss today. Of that, Grant was certain. He was a stickler for checking his schedule. He hated being caught unaware—even worse, he hated being caught unprepared.

Which is exactly how he felt now. They'd given Mr. Davenport an update last Friday. Today was only Monday.

"How are you doing, kids?"

Kids?

Grant shook his head, trying not to get distracted by the... the what? Diminutive? Endearment?

A sudden chill swept through the room as he took in the boss's strained expression. This was not a social visit.

"What's going on, sir?"

Mr. Davenport smiled, but it didn't mask the tension on his face or in his posture. "I knew I could trust you to get right to the point, Grant." He dropped into a chair across the table from Celeste.

Grant rotated his chair to face the boss. The man was almost a decade younger than his partners, hence the reason they had retired, and Davenport hadn't yet. But the sudden slump in his shoulders suggested Mr. Davenport might like to consider early retirement.

"I just got off the phone with Miles Armstrong." Mr. Davenport tugged at his collar. "He informed me the remodels on the hotels are two months ahead of schedule. So he wants to hear our proposal next Friday."

"Next week!" gasped Celeste. "That's two whole weeks earlier than we planned."

A sudden heat wave replaced the chill that swept through the room a few seconds ago. Grant resisted the urge to pick up his ever-present notepad and fan his face. He shifted his gaze to Celeste.

She stared at him with wide eyes, looking as overwhelmed as he felt.

"I tried to remind him how unprofessional it was to shorten a deadline like that, but he turned around and reminded me he's paying us a heck of a lot of money to do our job." Mr. Davenport scrubbed a hand over his face.

Grant's mind raced. They'd settled on the new logo designs and slogans. They even had commercial sketches drawn out, but there was still so much to do. They'd barely made a dent in the details of the overall launch plan.

If they couldn't pull this off, he could kiss the VP position goodbye.

"I know this throws a kink in things," Mr. Davenport continued, "but I'm confident you two can figure this out. Use any resources necessary. I'll have Sharon send out an email to all personnel that they are to drop anything they are working on and help you in any way you need. I'll approve paid overtime for everyone involved."

Grant sprang to his feet. "We can do this. It'll take a lot of work, but we've got this, right?" He looked to Celeste for a confirmation.

She nodded. "There's still a lot to do to prep for the pitch, but we are ahead of the schedule we set for ourselves. So I think we can manage."

"We'll bring in someone from the Productions Department right away. We're going to have to rely heavily on them to finalize the commercial sketches and see to the filming." He paced the room at the head of the table as he continued to rattle off the most urgent things they needed to worry about.

Celeste wrote as he talked, adding a comment here and there.

Mr. Davenport stood and smiled. His posture now more relaxed. "Armstrong threw us a curveball today, but I'm confident the two of you will knock it out of the park. I'm afraid I have another meeting in a few minutes but keep me apprised of your progress and let me know if you need anything."

After he walked out, Grant dropped into his chair and groaned. "Can we really pull this off?"

Celeste laughed, and the musical sound eased the tension in his body.

"What's so funny?"

"I think I figured out how to keep Mr. Davenport from throwing out sports analogies."

"What?" How could she be distracted by the boss's sports analogies at a time like this.

"He didn't use a single sports term while he was stressed about us being able to pull this off, but as soon as we started to develop a plan, he relaxed and started throwing around the sports terms again."

"Guess we fooled him, huh?"

Her brows furrowed. "Stop that. We've got this. By the way, that was totally amazing how your mind went right into problem-solving mode and you took control of the situation. It was kind of..." Her cheeks turned rosy as her words trailed off.

"Kind of what?"

"Never mind. I shouldn't have thought it, and I definitely shouldn't say it."

"Say what?" He leaned forward in his seat, propping his elbows on the table. Had he been too bossy and reminded her of her dad? "Come on, tell me. Please."

She stared at him for a long moment before speaking. "Fine, but you can't get mad at me." She dropped her gaze to the table as she spoke. "I thought you were kind of sexy."

Something warmed in Grant, and he laughed. "I like hearing you say that." He swiped a hand across his forehead in mock relief. "I was afraid you were going to say I looked bossy."

"You did, but apparently I like that." She kept her eyes downcast as she made the admission.

He bit back a smile. "Good, because I like you too. And you look kind of sexy all the time." He cleared his throat to rid it of the husky quality it had taken.

Her wide-eyed gaze jumped to his.

"It's true." He winked at her before turning back to his laptop. "Now we better get to work, or we might find ourselves out of a job."

"Is it question time yet?" Celeste bounced her leg as she waited for Grant to finish his lunch. She'd eaten only half of her salad before pushing it aside. The nervous energy zinging around inside her that caused her leg to bounce had affected her appetite.

Grant turned to her with a smile. "A little anxious, are we?"

She nodded her head in sync with her bouncing knee.

He chuckled. "I think it's my turn to go first, but I'm afraid you might hurt me if I make you wait." When she nodded again, he laughed. "Go for it."

"Yes!" The word, sounding like a hiss, was out before she could stop it. Celeste pulled the book she'd bought on Saturday—and spent the rest of the weekend reading—from her bag.

She'd planned to talk to him about it yesterday, but they had worked right through lunch with three extra people in the room. Those extra people had been here all morning too, but they'd taken off for lunch. Celeste and Grant had opted to stay behind, and she was determined to take advantage of the quiet.

"Okay, I want to ask you a series of questions today."

"Wait. I thought the rule was one question with possible follow-ups."

She hugged the book to her chest and gave him the puppy-dog look she'd always used on her dad to get her way. Of course, it only ever worked on the little things and never on the things that really mattered. "Can we bend our rules for one day? It's for a good cause, I promise."

Fine lines formed around his eyes, and the muscle in his jaw clenched. He shot a quick look over his shoulder at the open door, then looked back at her. He lowered his voice. "We bent the rules last Friday, and I haven't been able to stop thinking about you since."

Celeste dropped her gaze, trying not to think about what the intense look in his eyes meant. "Me too, but this is important." She rotated the book and showed him the cover. "I went to the bookstore on Saturday looking for relationship books and I came across this."

He leaned forward in his seat and read the title. "The Five Love Languages: The Secret to Love that Lasts" He sucked in a sharp breath. "Celeste," her name came out with his exhale, sounding like a caress.

Her pulse exploded like a firecracker. She loved the sound of her name on his lips.

"We—I can't—I'm barely keeping it professional, as it is."

Celeste's eyes widened, and warmth filled her body at his admission. It was nice to know he had as hard of time fighting the attraction between them as she did.

"No. That's not—This isn't about us. Unless... you want it to be."

"You know what I want." The pitch of his voice had dropped even lower, and warmth surrounded her like honey. Thick and sweet.

She gave herself a mental shake and struggled to gather the thoughts Grant's words had scattered. "I bought this book because I think it might help you with Reagan and Josh."

"Really?" The husky timber of his voice disappeared. He came around the table and dropped into the chair beside her. The side of his knee brushed hers.

This was the closest they'd been since he kissed her last Friday, and the proximity wreaked havoc on her blood pressure. The scent of his cologne hit her full force, and the temperature in the room suddenly felt tropical.

Pressing her heels into the carpet, she rolled her chair back a foot, putting a little space between them.

Grant's brow furrowed, and he pushed backward also, increasing the distance between them.

"Sorry. So, tell me what this book is about. I'm desperate for any help I can get. Reagan and I had another argument Saturday night."

Celeste passed the book to him. "It was written by a psychologist who believes there are five primary love languages. We all have a primary love language—this is how the actions of others speak to us to tell us they care about us. Most of us have a secondary love language as well."

She continued explaining about the five different love languages and how one's actions speak to those around them, depending on what their love language is. "No matter what you do to show Reagan and Josh you care, it'll never be enough if you aren't speaking the right language."

He flipped through the pages. "So this book isn't just about marriage relationships?"

"It's geared toward relationships between partners, but it works for all kinds of relationships."

Warmth filled her cheeks. She bit her tongue to keep from admitting that even though she went to the bookstore looking for a book that would help him with Reagan and Josh, Grant had been the only one on her mind when she'd picked up this book. It had intrigued her, so she bought it and read the whole thing by Sunday evening.

They lapsed into silence as he studied the table of contents. After a few minutes, he flipped a few pages, stopped, and read for a moment, then flipped a few more and paused again.

Celeste had done the same thing in the bookstore. She picked up her salad and took a bite.

Grant finally looked up again when he reached the section with the quiz. "Did you take the test?"

"Yes."

"What's your love language? No, wait. Let me guess." He leaned back in his chair and studied her. "Considering the conflict between you and your dad and the way you said he treated you, I'm guessing your love language is words of affirmation."

She gave him a tight smile, unsure whether she liked being so transparent. "You're right. He crushed me a little every time he told me I needed to do this better or that differently when I thought I'd earned his approval." Celeste put a hand on his arm. "Now do you understand why I want you to take the quiz? It'll help you understand yourself better, and it'll help you understand Reagan and Josh."

He looked at her hand on his arm. "It'll help me better understand you."

She pulled her hand away. "Um...yeah, I guess. But that's not why I want you to take the test. It's probably best we don't look at this in terms of... us."

"No, we shouldn't, but I can't help myself." He cleared his throat. "I don't need to take the quiz. I think I know what my love language is."

"I think yours might be quality time," Celeste said. When Grant looked at her with raised eyebrows, she went on. "I mean, your dad withdrew from you after your mom died, and that left you feeling lost."

"You're right, but his withdrawal was a lot more than no longer spending time with me." He placed the book on the table and stood. He stopped in front of the window and shoved his hands into his pockets. "I didn't realize it until I took your hand last week, but what I missed the most was the physical touch. I can't count the number of times I longed for him to pat me on the back and tell me it was going to be okay or put his arm around my shoulder and tell me he was proud of me."

"Why did you realize it last week when you held my hand?" Flutters filled Celeste's stomach.

"Before I answer that, let me explain something I'm coming to realize. Laney accused me of never really loving her and letting her in. I thought hugging her, holding her hand, and kissing her told her I loved her, but I was wrong. I think she needed... quality time—my undivided attention, talking with her, sharing with her."

Celeste bit her tongue to keep from interrupting him. She didn't want to hear about his ex-girlfriend. She wanted to hear what Grant realized when he held her hand.

"I thought I loved her because I felt something when she touched me or we kissed. I'm not talking only about the physical reaction, either." He shrugged. "The contact made me feel something."

Celeste gripped the armrests of her chair as jealousy swept over her. She did not like the direction this was headed.

He turned away from the window, and warmth filled his gray eyes as he gazed at her. "When I touched you last week, I not only felt a connection, I felt..." He pulled his hand from his pocket and placed it midway between his heart and his abdomen. "I felt something I haven't felt since my mother died."

She stood, wanting to go to him. She wanted to touch him, help him feel whatever it was he had felt again so he could define it.

He took a small step back and shot a quick glance at the open door.

She froze, her gaze following his. Thankfully, the cubicles were mostly empty. "What did you feel?" The words came out little more than a whisper.

"I felt complete. Your touch filled something deep inside of me. Something, I didn't know I'd been missing." He shoved his fingers into his hair and shook his head, giving a rueful laugh. "Every time we touched, it turned my world upside down. It has me questioning all the rules and breaking them. We've already discussed why that's not a good idea."

The air in the room fairly crackled with electricity, and it was all Celeste could do to stand still.

"Grant—"

He held up a hand. "But this isn't about us, is it? It can't be. Not yet anyway." Grant stepped to the end of the table and folded up his laptop. "I wanted you to know what I felt when you touched me. What you... mean to me." He gave her a longing look before sliding his computer and note pads into his bag. "Please don't take this personally, but I'm going to spend the rest of the day in my office before I do or say something inappropriate for the workplace." He looked at the laptops left behind by their coworkers. "We all have our own tasks to work on, but if anyone needs me, send them to my office."

Celeste wanted to beg him to stay, but it was a good thing he was leaving. The tension between them was way too high right now. One of them was bound to say or do something that crossed the line of appropriate workplace behavior. It would raise all kinds of questions if that tension still lingered when their coworkers returned.

He shouldered his bag and stepped to her end of the table. He reached out for the book. "May I?"

She pushed it toward him. "Of course, I bought it for you."

"Thank you, Celeste. For everything."

Her chest tightened. Despite Grant's declarations, she couldn't help feeling like she was losing him. Which was silly because she'd never really had him.

But she wanted him.

He paused in the doorway. "Don't worry, I'll be here tomorrow, and I will be in complete control of my faculties, including my tongue." He gave her a tight grin.

Celeste returned his smile, but hers didn't reach her eyes either. Grant shouldn't have to take sole responsibility for what was happening between them. She needed to be more careful about what she said and did around him too.

She returned to her chair with fresh resolve. She wouldn't make things more difficult between them. She wouldn't flirt with him. She couldn't keep herself from thinking about their kiss, but she certainly wouldn't remind him about it.

Keep it professional, C!

CHAPTER 10

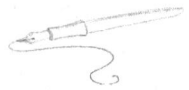

G rant stood behind his golf ball and positioned his putter. He eyed the small hole to the tunnel his ball was supposed to go through. He was not scoring well, and it was going to take all his focus to finish the final four holes without coming in dead last.

He pulled his club back.

"So, tell me, Reagan, what is the worst thing Grant has ever cooked?" Celeste's playful voice came from behind him.

Grant swung, barely hitting the ball. It rolled to the right of the hole, hit the Styrofoam rock wall, and rolled right back to where he'd started. Three putts ago.

Celeste, Reagan, and Josh all laughed.

He swung around and pointed his golf club at Celeste. "That's not fair."

"What? I just asked Reagan a simple question."

"Simple, my foot. You were trying to distract me. Again."

This was not the first time she'd done this when it was his turn to putt. And it had led to Reagan and Josh telling embarrassing stories about him. Celeste now knew his closet was color coordinated and he insisted on wiping down the entire kitchen before he cooked. Never mind that he sanitized it after he last cooked.

"Why would I need to distract you?" She waved her hand back and forth between herself and Reagan with an air of innocence. "We're winning."

Somehow this had turned into a guys against girls' thing, and Josh was not impressed with Grant's golfing skills.

"Because you're sneaky and conniving." He stepped closer until he loomed over her. Her perfume hit him full force, and he realized he'd made a mistake, but he stood his ground. "You're not playing fair."

"I haven't broken the rules," she said, her voice low.

Was it his imagination or did she sound a little breathless? At any rate, she sounded downright sexy.

Grant had been careful this past week to make sure he neither said nor did anything that could be deemed inappropriate at work. Celeste seemed committed to keeping things professional, too. It helped that they frequently had other coworkers around.

"No, but you're finding out all kinds of stuff about me. It's not fair, because I don't get to do the same with you." Now he sounded like a whiny brat when all he wanted was for Celeste to stop driving him crazy. It didn't matter if she was asking a question or flipping her hair over her shoulder before putting. Just being around the woman in another social setting was making him crave more than friendship.

He was surprised they all ended up going out tonight at all. When Celeste had suggested it at lunchtime to let off steam after their stressful week, they had decided it wouldn't be a good idea, because it would make things harder for them. Grant had been disappointed, but he'd hidden it and agreed.

Neither Reagan nor Josh's friends could hang out tonight though, so Grant had suggested doing something together in an effort to spend some quality time with them. They had agreed, but only if he invited Celeste to join them.

So he'd called Celeste, and they'd met up at a Mexican restaurant where he felt like a jerk for letting her pay for her own dinner. He'd tried to tell her it wouldn't be a big deal for him to pay for her too, but she'd insisted on following the rules. And she'd done so again when they all decided to go miniature golfing.

Both Reagan and Josh scowled at him when he stepped back and let her pay for herself again.

"I'll give you my friend Amy's number, and you can call and ask her anything you want about me," Celeste said, drawing him back to the present. She looked up at him with wide, innocent eyes, a smile playing at her lips.

He stepped away. If he didn't put some space between them, he'd end up kissing her. In front of Reagan and Josh—who didn't believe him that he and Celeste were just friends—and everybody else out enjoying the spring weather at the miniature golf course.

Grant stepped up to his ball again and prepared to putt. *Ignore her.*

"I'm serious guys, what is the worst thing Grant has ever cooked?"

He did his best to tune out the annoying, beautiful woman, who wreaked havoc on his life, and focused on his golf game while Reagan and Josh told Celeste how he'd once started a grease fire on the stove when he'd been attempting to fry chicken. Now, he stuck with Shake-n-Bake.

His golf game didn't improve, and somewhere along the way, a wager was made that the losers would treat the winners to ice cream.

That's how Grant found himself sitting next to Celeste in a small ice cream shop down the street from the miniature golf place he vowed to never visit again. He turned away from the counter after paying for their ice cream—thankfully Celeste let him pay without an argument—to find Reagan pushing Josh into a booth. Then she slid in beside him, leaving Celeste and Grant to share the other way too small bench seat.

She kept her shoulder pressed against the wall, and he sat as close to the edge of the seat as possible without making it look like he was intentionally avoiding her.

He could hear Reagan now: "No wonder you're still single. First, you refuse to pay for Celeste's food, then, you act like she's got cooties."

He didn't look forward to having to explain himself to his sister, who had no clue what he was going through.

Celeste's leg bumped his under the table for the third time. She shot him an apologetic look before shifting closer to the wall.

The warmth of her body beside his and the innocent brush of her leg or arm filled him with desire. He took a big spoonful of ice cream. The sooner he finished his dessert, the sooner he could move away from her. He should have gotten a single scoop instead of a double.

The cold mint chocolate chip ice cream sliding down his throat did nothing to cool the heat building in him.

"So, Reagan, do you play any sports?" Celeste did a good job pretending their proximity didn't affect her as she drew both Reagan and Josh into conversation.

Maybe she wasn't affected. Not as strongly as he was, anyway. He took another big bite of ice cream.

Sure, she admitted she was attracted to him and cared about him, but physical touch wasn't her love language like it was his. Being so close but not able to really touch probably wasn't as torturous to her as it was to him. Tonight, though, the innocent brush of her leg or arm was doing a lot more than filling up those empty places inside him. It was starting a slow burning forest fire.

He took another huge bite of ice cream.

Did Celeste feel the same level of attraction and desire he did? Or was he the only one letting himself get carried away with dreaming about a relationship that didn't have a future? Not an immediate one anyway.

The warmth building in him suddenly shifted to his chest and head and burst into such a powerful burning sensation, Grant thought he might die.

"Ahh!" he groaned, pressing one hand to his chest and the other to his forehead.

Laughter erupted around him.

"Brain freeze!" Josh said.

"Are you okay?" The hand Celeste placed on his shoulder shook as she continued to laugh.

He stayed curled in on himself, trying not to read too much into her touch. As the brain freeze subsided, the warmth of her hand seeped through his jacket and shirt. He knew Celeste meant for the touch to be comforting and nothing else, so he focused on that. Instead of letting himself get carried away with a desire he couldn't afford to be feeling right now.

"I'm fine." He shrugged, and she removed her hand like he'd hoped she would.

Relief filled him when conversation resumed around the table, and he focused on taking smaller bites. Two scoops of his favorite ice cream had never been so difficult to choke down.

Grant sprang to his feet as soon as he finished his ice cream. He threw his cup away and returned to the table to find the others still eating. He stood next to the table, hands in his pocket. No way could he sit by Celeste again.

She stood and threw the last of her ice cream away. Aware of his impatience, Reagan and Josh headed to the door with theirs. Normally he didn't allow open food in his car, but he'd make an exception tonight.

As they made the short walk back to the parking lot of the miniature golf place, he walked beside Celeste.

Reagan and Josh hurried ahead. He wasn't sure whether to be grateful or wring their necks.

"Thanks for inviting me tonight, Grant. I had fun."

"Me too." The words came out tight.

"Really? You seemed kind of tense all night."

Grant wasn't sure how to answer. Of course, he'd been tense all night because it had taken every ounce of his self-control not to reach out and take her hand or pull her into his arms and kiss her.

When he didn't respond, she stepped in front of him and turned to face him. "Is something bothering you? Do you need someone to talk to?"

He stopped, barely avoiding running into her. They were almost to their cars. He reached in his pocket for the key fob and unlocked the doors so Reagan and Josh could get in. He didn't want them to hear what he was about to say to Celeste.

"Thanks for hanging out with us tonight, but I can't do this again." He took a step back.

Confusion filled her face. "Why? Is it because I teased you so much?"

"No." He raked his fingers through his hair. "Actually, yes. It's that and everything else."

"Everything else? Are you upset because you always lose when we play games together?"

Being a competitive person, losing to Celeste drove him crazy but not nearly as much as simply being around her. Grant needed control and order. He'd always been disciplined and deliberate about everything he did. But when he was around Celeste, he wanted to be impulsive and do things he hadn't carefully planned out. Being around her made him feel so reckless and out of control.

It scared him. And the fear that she didn't feel as strongly as he did scared him even more.

"Celeste, please tell me I'm not the only one who feels..." He wasn't sure how to finish his question.

"Grant." She took a step toward him, hand outstretched. She stopped and shoved her hands into her jacket pockets. "I felt all kinds of things tonight. Things I really liked. Things I want to feel more of."

He bit back a groan and shoved his hands into his own pockets. "Don't say stuff like that."

"Like what? That I'm attracted to you? That I wish it had been just the two of us? That the sexual tension between us drives me crazy?" She sucked in a sharp breath as though she hadn't meant to say those last words out loud.

Grant drew in his own sharp breath. Those were the exact things he'd been feeling.

"That's why I tease, you know. And make jokes. It's my way of trying to diffuse the tension."

"It doesn't work. In fact, it has the opposite effect." He looked down at his feet for a long moment before returning his gaze to her. "That's why we can't go out like this again. Keeping things professional at work is hard enough. If we get too close outside of work, I'll never be able to maintain an appropriate working relationship."

"Remind me again why dating a coworker isn't a good idea."

"Celeste." He ground out the word.

"I'm serious. My wants are trying to take over here, and I need you to help me remember why we can't date."

"Working with someone you're emotionally involved with creates distraction in the workplace." He pulled his hand from his pocket and held up a finger.

"Right. And our trying not to become emotionally involved isn't at all distracting at work."

He scowled at her and held up another finger. "If we had a relationship, and things didn't work out between us, that would negatively affect our work. And we both know if the Armstrong project—the biggest project of our careers—goes south, we'd both be looking for another job."

"You're right. I'm sorry." Her face filled with contrition. "I hate that it has to be like this."

"Me too but being near you drives me crazy. I'm afraid I'm going to lose control one of these days."

A wistful look crossed her face before an impish grin took over.

Grant braced himself for a teasing remark about her wanting to see him lose control, but it never came. He wanted to be grateful, but disappointment filled him. He agreed with Celeste. He hated this. They should be able to tease and flirt and be themselves. But they couldn't.

She cleared her throat and took a step back. "Okay, no more social outings. We'll keep things professional at work, and we won't talk about feelings and attraction. And especially not sexual tension." She gave him a small smile. "But if you ever need to talk to someone about Reagan and Josh... or anything really, promise me you'll call or text."

"I promise."

Grant stayed rooted twenty feet from his car as he watched her get into her car and drive away. Why did he feel like he and Celeste had broken up?

It was ridiculous because they had never been together, but watching her drive away felt so final. He knew he'd see her on Monday morning, but he had a feeling it wouldn't be the same.

GRANT'S HEART rate kicked up a notch when Reagan walked through the front door. He'd been working on a list of tasks for the new team he and Celeste had assembled while he waited for Reagan to get home.

He was anxious for her to find the gift he'd left on her bed. He wanted to see her reaction when she found it, but he was too big of a chicken to give it to her in person. If she didn't show enough enthusiasm, he'd be disappointed.

"Hey, how was your afternoon with Shelby?" He looked up and gave Reagan his undivided attention.

"Fine." Reagan got a glass of water and sat at the dining table. She pulled out her phone.

"So, what did you guys do?"

"Not much." Her eyes never left her phone.

"What does 'not much' look like?" He tried again to engage her in conversation.

"If you must know..." Reagan lifted her eyes so she could roll them. "We took a walk, painted our nails, and listened to music." She finished her water, put her glass in the dishwasher—like Grant had trained her to do—and walked out of the room.

Her love language obviously isn't quality time. He'd given her plenty of opportunities to talk about anything she wanted, but she always walked away.

He'd already tried lavishing words of praise on both Reagan and Josh. Josh had responded better than Reagan. The boy's eyes practically lit up when Grant told him he was proud of him for getting an "A" on his last math test. Reagan just gave him a strange look when he complimented her on her outfit and thanked her for doing the dishes without being asked.

He'd tried to spend some quality time with each of them, but Reagan had made that feat difficult, since she spent most of her time in her room. Josh had looked confused when Grant asked if he could play Fortnite with him, but he'd agreed. He'd even shown great patience in teaching Grant how to play.

Reagan's footsteps came back down the stairs a few minutes later, and Grant braced himself.

She walked around the corner with the small decorative crate in her hand. "Where did this come from?"

"What?" He feigned ignorance.

She came closer and set the box down on the table so he could see what was in it. But Grant didn't need to look in the container to know what it held. Despite Celeste's help last week, before they'd decided they needed to cool it socially, he'd deliberated over every item in that box.

She'd met him at the grocery store last Saturday morning and assembled the box for him. He'd insisted on putting half the items back because he didn't even know what many of them were and would never have chosen them himself. He didn't want it to look like someone else had handpicked the gift for Reagan, even though that was the case.

Grant had finally gotten a smaller container and kept the chocolates, scented candle, and gel pens with a small journal, because Reagan liked things like that. Celeste kept insisting he needed to get the lip balm, bath bombs, and face masks too, so he'd relented, but he hadn't included them in this basket. He felt like he was going overboard as it was. That's why he'd waited a whole week to give it to her.

He glanced at the basket. "Oh, that. Yeah, I picked up a few things for you while I was at the store." He shrugged his shoulders like it wasn't a big deal even though he watched her face for a reaction.

"Why?" Reagan's eyes narrowed.

"Why what?"

"Why did you buy these things for me?"

He hadn't expected Reagan to call him out on his unexpected behavior.

When he tossed the Xbox gift card he'd bought for Josh at him saying, "Hey, I thought you might like this." Josh hadn't looked at him weird, as though Grant had ulterior motives for the gift. He'd simply said, "Cool, thanks," then added that now he could buy something that made him sound like he was speaking in a foreign language. Grant had no idea what Josh was talking about, but he assumed it was a weapon of some sort for his game.

He shrugged again, but the motion felt stiff. "I thought you'd like them. If you don't want it, I can take it back." He'd do no such thing, but he'd never admit that to her. If Reagan called his bluff, he'd give the basket to Celeste and tell her this experiment had failed.

Reagan picked up the basket. "No, I want them. I just don't understand why you're being so nice lately."

Grant decided honesty was the best policy here. "Things have been strained between us for a while now, and I know that's partly my fault. I can see you're trying to follow the rules, so I wanted you to know I appreciate your effort."

"Hmm... well thanks." And with that, Reagan walked out of the room with the basket.

He leaned back in his chair, frustrated. He picked up his phone and texted Celeste.

Grant: *I'm not sure Reagan's love language is gifts.*

Celeste: *Why? How did she respond?*

Grant: *She asked me why I bought her those things and looked at me like I had lost my mind.*

Celeste: *Hmm... sounds like you're right. Her love language isn't gifts.*

Grant: *And I don't think it's words of affirmation or quality time either.*

Celeste: *So that leaves physical touch and acts of service.*

Grant: *What am I supposed to do for those?*

He didn't know an appropriate way to show his sister physical touch. He tried patting her on the shoulder once last week, but she'd given him one of those strange looks, so he hadn't touched her again. He couldn't remember the last time he'd intentionally touched Reagan or Josh before last week. With his love language being physical touch, he expected it to come naturally to him, but it didn't.

Maybe because he went so many years without hardly being touched.

Romantic love was obviously different from familial affection, though. Because as he experienced last night, it was all he could do to keep his hands off Celeste.

His phone dinged.

Celeste: *Let me think about it and we'll discuss it on Monday. I've got to go. I'm shopping with my friend Amy.*

Grant: *Okay, have fun.*

He set his phone down, wishing he had a guy friend to hang out with.

Maybe it was time he reached out to some of the friends he'd alienated over the past year.

CHAPTER 11

Grant's gaze drifted across the crowded conference table in 3D's largest conference room to look at Celeste. Her left eyebrow was quirked, and he didn't blame her. He fought to hold back a smile.

After two stressful weeks, they were all set to present their campaign ideas to Miles Armstrong and four of his board members, but before they could get started, Miles rose from his seat at the head of the table, saying he wanted to take a minute.

The man had been going on for five minutes now, and with each passing minute, Celeste's brow inched higher. Miles had started with how the chain of Livingston hotels had been in his family for generations and how his father had worked hard to build it into an empire.

Her brow had first risen when miles declared, "And I refuse to let my father's action and a bunch of bad publicity destroy such an incredible legacy."

It had inched up again when Miles insisted that, "No matter what it takes, I will make the Livingston—now Armstrong—hotel empire great again."

What a stuffed shirt!

Celeste looked at Grant as Miles droned on, and he couldn't help himself—he winked at her. He reached a finger up and smoothed his own brow, figuring she wasn't aware of how high her eyebrow had risen.

She grinned and lowered her brow.

"And I'm prepared to stay here all day if necessary, until we agree on a suitable campaign that meets my expectations and helps me reach my goals."

And there went Celeste's eyebrow again.

He stifled a chuckle and silently applauded her as she sprang to her feet.

"Well then, let's get to the presentation, shall we?"

Miles dropped into his seat as Celeste stole everyone's attention.

Grant watched the room and especially Miles Armstrong's face as Celeste used their PowerPoint to present the logo design options and slogans they had come up with.

An appreciative smile formed on the other man's face, and his head slowly nodded as Celeste talked. His eyes followed her every move, and a surge of irritation filled Grant.

Ignoring it, he leaned back in his chair and relaxed. The closer this deadline loomed, the more uptight he'd become. He'd hardly slept this week as he stressed over every little detail.

Grant had learned Celeste was an introvert and hated being the center of attention, but she was killing it right now with her cheerful smile that lit up her face. She'd dressed to kill in a black pencil skirt and ruby-red blouse that accentuated her dark eyes and hair. Her red lipstick matched the exact shade of her shirt. It also ramped up his desire to drag her to the stairwell and steal a kiss.

He'd had a hard time taking his eyes off her all morning, so he wasn't surprised Miles was so taken with her. She'd been tireless in helping prepare for this presentation from the logo designs, the PowerPoint, and printed brochures to the centerpiece and the danishes that graced the conference room table. The other coworkers they'd pulled in to help last week had come through for them also.

Grant pulled his gaze away from Celeste and studied the other occupants surrounding the conference table. Miles had brought four board members with him—three men and one woman. They all looked equally impressed so far.

He shifted his gaze to Mr. Davenport. It wasn't hard to read the boss's reactions. He grinned from ear to ear.

Celeste controlled the room masterfully while Armstrong's people decided on which logo design and slogan they wanted to run with, then she looked at Grant, a smile playing at her lips. "And now, Mr. Foster will present the step-by-step process of your rebranding campaign."

He gave her a quick wink and a subtle thumbs up as he stood and buttoned his suit coat. "Thank you, Miss Hightower. Unfortunately, the rest of our presentation isn't as entertaining as discussing designs, but the sooner we agree on a launch strategy, the sooner we can get your campaign up and running."

He gaged the mood of the room as he glided through his presentation. Every time he looked at Miles, the other man's eyes were on Celeste.

Grant made it a point to move around during his presentation, and more than once, he stood directly behind Celeste so he could make eye contact with Miles. He tucked his hand in his pocket to keep from resting it on her shoulder in a possessive gesture.

He'd never thought of himself as a jealous man, but he did not like the way Miles ogled Celeste. Sure, the man was good looking and a billionaire, but the media also painted him as a playboy. Celeste was too good for him. Not to mention he was fourteen years her senior.

Grant focused on his presentation so he wouldn't blow it. He couldn't afford to mess this up because he was jealous.

After he finished his presentation, Celeste stood beside him as they fielded questions. He felt ten feet tall with her beside him as his partner. He liked the idea of having her as his partner for life even more.

Would they be able to find a way to work together *and* have a relationship?

Calm down, man. Stay focused.

Mr. Davenport beamed at Grant and Celeste the entire time, remaining quiet throughout the whole thing. He didn't throw out a single sports analogy and only spoke when someone asked him a direct question.

Once Miles and his board members agreed on a logo and a slogan —with slight modifications—and a launch strategy, they ironed out a handful of other details for the campaign itself, then Grant brought the meeting to a close. A whole hour earlier than he'd expected.

"Ladies and Gentlemen, we have a plan in place. Our team is ready to run with this, and you will receive weekly updates on our progress. Watch your inboxes for the updated logo and slogan designs. Within a few weeks, you'll receive the new commercial sketches and sample brochures. We'll continue to meet monthly in person to iron the details until the grand opening of Armstrong Hotels. Remember, our door is always open. Communication is the key to your and our success."

The occupants in the room all rose, and Miles Armstrong beelined to Celeste. He held out his hand even though they already shook when introductions were made. "Miss Hightower, I was very impressed with your presentation today."

Grant gave an eye roll that would make Reagan proud. *What am I? Chopped liver?*

Miles didn't release Celeste's hand after the lengthy handshake. In fact, he covered their hands with his other one. "You have great artistic talent."

"Mr. Armstrong, will you allow me to buy you and your colleagues lunch?" Mr. Davenport stepped close to Miles and held a hand out toward the door.

Disappointment filled the billionaire's face as he relinquished Celeste's hand.

Grant had never wanted to hug a superior more than he did today as Mr. Davenport effectively guided Miles and his board members from the conference room. He was about to let out an enormous sigh when Mr. Davenport stepped back into the room.

"Phenomenal job! Both of you!" He held two thumbs up. "Take care of your stuff and meet us at the restaurant." He rattled off the name and address of an expensive Italian restaurant.

The boss disappeared through the door, and the room fell silent. He turned to Celeste, who stood near him. She smiled, and he couldn't help himself; he swept her up into his arms.

"You were amazing!" he whispered.

She wrapped her arms around his neck. "Me? You totally commanded the room! It was so inspirational to watch you."

He loosened his hold on her enough to pull back and look at her. "You really think so?" When had this woman's praise come to mean so much to him?

"Absolutely, you were incredible, and you're going to make a great vice president."

Celeste's tropical floral scent surrounded him, and desire surged through him. His gaze fell to her ruby-red lips. He loved the words coming from her mouth, but there were other sounds he'd rather hear from her lips right now. Like a sigh or a moan as he kissed her.

"Um..." He cleared his throat and dropped his arms. "I'm having some very unprofessional thoughts right now, so I need to step away."

Her cheeks turned rosy as she backed away and wrapped her arms around herself. "Yeah, that's probably for the best."

He shoved his hands into his pockets to keep from pulling her into his arms again.

Silence filled the room again.

"Sorry, I didn't mean to make things awkward." He gave her a tight smile and shrugged. "But I figured I should be honest with you."

She cleared her throat. "I appreciate the honesty... and restraint."

Grant scoffed. "Restraint. Definitely not one of my strong points."

She grinned and started gathering her things, so he did the same.

Instead of joining Mr. Davenport and the stuffed shirt for lunch, Grant would rather take Celeste somewhere quiet and private for lunch.

He wished he'd followed through on that urge twenty minutes later when they walked into the restaurant to join the others, and Miles made one of his board members shift to another chair to make room for Celeste beside him.

Grant took the last vacant seat at the table. Directly across from

Celeste and Miles. He did his best not to look at either of them and managed to succeed until after they had placed their orders. Without a menu in front of him, his gaze was drawn to Celeste like a magnet.

She laughed at something Miles said, and a tight, heavy sensation filled Grant's abdomen. He welcomed the distraction when one of the board members asked him a question about the launch. It didn't keep him from noticing, however, that Armstrong frequently leaned toward Celeste and bumped shoulders with her or touched her hand. The man seemed bent on impressing Celeste, and judging by the smile on her face, he was succeeding.

By the time their food arrived, the tangled ball of jealousy in his stomach had expanded to his chest, and he lost his appetite. He couldn't blame Celeste for being swept away by the handsome billionaire, but that didn't mean he liked watching the playboy move in on his girl.

Except she's not my girl... yet.

And she never would be if he wasn't willing to be the talk of the office. If he and Celeste got involved in a relationship, the whole company would know about it in no time. Plenty of people already suspected something was going on between them, since they both continued to work in the conference room. Mostly alone.

That would all change come Monday, though. They would bring in the launch team, and he would have very little time alone with her. His chest tightened, and a heaviness took over his body at the thought.

He recalled how people gossiped about Ian and Olivia last year. Just when it looked like they were about to get engaged, something happened, and Olivia dumped Ian. All kinds of ugly rumors flew around the office about both of them, and people were suddenly taking sides against their coworkers. Grant would hate for anyone to spread rumors about him, but he'd detest it even more if someone talked bad about Celeste behind her back.

Armstrong put his arm on the back of Celeste's chair and held a bite of his lasagna in front of her face. "You have got to try this. It's amazing."

Grant gripped his fork so tightly, he feared he might bend it. Over the past month, he'd frequently worried he wouldn't make it through the Armstrong project without doing something that might cost him not only the VP position but maybe even his job. And if that happened, he'd probably lose Celeste too.

He clenched his teeth, reminding himself punching Armstrong would definitely cost him the VP position and his job. But if he didn't do something to let Celeste know how he felt, he might lose her anyway. To this stuffed shirt, playboy, billionaire. Miles was so confident and persistent that sweet, innocent Celeste didn't stand a chance.

Before he could drag his eyes away from the intimate scene across the table, Celeste's left eyebrow rose. She pulled back and gave a tight laugh. She handed Armstrong her fork. "Sorry, I'm a bit of a germaphobe. I'll try a bite off my own fork."

Armstrong's smile disappeared, and his eyes narrowed before he took Celeste's fork and filled it with lasagna.

Since when is Celeste a germaphobe? She usually enjoyed teasing Grant about being one.

He caught her gaze across the table and almost burst out laughing when she rolled her eyes. The massive, tangled knot of jealousy in his stomach eased a little. She wasn't enjoying the playboy's company as much as Grant feared. At least, that's what he hoped the eye roll meant.

He couldn't wait for this lunch to be over, especially since Mr. Davenport had started talking sports with two of Armstrong's board members.

As soon as his boss pocketed his credit card after paying the bill, Grant sprang to his feet. Celeste followed suit, as though she feared he might leave her, and she'd be right. He made himself pause and shake hands with Miles and each of his board members, saying he looked forward to working with them.

Celeste did the same, and when it looked like she might leave without shaking Miles's hand, the billionaire captured her hand and raised it to his lips.

"I'm looking forward to working with you, Celeste. I can't wait to get to know you better." He still held her hand in his. "Would you have dinner with me tomorrow evening?"

The man certainly didn't waste any time or beat around the bush.

Celeste's eyebrow jumped higher than Grant had ever seen it raise. He'd come to enjoy watching it do that, but there was nothing enjoyable about watching the billionaire ask the woman he was falling in love with out on a date.

Celeste's smile tightened as she tugged her hand away from Miles's grip. "I'm very flattered, Mr. Armstrong. But I don't date clients. Besides," her gaze darted to Grant and back to Miles again so fast, Grant wondered if he'd imagined it. "I'm kind of involved with someone right now."

Grant sucked in a sharp breath. He pushed his chair under the table to keep himself from wrapping his arm around her shoulder, staking his claim.

"Maybe I can talk you into reconsidering after our grand reopening. Until then, I'll look forward to seeing you at our monthly meetings."

After a final wave to the group, Grant and Celeste made their way to the door. He resisted the urge to take her hand as they exited the restaurant. It took every ounce of his willpower not to open the car door for her. His mother would be so disappointed in him.

He hesitated before starting the car. Once they made the short drive back to the office, they would have to go back to pretending they weren't attracted to each other and wanting so much more than a working relationship.

"Is something wrong?" Celeste's quiet voice filled the car.

"Did you mean it?" His voice was gruffer than he intended. "Did you mean what you said to Armstrong?" He studied her beautiful face, looking for clues that she felt as strongly about him as he did her.

"Yes, even though we can't... you know." She gave him a heart-stopping smile before lowering her gaze.

"I know." The words came out a growl. "Believe me, I know." He started the car then laid his hand across the console, palm up. "But I wish we could."

The invitation broke so many of the rules they'd set for themselves, and he'd hate himself later, but he wanted to make the most of these few minutes with Celeste.

She looked at his hand for a long moment before lacing her fingers with his. "Me too."

CHAPTER 12

Celeste was much quieter Monday morning than Grant had expected. The V between her brows deepened with each passing hour as they discussed the details of the Armstrong project with the newly assembled team. She hardly said a word all morning.

He'd frequently asked her questions, trying to draw her into the discussion, but she answered as briefly as possible and passed the ball back to him. At least she hadn't dropped the ball altogether. Grant shook his head at the sports analogies rolling around inside his brain.

He'd watched her eyebrow carefully, to see if she thought he was being overbearing, but it didn't raise. At all.

As soon as the team filed from the conference room for lunch, Grant blocked Celeste's escape. "Alright, what did I do?"

Did this have something to do with the hug they shared after their presentation last Friday? Had someone witnessed it and reported it to HR? Had someone said something to Celeste?

"What do you mean?"

"I obviously said or did something wrong, since you scowled at me all morning." Her perfume and the warmth of her body so close to his made it difficult to focus.

"You did nothing wrong. In fact, you did great. You're a born leader." She smiled, but it didn't reach her eyes.

"Then why are you all scowly?"

"I'm not scow—" Celeste let out a huff. "Okay, fine. I was scowling, but it wasn't aimed at you."

"Is this one of those situations where you're trying to tell me, 'It's not you, it's me'?" Grant joked, but something tightened in his chest.

"It's not you, really. I need to make a decision I never thought I'd have to make. And I'm afraid of making the wrong choice."

Grant avoided touching Celeste at work. It wasn't appropriate behavior between coworkers, but she needed a friend. He wanted to be that friend.

He put a hand on her shoulder. "Let me buy you some tacos, and we can take a walk through the park."

Even though they'd taken many walks since, suggesting a walk through the park always brought to mind the kiss they shared there weeks ago.

"To talk," he promised.

She deliberated for a long moment before answering. "Okay, I would like your input."

Fifteen minutes later, they sat on the same bench where they had shared their most heart-wrenching secrets. Grant tried not to think about what had happened after those intimate moments.

Despite the walks they'd taken since, he'd been careful to never get close enough to Celeste to even hold her hand, let alone kiss her. It was hard enough maintaining a professional relationship and a platonic friendship. He didn't need to muddy the waters by letting temptations run too strong.

When she hadn't told him what she was struggling with by the time he'd finished his second taco, Grant considered asking outright what was bothering her. But he remembered how difficult it had been for both of them to share the traumatic details of their lives with each other.

He consumed another taco while Celeste worked on her first. He set his last two tacos aside and leaned back. "I can't give you input if you're not willing to trust me with whatever is bothering you."

Celeste set her taco in her tray and looked at him. "My dad wants to have lunch with me."

"Wow. I did not expect that."

"Me either. I mean, he reached out to my friend Amy a couple weeks ago, but I thought if I ignored him, he'd go away. But he showed up at Amy's work again last week, wanting her to ask me again to have lunch with him."

"And I take it you don't want to?"

"Why should I? He'll be judgmental and critical. He's looking for an opportunity to tell me I'm not successful."

"But you are successful, Celeste, and crazy talented. Any label he may give you will only stick if you let it."

"You're right. I don't need to prove anything to him anymore."

"Why does it sound like you've decided not to see him then?"

"Why should I?" she asked again.

"Because he's your dad, and he has taken the first step at reconciliation, which I'm sure wasn't easy for him."

She set her tacos aside and folded her arms over her chest. "I should have known you'd take Amy's side."

"I'm not taking Amy's side. I'm taking your side. I've never even met Amy. That's a situation we need to rectify, by the way." He pointed his finger at her.

"If you were taking my side, you wouldn't be pushing me to subject myself to my dad's critical, domineering—"

Grant pressed a finger to her lips. A mistake, but he needed to calm her down. "Listen, if my dad were alive, and he reached out to me for any reason, I'd meet him for lunch tomorrow."

"Can I talk now?" Warm air rushed over his finger, and a spark of desire lit in him.

"Sorry." He dropped his hand and balled it into a fist to keep from reaching out and grabbing her hand, or worse yet, pulling her into his arms and putting his lips where his finger had just been.

"Amy said the same thing," Celeste said, oblivious to the turmoil inside him. "She'd be ecstatic if her mother who basically ignored her all of her life reached out to her."

"All I'm saying is maybe he's changed, and you should give him a chance."

Celeste tapped a finger against her lips, making Grant jealous of that finger.

"Maybe you're right. But I don't want to go alone to meet him. I'd ask Amy to go with me, but she's got a lot—"

"I'll go with you," he said without hesitation.

"But we decided we shouldn't see each other outside of work."

"This is different. You need moral support from a friend. I want to be that friend."

"Really? You'd do that for me?"

"I'd do anything for you, Celeste."

Her gaze jumped to his. He probably shouldn't have said that with so much fervor, but if there was one thing he'd learned about himself while enduring the sweet torture of working with her this past month, it was that he was falling madly in love with her.

She reached over and squeezed his balled fist. "The feeling is mutual." Then she removed her hand again before he could relax his fist and clasp her fingers in his.

Wait. Did she mean she'd do anything for him? Or had she read the love he had for her on his face, and her reply meant she loved him too?

He didn't dare ask for an explanation, because they still had to work together for another five months. Even once the Armstrong Project was complete, Grant wasn't sure dating a coworker was wise.

CELESTE PARKED her car in front of the Italian restaurant where she'd told her father she'd meet him for lunch. She looked at Grant beside her.

He'd offered to meet her at the restaurant, but she'd been half afraid he wouldn't show up, and she would have to face her father alone. Unwilling to take any chances, she'd insisted on picking him up.

"What time did you tell your father we would meet him?"

"I didn't actually talk to him." She licked her dry lips. "I left a message with his secretary that I would meet him for lunch at Lombardi's at one o'clock, and that I would be bringing a friend."

Grant checked the time on his phone.

"Yes, I know we're early. But he's bound to be early, too. He uses it as an intimidation tactic."

"Why did you leave a message with his secretary instead of talking to your dad directly?"

"Because, I didn't want to give him the upper hand. I needed to feel like I was in control of this meeting." She waved a hand toward the restaurant. "That's why I pick Lombardi's. It's high class enough he won't criticize my choice but still affordable on my budget."

Grant took her hand, sending waves of warmth radiating up her arm. "You have nothing to prove, Celeste. If it helps, think of this as you doing him a favor."

"You're right. And if I don't like the way things are going, I can always leave. I'm an adult, and he doesn't control me anymore."

"Exactly. You are a successful, talented, competent, beautiful woman."

Her eyes widened as he piled on the compliments. Was he saying them because he actually meant them? Or had he said them because he knew words of affirmation was her love language?

As though he read her mind, Grant squeezed her hand before letting go. "I meant every word."

Celeste's heart expanded. She loved the way he made her feel. Like he believed in her, no matter what she did. Hopefully, they'd find a way to have a relationship once they finished the Armstrong project.

She toyed with the idea of quitting her job altogether and pursuing her dream of writing and illustrating children's books. But quitting her job without another source of income terrified her. She needed to get over her fear of failing and send her first book with the series idea to Penny at Hi-Lo Publishing.

"So, are we going in? Or are we going to sit here and wait for your dad to get there first?"

"We're going in." She reached for her door handle. Her dreams would have to wait for another day.

Five minutes later, Celeste grabbed Grant's hand under the table. "He's here."

She watched the man she loved—but couldn't tolerate—walk toward her. Owen Hightower was a tall man with an imposing presence, but she agreed with Amy. Her dad had aged. His shoulders now had the slightest curve to them, and even though he had a full head of hair, his temples were silver. Faint wrinkles framed his eyes.

Grant stood as her father approached, so Celeste did the same. She had no idea how to greet the man who'd told her if she walked out the door to never bother coming back.

Her father appeared to have the same struggle, because he stopped next to the table and smoothed his hands down his sports coat.

When the silence lengthened, Grant stuck out his hand. "Mr. Hightower, I presume? I'm Grant Foster, Celeste's friend."

Owen looked relieved to have something to do with his hands. He shook Grant's hand, and before things could get awkward again, she stuck her hand out. "Father."

"Celeste." Disappointment filled her dad's eyes, but his handshake was as firm as ever. "You look good, honey."

The term of endearment surprised her. Her dad had never been the sensitive and tender type, so to hear him call her honey after seven years of estrangement left Celeste reeling.

"Th-thank you. You look good too." She thought about adding *"Dad"* at the end but couldn't make her tongue form the word.

They took their seats, and thankfully the waiter showed up right away to take their drink order. She needed a Diet Coke.

Heavy silence settled over the table as they studied their menus. Celeste knew what she wanted—she always ordered the Chicken Carbonara when she came here—but she took her time studying the menu so she wouldn't have to make conversation.

Once they placed their orders, Grant turned to her father. "So, Celeste tells me you're an attorney. What type of law do you practice?"

Celeste wanted to kiss Grant as her father explained the intricacies of corporate law. Not because she cared one whit about lawyer talk, but because Grant made what could be a completely unbearable situation bearable.

Grant asked follow-up questions that kept her dad talking until their food showed up.

Once again, silence—though not as tense as before—descended on their table as they ate. After several long minutes, her father cleared his throat. "So Grant, what do you do?"

Grant brushed his napkin across his mouth before speaking. "I'm the Director of Content and Development for a leading advertising firm here in Portland."

Celeste bit back the urge to brag that he was months away from being made the Vice President of Marketing.

He and her father talked a little more about Grant's work, then her father asked a question that left her speechless—not that she'd said much.

"So, are you two a couple?"

Grant tensed beside her.

She reached for her Coke. "It's... uh... it's complicated." She wanted to say, "Yes, he's my boyfriend." Not because she wanted her father's approval—knowing him, he wouldn't approve of her dating a coworker. She wanted to claim Grant as her boyfriend because she liked him that much. After the way he'd handled her father, she was more than half in love with him.

He took her hand, sending a warm tingling sensation racing up her arm. "I like your daughter very much, Mr. Hightower, but since we're working together on an important project, we're taking things slowly. Dating a coworker is never ideal, but we can't always be in control of when these things happen."

Yep. She wanted to kiss him alright. And she was more than half in love with him. They had avoided personal talk that might be deemed inappropriate for the workplace, so she had no idea Grant felt that strongly about her.

"Wise move," her father said, then he looked at her. "That's why I was glad your mother worked at a different law firm. I wouldn't have felt right about dating someone from my firm. A subordinate at that."

And there it was. It was subtle, but it was disapproval all the same. Celeste couldn't tell if he referred to her mother as a subordinate because she was a few years behind him in her career or if he just thought of her mother as subordinate in general. Deciding it wasn't worth analyzing, she let it go. It wouldn't change anything in the past or now, except to make her more wary of her father and his intentions.

Whether her father approved of her relationship with Grant or not —not that they were in a relationship—didn't matter. She didn't need his approval.

"I see the Carbonara is still your favorite, Celeste. Does it taste as good as it used to?"

The air whooshed from her lungs as surprise swept over her. After her mother passed away, they had come here every couple of months —at Celeste's insistence—but she didn't realize her father had ever noted what she ordered.

How does he still remember after seven years?

"Yes, it's as good as ever. And how is your ravioli?"

"Good." Quiet fell over the table for a long moment before her father spoke again. "How are you enjoying your work at 3D Media?"

"How did you know I work for 3D Media?" This visit with her father was full of all kinds of surprises.

He cleared his throat. "I've kept tabs on you. That's how I knew you worked with Grant before he mentioned it."

Heat flushed through her body. "You're spying on me?"

"No, of course not." Her dad tugged at his collar.

Celeste had never seen her father display any type of nervous behavior before. It should have comforted her, but it didn't. She needed to know how he knew she and Grant worked together.

"I have friends in influential positions who I've asked to... keep tabs on you. You know, in case you needed something."

"You mean to see if I've failed in my career so you can say, 'I told you so'?" She bit her tongue to keep from adding, *even if I needed help, I wouldn't ask you.*

"No, of course not." Her father sounded like a broken record. "I only want you to succeed, like any father who wants what's best for his daughter."

Every muscle in Celeste's body tensed and she felt Grant do the same beside her. He set his fork down and a split second later his hand squeezed her knee. His touch should have been a welcome distraction, but she refused to back down and let her father continue to think he knew what was best for her.

"So help me... if you mention law school, I am walking out that door, and I'll make sure we never meet again." She jabbed a finger toward the front door.

"No, of course not, honey." Yep, he was a broken record. "I realized once you graduated with your art degree that you were as stubborn as your mother, and there was no changing your mind."

"I did not get my stubbornness from Mom." She ground out the words.

"Perhaps you're right. But regardless, I did everything in my power to make sure you succeeded in your chosen career."

"You did everything in your power? You had no control over my career. I got where I am on my own."

"I agree, you've done well in your career. But if it wasn't for me, 3D Media would never have looked at you."

A cold chill swept through the room, yet Celeste's temperature rose, and her heart raced. "What do you mean?"

"Corporations like 3D don't offer internships to students with degrees from community colleges." The smug look on her father's face made her stomach churn.

Corporations like 3D? Now it was clear. Her father's firm, Burkhart, Hightower, and Aldridge no doubt provided legal counsel for 3D Media.

"Are you saying you forced 3D to offer me an internship?" A strange vibrating sensation consumed Celeste's body as perspiration pricked between her breasts.

"No, of course not."

Wow. Her father, who was usually so articulate, had a limited vocabulary today.

"I only suggested to 3D's partners that they reach out to the community college the year you graduated." His cheeks flushed. "I will admit to mentioning you by name."

She sat back and folded her arms across her chest, reminding herself to breath. Her gaze narrowed on her father. "I'll bet you offered them a discount on their legal fees if they hired me."

Owen Hightower mimicked her posture. "So what if I did? I only did it because I wanted to see you succeed."

"Right, because I wasn't talented enough to succeed on my own?" She tossed her napkin on the table. She needed to leave before she started hurling insults at her father about how controlling and over-bearing he was. "I don't know why you bothered to reach out to Amy to get a hold of me. You apparently know everything about me. You know where I work, you probably even know where I live. Please tell me you had nothing to do with me getting into my apartment."

"Of course not."

Did the man not know how to say anything else?

"If I'd had anything to do with it, you'd be in a much nicer apart-ment building than that... roach motel."

"It's not a roach motel. And I like it there, more than I do here." She sprang to her feet. "Grant, we're leaving." Tears pricked her eyes. She'd been so stupid to think her father would ever change.

"Wait, Celeste!" Her father grabbed her arm. "I went to Amy because I was afraid you'd never agree to meet with me. You and Amy have always been so close. I thought maybe she could help persuade you to meet with me."

"You asked Amy to convince me to meet with you?"

He shrugged. An admission of guilt as far as Celeste was concerned.

That does it!

She headed for the door. It took her several seconds to realize Grant wasn't behind her. She turned to see him pull his wallet from his pocket and drop some bills on the table. Guilt washed over her. She'd have to remember to pay him back.

"For your information, Mr. Hightower, *I* persuaded Celeste to meet with you as much or more than Amy did. I thought working things out with you would be good for her. It looks like I was wrong. Celeste is so talented; I know she'd have succeeded on her own. I'm sorry you can't see what an amazing woman your daughter is and accept and love her for who she is instead of who you want her to be."

Celeste's heart melted. Grant really was the most amazing man.

CONFLICTING EMOTIONS SWIRLED around in Celeste like a tornado as they made the drive back to Grant's house in silence. The cold front fueled by anger kept tangling with the warm front created by Grant's defense of her.

Grant must have read the tension in her, because besides saying, " I'm sorry," when they first got in the car, he made no attempt to make conversation.

Even though she and Grant needed to maintain a platonic relationship for work, she felt like they'd crossed some sort of invisible barrier today. He'd had a front-row seat to the type of controlling Celeste had lived with for so many years, and it had strengthened the bond between them. It would be interesting to see what happened between them from now on.

When she pulled to a stop in front of his house, he turned in his seat and took her hand. "I'm sorry things turned out the way they did today. I think your dad really cares about you. He just doesn't understand that trying to control your life is not the way to show it."

She held up her other hand. "I appreciate your support today, but I really can't handle you defending him right now." She was barely keeping it together as it was.

"I know. I'm sorry. For the record, I think if you had applied to 3D on your own, you would have gotten the job. I don't think it matters how it came about." He reached up to stroke her cheek with his thumb, sending warmth flooding over her. "Also for the record, I meant everything I said about you... about us. Unfortunately, even though I feel like something shifted between us today, I'm afraid things can't change as far as work goes. Not as long as we're working the Armstrong project together."

She nodded despite the disappointment that filled her. He was right, of course. No matter how much she wished things could be different, they needed to keep things professional.

Grant's voice dropped to a husky whisper as he leaned a little closer. "That's why after I kiss you, we'll both show up to work Monday morning and pretend I'm not a weak-willed man when it comes to you."

Despite her racing heart, Celeste laughed. "How romantic. That's just what every girl wants to hear before a guy kisses her."

"Hush." He leaned closer still but paused with his lips an inch from hers. "You make me feel so out of control sometimes." His breath mingled with hers, and her mouth grew moist. His lips brushed hers in a brief, feathery, not-at-all-satisfying kiss. "I hate feeling out of control." His mouth met hers again. This time with more pressure, lingering longer but not long enough. "But I love how I feel when I'm with you." Grant slid the hand that had been caressing her cheek into her hair as his mouth claimed hers.

There was nothing brief or timid about this kiss. His lips moved against hers, encouraging them to part. Celeste was all too eager to comply. She grabbed the front of his button-down shirt and pulled him a little closer as her mouth kept tempo with his.

A sense of wholeness washed over her, leaving her feeling complete. This was what she'd been missing her entire life.

With a groan, Grant released her head and pulled back. "Woman, you drive me crazy."

"The feeling is mutual." She couldn't fight the smile that took over her face.

He reached for the door handle with one hand while pointing a finger at her with the other. "Remember, we will not speak of this on Monday." Then his voice lowered, taking on a tortured tone. "And we will not repeat this until the Armstrong Project is complete."

She nodded and gripped the steering wheel to keep herself from pulling him back into the car.

Celeste didn't know if Grant really was weak willed or if he'd just been trying to distract her from the crappy lunch with her dad, but she spent the afternoon floating around her apartment, attempting to clean. She was way too distracted to be effective, however.

It wasn't until her phone chimed with an incoming text, that her elation dissipated.

Amy: *How did lunch go with your dad?*

Celeste debated giving Amy a piece of her mind through text, but Amy was too good of a friend for that. She hit the call button.

Amy answered after the first ring. "You calling me back this fast means it either went great, or it went terrible."

"Did my dad bribe you to convince me to have lunch with him?" The question came out clipped and sharp.

"What? No." Amy's tone was defensive. "He said he hoped I could help persuade you, because we've always had such a strong influence on each other."

"Yeah, that sounds more like judgment than bribery."

Because of Amy's difficult home life, Owen Hightower had always welcomed her into their home. But Amy moved out on her own a few months before turning eighteen. And that coincided too closely with the law school conflict between Celeste and her father, so he blamed Amy for being a negative influence on Celeste.

"I suppose, but he was nice enough about it. He left me a big tip. Both times."

Did he tip generously, hoping it would sway Amy to convince Celeste to go to lunch with him?

"So tell me. How did it go?"

Celeste started with how glad she was she'd taken Grant along and her surprise at her father remembering that Chicken Carbonara was her favorite dish. She paced her tiny apartment, vigorously fluffing the throw pillows as she told Amy her dad had basically been spying on her for the last seven years.

"Not only does he know exactly where I live, he suggested the partners at 3D offer an internship to the community college the year I graduated, meant specifically for me."

"He didn't!"

"He promised them a discount on their legal fees if they gave me the internship."

"So, even after all these years, he's still trying to control you?"

Sarcasm filled Celeste's voice when she spoke again. "He said he just wanted what's best for his daughter. Like he knows what's best for me. What he really wants is for me not embarrass him."

"I get where you're coming from, but I think it's kind of sweet that he cared about you enough to help you succeed."

Amy would have loved that kind of attention from her mother. But Celeste saw her father's actions as for what they were; an attempt to control his rebellious daughter.

"That's basically the same thing Grant said, but I'm not ready to hear it. My dad called my apartment complex a roach motel."

"What? Your apartment may be small, but it's nice, and it's in a decent neighborhood." Amy let out a sigh. "I'm sorry things turned out like that, C. I'd hoped he had changed, you know."

"Me too, but I should have known better." All the angry and confused feelings Celeste felt after leaving the restaurant had returned and tears stung her eyes. "I just don't know if I'm good enough to make it on my own, Aim." She looked at the scattered pieces of artwork and snippets of stories that littered her coffee table.

"Of course you are. You never would have been kept on at 3D after the internship if you weren't a valuable employee."

"I suppose you're right, but I feel like I've been living a lie for the past four years. That internship sounded great when I was facing thousands of dollars of student debt, so I took it. I mean, I like my job —some projects are really rewarding—but I feel like I took the easy route, you know. Instead of really chasing my dreams, I settled into a career that wasn't really on my radar until my guidance counselor suggested I apply for the internship."

"So, what are you going to do about it?" Amy's tone held a challenge.

Celeste's chest tightened, and her breathing sped up as she looked at her drawings of fairies and trolls. Images from a whole new set of stories about an independent, strong-willed girl with a stubborn, hard-headed father filled her head. Dozens of story ideas swam through Celeste's head, complete with conflicts father and daughter might face. She would make sure the father always learned a lesson as well as the daughter.

"I'm going to follow my dreams!" Celeste gathered her sketches from the coffee table. She loved the characters she'd created here, but she knew from experience the ideas dancing through her head would not leave until she put them on the paper. Promising she would someday return to her beautiful little fairies, she tucked them away in a portfolio.

"That's my girl," laughed Amy. "Do I need to bring you some dinner tonight?"

"No, because you'll distract me, and I've got work to do."

Celeste ended the call with Amy and pulled out a new sketch pad. She settled on the couch, her legs curled beneath her, and let the turmoil rolling around inside her fuel her creativity.

CHAPTER 13

*M*onday morning, Celeste looked at the stack of stories on her coffee table. She'd spent the rest of Saturday and all day Sunday writing and sketching. Most of the drawings still needed a lot of work, but she'd completed six separate stories, with another six outlined. She was more excited than ever to follow her dreams.

She stared at her reflection as she brushed her teeth. She didn't look any different, but she felt different. She felt like an explorer on the verge of a major discovery. Now all she needed to do was get over her fear of rejection, of failure, and send out a query letter to Hi-Lo Publishing.

She dropped her toothbrush into its holder and applied her lipstick. She looked her reflection in the eye. "I promise to email Penny before the week is over. But first I need to quit my job."

She stepped out of the bathroom and grabbed her purse and cell phone. Looking up Sharon's number before walking out the door.

Fifteen minutes later, as Celeste walked through the front door of 3D Media, her phone rang. She pulled it from her purse and answered without bothering to check the caller ID.

"Hello."

"Miss Hightower? This is Sharon, Mr. Davenport's secretary. Your message said you'd like to meet with Mr. Davenport at his earliest convenience. I'm afraid his schedule is pretty packed for the next two days, but he is available right now."

Celeste froze. "Right now?" her voice squeaked.

She needed to take this step before she chickened out, but when she left the message on Sharon's voice mail, she thought she'd have a few hours to psych herself up.

"He's available until eight forty-five."

"Okay, I just walked in the building. I'll be up in a few minutes." Celeste took a deep breath as she dropped her cell phone back into her purse.

It's time to chase my dreams.

All too soon, she sat opposite Mr. Davenport, his enormous mahogany desk between them.

"Miss Hightower, I never really took the time to tell you and Grant... er... Mr. Foster, how impressed I was with your presentation of the Armstrong project. The two of you were like a well-oiled machine. Miles was blown away as well. I knew you two would be an unbeatable team. You are both destined for big things."

Celeste's breath caught in her throat. What did he mean by that? Was he saying she had more of a future here than only as an artist in the graphic arts department?

It doesn't matter. This isn't your dream, remember.

She wiped damp palms on her skirt. "Thank you, sir. It has been a pleasure working with Grant, uh, Mr. Foster. He's a dedicated, hard worker."

"Why do I feel you're about to throw a flag on the field?" Mr. Davenport leaned forward and braced his elbows on his desk. Sitting down, the much taller man wasn't nearly as imposing as when he was standing, but the look on his face was anything but happy.

"But... I need to give my two weeks' notice." *There, I said it.* No going back now.

Mr. Davenport leaned back in his seat, as though the wind had escaped from his sails. He suddenly looked much older.

"I did not see that coming. You and Grant make a perfect team." Then he leaned forward again, his eyes scrutinizing her face. "Has he committed a foul?"

"No. Nothing like that. He's been completely professional." *At work, anyway.* Her face warmed as she remembered the toe-curling kiss he gave her last Saturday.

Since 3D didn't have a policy against its employees dating each other—at least, she didn't think they did—what happened away from work was none of Mr. Davenport's business.

"I have thoroughly enjoyed working with Grant. He is a born leader who is not too proud to listen to his peers and take their opinions into consideration. He's doing an excellent job"

"I don't understand then. Is this about money? I'm prepared to offer you a raise. I know I promised you a bonus at the start of this project, but you and Grant have exceeded my expectations."

A raise? That was tempting.

No, stay focused. On your dreams.

Celeste cleared her throat and squared her shoulders. "I don't know if you're aware or not, sir, but my father and I have been estranged for the past seven years."

Mr. Davenport's brows creased as he gave a slight shake of his head.

"My father was... *is* a very controlling man. I recently found out that four years ago—when I was about to graduate with my bachelor's degree—my father offered 3D a discount on their legal fees if they would award an internship to a specific graduate from Portland community college."

Mr. Davenport lowered his eyes, a flash of guilt crossing his face.

"Even though my father and I weren't on speaking terms, he found a way to control my career choice."

"Look here, Celeste. I don't regret for a single minute making that play, offering you that internship, I mean. You have more than proven yourself. In fact, we now offer regular internships to the community college."

"I'm glad to hear that. But it doesn't change the fact that my father hijacked my career because he didn't think being an illustrator of children's books was a worthwhile career for his daughter."

"I understand your disappointment and frustration, but I hate to lose your talent here at 3D, especially with the Armstrong contract on the line."

She held both hands up, palms out. "I promise I'm not dropping the ball, sir. Grant is a fantastic coach with an excellent team in place. The players are already running their respective balls."

Mr. Davenport's eyebrows raised. He looked impressed with Celeste's ability to pull off a sport's analogy.

She took a deep breath, relieved it hadn't fallen flat. She'd come up with that one in the elevator but wasn't sure she should use it.

Mr. Davenport picked up a monogrammed pen, rolling it between his fingers. "Is there anything I can say to make you reconsider?"

"No, sir."

He gave a slow nod. "When an employee gives two weeks' notice, I don't normally ask them to stay the two weeks. Quick and clean is usually best, but for the sake of the Armstrong project, I'd like you to finish out the two weeks. I want you and Grant to get every minute detail ironed out before you leave."

She nodded.

He pointed a finger at her. "And *you* get to break the news to Foster."

Celeste swallowed hard. The sting of tears pricked her eyes as she realized she was about to let her partner down.

Grant would not be happy.

GRANT WALKED into the conference room he'd shared with Celeste the last five weeks, surprised he'd beaten her here. They usually arrived about the same time most days, but he had a hard time getting Reagan and Josh moving on Mondays, so she usually beat him.

Would things be awkward because he kissed her on Saturday? Hopefully not, but Celeste would definitely be distracting. As usual.

He couldn't wait for the Armstrong project to end. It wouldn't be ideal dating while they both worked at 3D, even though they worked in different departments. But he wasn't willing to let her go. He'd hate to turn down the VP position, but maybe it would be a good idea to look for a job elsewhere.

Grant set up his laptop and started going through his email. Celeste still hadn't arrived by the time he'd finished, so he turned to the list of tasks they needed to assign. He felt good about the team he and Celeste had assembled and their abilities to meet their deadlines.

He looked at the clock. It was eight thirty already, and she still wasn't here. Even on her latest days, she'd never arrived later than ten after eight. He pulled out his phone and texted her: *Where are you? Is everything okay?*

When she hadn't responded after another ten minutes, his stomach hardened. Finding out her father was responsible for her getting a job at 3D had upset her, but surely, she hadn't done something drastic. Had she?

He sent another text: *I'm worried about you. Please let me know you're okay.*

He walked to the door of the conference room and looked out across the cubicles. Maybe she got caught up talking to someone.

His chest grew tighter by the second as he scanned the open room.

She wasn't out there.

He returned to his desk and opened the inter-office group chat he'd created specifically for the team they'd put together for the Armstrong project. Maybe she'd gotten here early and was following up with one of their team players. Most days, the team members returned to their own offices to work. Other days, they all worked together all day.

In the chat, he typed the words: *Has anyone seen Miss Hightower this morning?*

His mouse hovered over the send button. Would he look incompetent because he lost his partner? His assistant coach.

A sharp twinge of pain pierced his chest. He couldn't lose Celeste.

He picked his phone up off the table to make sure he hadn't missed a text from her.

Nothing.

"Come on, Celeste. Where are you?" he mumbled.

"I'm right here. I'm sorry." Celeste breezed through the door, looking gorgeous as usual.

His breath hitched. *She's okay.* He bolted from his chair and took a step toward her. It was all he could do to not crush her in his arms.

"Where have you been? Is everything okay? I've been worried sick about you."

"I know. I'm sorry. I honestly didn't expect to be in Mr. Davenport's office that long."

Mr. Davenport's office? Did I miss a meeting? He mentally reviewed his calendar, knowing he hadn't overlooked an appointment.

Had she gone to complain about him? Had he fouled everything up by kissing her last Saturday?

He studied her beautiful face, trying to read the emotion there. He spotted a hint of sadness, and her eyes looked a little red. His stomach bottomed out.

"Why were you in Mr. Davenport's office? And why does it look like you've been crying?"

Celeste cast a glance at the open door before she set her bag down and lifted her laptop out. "Sit down and relax. I'll explain everything."

Grant didn't want to sit down. He wanted to take Celeste by the hand and take her to the park—or maybe his car since it was rainy today. He wanted to wrap her in his arms and convince her not to tell him the bad news he had a feeling was coming.

He sank into his chair, every muscle in his body tensing. "Please tell me I didn't mess up everything by kissing you on Saturday." The words came out a hoarse whisper.

She smiled. "I'm pretty sure we agreed not to talk about that today."

"You're killing me here. Why were you in Mr. Davenport's office, if it wasn't to complain about me?"

"Is that what you think?" Her brow furrowed, forming the deep V he'd come to love almost as much as he loved her arched eyebrow and dimples. "It's the opposite, actually. I've been singing your praises for the last half hour."

"Singing my praises? Why?"

"I wanted Mr. Davenport to know that you are perfectly capable of managing this project by yourself."

"But I'm not managing it by myself. You're my partner. I need you." A note of desperation filled his voice, but he didn't care.

"You don't need me, Grant. We have a great team in place to help carry this project out. You'll be fine."

He leaned toward her, even though a conference table sat between them. "What are you not telling me?"

"I'm quitting. I gave Mr. Davenport my two weeks' notice."

"What?" He sprang to his feet. "You can't quit!"

Celeste looked at the open door. "Sit down and lower your voice."

"Sorry." Grant dropped into his chair again. "It's because I kissed you, isn't it? I knew I shouldn't have given in to the temptation."

She hurried over to the door and closed it before returning to her seat. "Okay, you really need to stop talking about that kiss, or everyone is going to know what a weak-willed man you are when it comes to me." She gave him a teasing grin.

But Grant didn't smile. There was nothing funny about Celeste leaving.

"I did not quit my job because you kissed me. I quit my job because I was tired of my father pulling my strings. I refuse to be his puppet any longer."

"He may have gotten you the internship, but you're the one who proved yourself. You're the one who earned the permanent position."

She held up her hand. "You're right; I did. But I haven't chased my own dreams. I'm living my dad's modified dreams for me. I've enjoyed working here. I'm grateful for everything I've learned in this job and the people I've met..." Her eyes held his. "But I need to move on."

Grant's throat tightened. He felt like he was about to lose his best friend.

When did Celeste become his best friend?

She's been there for me every time I needed her.

"I need you, Celeste. I don't want to lose you."

"You're not losing me. In fact, if I'm no longer working here..." A twinkle lit her eyes as she smiled. "Then there's nothing to keep us from seeing each other socially. If we want to, that is."

"I want to. But..."

"But what?" Her face fell.

He sat back in his seat and shook his head. "I don't know. I'm still in shock, I guess. I can't imagine showing up here every day and not seeing your beautif— your face across the table. Who will I talk to when I need to bounce ideas around? And who's going to call me on my BS when I get bossy?"

"I'll only be a phone call or text away. And you can bounce ideas off me in the evenings while I we have dinner together." Was it his imagination or had Celeste's voice taken on a seductive quality?

"I like the sound of that." Boy, did he like the sound of that. "But I don't understand why you would walk away from a successful career just because your father orchestrated it." He studied her face. Those gorgeous dark eyes that sparked with passion when he kissed her held a gleam he'd never seen there before. "What dreams do you want to chase?"

She lowered her eyes, and a blush tinted her cheeks.

Warmth filled him as he looked at the beautiful woman across the table. Somewhere along the line, Celeste had become his dream. He wanted her by his side. Forever.

"Share your dreams with me, Celeste." He held his breath. Would she trust him with her dreams?

"Ever since I was a little girl and my mom used to read bedtime stories to me, I've wanted to be a children's author and illustrator."

"You'd be amazing at it." He could totally see Celeste as a children's author.

"You really think so?" She gave him a shy smile.

"I know so. I see how amazing you are with Reagan and Josh, and I imagine you would be equally amazing with younger kids. And you're so talented with words as well as art."

"Thank you. That means a lot to me."

He glanced over his shoulder to make sure the door was still closed. "You mean a lot to me, and I want to help you chase your dreams."

CHAPTER 14

*C*eleste pulled the mail from her slot and made her way to her apartment. It had been another long day at work, and she was eager to get back to her stories.

One week down, one more to go. Grant was the one thing that made work bearable nowadays. She woul miss working with him, but ever since she'd given notice and started chasing her dreams, she couldn't wait to return home each night and work on her stories.

She'd written two more this week and finally finished the artwork on the first one. This weekend, she hoped to get started on the illustrations for the second book.

She dropped the mail on the counter while she slipped off her jacket and kicked off her shoes. Stepping back to the counter, she picked up the pile of mail. Mixed with the ads from pesticide companies and dentists were two bills. Bills she'd have a hard time paying if she didn't get a contract on her stories soon. Her meager savings would not last long, especially since she needed to pay rent next week.

Of course, she couldn't get a contract on her stories if she didn't get some queries sent out. Despite promising herself on Monday to send out a query to Hi-Lo this week, she'd dragged her feet. The perfectionist in her needed to make sure the first story was fully illustrated before submitting, even though publishers didn't usually require full illustrations. But that first story was complete now, so she had no more excuses.

Tomorrow. I'll email Penny tomorrow.

Celeste's hand froze as she looked at the last envelope. Her name—written in her dad's unmistakable, perfect print—caused her chest to tighten. Had he heard she'd quit her job and written this letter because he knew she wouldn't listen to verbal censure?

She dropped the rest of the mail and walked to the couch, the letter clutched in one hand, her cell phone in the other. She stared at the envelope for a long time, both afraid to open it—she didn't want to read what was inside—and afraid to let it go. In case, if by some miracle, this wasn't a censure, but an olive branch.

Finally, she dialed Grant's number. In the past, she would have called Amy, but Grant was there at lunch with her father last week, and he was now involved in this. Part of her wanted him to tell her to throw it in the garbage, or better yet, return to sender. The other part wanted him to tell her it was okay to open it. To assure her that whatever her father wrote wouldn't hurt her yet again.

"Hello?"

Just the sound of his voice was enough to send her pulse skyrocketing. She'd only left work half an hour ago, but already she couldn't wait to see him again.

One more week.

"Celeste? Are you there?"

"Yes, sorry." Heat filled her face, even though he couldn't see her. "I um... got a letter from... my dad."

"Really?" Surprise filled his voice. "What does it say?"

"I don't know. I haven't opened it yet."

"I see. Do you want me to come over and hold your hand while you open it?" His voice sounded like he was smiling, and the thought of holding his hand tempted her more than it should.

"No, I just... don't know if I should open it... or not."

"Fine." Grant's voice sounded disappointed. "Let's look at the worst-case scenario: the letter might be negative. Maybe for walking out on him at lunch, or maybe he's heard about you quitting your job. Either way, you do not need to explain yourself to him anymore, Celeste. You don't owe him anything, remember?"

"You're right." She nodded her head. Grant understood her so well. No wonder she loved him so much.

Floored by the revelation that she was head over heels in love with Grant, she sucked in a deep breath and bit her tongue to keep herself from blurting it out. They hadn't even gone out on a date yet. She couldn't admit she loved him already, no matter how true it was.

"On the other hand," Grant's voice pulled her back, "if it's some sort of an apology... well, wouldn't you want to read that?"

"Yes, but..."

"But you don't think your father will ever change, so it can't possibly be an apology."

"Exactly." He knew her so well.

"There's only one way to find out, honey." Grant gave a quick cough, and before Celeste could get excited about the term of endearment that slipped from his mouth, he continued. "Sorry, I didn't mean to say that... yet." A soft groan came over the line. "Can't we forget I said that, please?"

"Nope," she laughed. "I mean, I could say I'll forget you said it, but then I'd be a liar." She lowered her voice, even though there was no chance of anyone overhearing her. "I don't want to forget it."

A sound resembling a hiss came over the phone. "You are not making this any easier on either of us."

"Me? You're the one who called me—"

"I know what I called you. Just... please don't tell anyone I called you that. Especially not anyone from work."

"I promise." She bit back the laughter that threatened to bubble out. She couldn't believe Grant was still so adamant about keeping their relationship separate from work and the Armstrong project, but it was just the way his mind worked.

"Celeste?"

"What?"

"Open the da— darn letter already."

She chuckled. Trust Grant to distract her from her problems with her father. She put the phone on speaker and set it on the couch beside her. Taking a deep breath, she ripped the envelope open. If it looked like an apology, she'd keep reading. If not, she'd throw it in the trash.

She held her breath as she pulled the single sheet of paper from the envelope. The hand-written letter carried the official letterhead from her dad's law office.

My dearest daughter,

I'm sorry.

"It's an apology." The words rushed out, half sob and half laughter. "A long one by the looks of it."

"Good." Grant's smooth, deep voice filled the room. "Take your time reading it. Then call me back if you want to talk about it. I need to go tell Reagan to turn down her music."

"Thank you, Grant. I lo—uh... I appreciate it." Celeste clapped a hand over her mouth. She'd almost told him she loved him.

"What are friends for? Bye, Celeste."

Friends? She wanted to be a whole lot more than friends.

The phone clicked, and her screen displayed "call ended".

She blew out a deep breath. She would have to be extra careful while they worked together next week. Turning back to her father's letter, she braced herself.

My dearest daughter,

I'm sorry.

I'm sure you know how hard those two words are for me to write. You know I don't like to admit when I am wrong. I couldn't bring myself to do it seven years ago, and I couldn't do it last week at the restaurant.

I never meant to make you feel like I was trying to control your life. I only mentioned my part in the internship with 3D Media to let you know how much I care about you, despite all that happened between us. I've only ever wanted you to be successful.

But now, I recognize that my idea of success may not be right. Well, not right for you anyway. I truly am proud of the beautiful woman you have become. I see your mother when I look at you. And it hurts that I've lost both of you.

I can't bring her back, but I would very much like to have you back in my life. In whatever capacity you deem acceptable.

If you choose to ignore my request... well, I guess I understand why, and I promise not to bother you again. But I hope you will let me be a part of your life again, because I still love you dearly.

Please forgive a stubborn, lonely, old man.

Love,

Your Father.

Celeste wiped the tears from her eyes. Never in all her life had she ever heard her father apologize. Writing the words was surely easier than saying them to her in person, but this was a tremendous step for him. She wasn't sure she was ready to let him waltz back into her life yet. He needed to earn her trust, but the thought of having a relationship with her father again appealed to her.

Would he freak out and regret his decision to be a part of her life when he found out she'd quit her job?

Maybe she'd wait a while to respond to his letter.

A FLOCK of wild geese took flight through Grant's stomach as he brought his car to a stop in front of Celeste's apartment building. He checked his hair in the rearview mirror before climbing from the car. It had only been twenty-four hours since she walked out of 3D's doors for the last time, but he felt like it had been a month.

He'd made the most of working with her these last two weeks as they ironed out all the kinks for the Armstrong project. They'd kept things professional, but his eyes had frequently strayed to her across the table from him. He was going to miss working with her. Not only was she incredibly talented, she was funny and quirky. She didn't put up with any of his garbage either.

While he would miss working with her, he was glad they didn't have to fight their feelings for each other anymore.

He knocked on her apartment door and wiped his sweaty palms against his jeans. *Why am I so nervous?*

The door opened, and the air whooshed from his lungs. The raven-haired beauty who frequently took his breath away at work in her jewel-toned blouses that hinted at her curves, stood there in a formfitting, fuchsia t-shirt. Remembering how cute she looked in her yoga pants and baggy sweatshirts, he'd told her to dress casually. But he was unprepared for how sexy she looked in the snug t-shirt and jeans that hugged her curves.

"Hi, come in. I'm almost ready. I just need to get my shoes on."

Grant walked into the small, simply furnished apartment, spotting touches and splashes of color here and there that fit Celeste's personality.

She disappeared into what he assumed was her bedroom, and his gaze shifted to the stacks of colorful pages on the coffee table.

Her story.

Like a moth drawn to flame, he sat on the sofa and reached for a stack of pages. He should ask for permission to read her stories, but he was afraid she might say no. Deciding he'd rather seek forgiveness than permission, he flipped the vibrant cover of the stack he held.

His eyes quickly roamed over the page, scanning the colorful images, and reading the text. He turned the page and read the story of the little girl who wanted so badly to prove herself but couldn't seem to please her father. He lifted another page, then another, chuckling at the predicament the little girl found herself in. Tears pricked his eyes when her father came to her rescue in the end, apologizing to his daughter for not being there for her when she needed him.

Grant blinked the tears away and looked up to see Celeste leaning against the bedroom doorway, a fingernail trapped between her teeth.

"This..." He held the pages up. "It's amazing."

"Do you really think so?"

"I'm not an expert on children's books, but I love this." He put the pages back on the table and stood. It only took two steps to bring him close enough to touch her. "Please tell me you're going to get them published."

"I sent a query to Hi-Lo Publishing this morning. I've done some illustrating for them in the past."

"Who else have you queried?"

"Only Hi-Lo."

"No. No. No. You have an incredible book here." He looked back at the table that held multiple stacks of papers. "Books. You can't send it to only one publisher and hope for the best. You need to send it to everyone. And then when they all want it, you can take your pick of who you want to publish your books."

"Whoa, slow down. You're being a little too intense for me right now. I'm taking baby steps here. This is the first time I've put my writing out there for anyone to read."

"Not true. I've read lots of your writing at work."

"That's different."

"How so?"

"You read the story. This is a piece of me." She waved toward the coffee table. "This isn't work. It's a passion project."

Grant grabbed the hem of her t-shirt and tugged her toward him. "Honey, you can't chase your dreams if you're taking baby steps. And I get why you're hesitant to share your passion project with the world, but if you want to be a successful writer, you need to think of writing as your business and let the passion shift to other areas." He smiled as he slid his hands around her waist, pulling her closer.

"You think so?" She slid her arms behind his neck. "You don't think I should devote all my passion toward launching my career as a writer?"

"Not all of it." He leaned a little closer, pushing her up against the wall. He dipped his head until his mouth was inches from hers. "I think you should save the bulk of your passion for me."

He closed the gap between their lips, and a soft moan escaped her. He bit back a groan of his own. The last two weeks had felt like an eternity as Grant dreamed of pulling Celeste into his arms and kissing her with an abandon that wouldn't be appropriate if she was still a coworker.

Her lips parted, inviting him in, and he accepted the invitation.

Her mouth moved with his, keeping a perfect rhythm that turned his brain to mush and lit a fire deep inside him. He could get lost in this woman's kiss.

He finally broke the contact after another long moment. "Wow! I think that might have been a mistake."

"What?" a surprised and offended look crossed Celeste's face.

"I hadn't planned to kiss you like that until the end of the night, because I knew once I did, I wouldn't want to stop. And I was right."

She pushed against his chest, shoving him away. "You promised me dinner, so you'd better deliver buddy. Or no more kisses for you."

"Fine, but after dinner, I want to come back here and finish reading your stories."

"You don't have to do that." Her cheeks flushed.

"I know I don't have to, but I want to. I wasn't kidding when I said I loved it. And tomorrow I'm going to do some research and help you find some more publishers to submit to."

Celeste stopped halfway through the door and gave him a puzzled look.

"I meant it when I said I want to help you chase your dreams."

As long as your dreams include me.

GRANT PULLED up in front of the restaurant one of his coworkers had recommended. He looked at the line that flowed out the front door.

"We're eating at Charly's?" Celeste asked, her voice full of surprise.

"Have you been here before? I've heard it's good, but I haven't eaten here yet." He looked at the line again. "It looks popular. We can go somewhere else though if you don't want to wait in that line."

"I have eaten here, and it is fantastic. Best barbecue in Portland. Trust me; it's worth the wait." A bright smile lit her face. "Besides, it's Saturday night—everywhere is going to be busy."

"True. It'll probably take me a while to find a parking space. Do you want to get out here, so you don't have to walk?"

"I don't mind walking with you."

Two long minutes later, Grant opened Celeste's door for her. As they started the lengthy walk to the restaurant, he slipped his hand into hers. Warmth exploded through him as she curled her fingers around his.

That kiss they shared back at her apartment had nearly driven him crazy. It felt so good to let loose with her and not have to worry he was making a mistake that could negatively impact his career. He hoped he could maintain a little restraint, because he didn't want to scare her off by coming on too strong.

Celeste fairly bubbled as she pulled him through the crowd to the hostess' desk.

She must really like the food here. Hopefully it would be worth the wait. Grant expected the hostess to tell them it would be a full hour before they could be seated.

Behind the hostess' stand stood a burly African American man whose face split into the biggest grin Grant had ever seen as they approached the desk. In a flash, the man rounded the stand and swept Celeste into a hug that pulled her hand from Grant's and lifted her off the floor.

"C! I haven't seen you in forever. Where have you been, girl?"

"I've missed you too, Chuck, but I've been busy," she said after he put her down.

Obviously, Celeste has been here more than once. Grant felt like he'd been swept into an alternate dimension where everyone knew what was going on except for him.

"I'll bet. Amy said you were working on some big-wig project." Concern filled the big man's eyes. "But then she told me you quit your job." He took both of her hands in his. "You're really going to go for it with your stories, huh?"

Celeste nodded, but Grant could see the trepidation hidden behind the smile she gave Chuck.

"It's about time, girl!" Chuck pulled her against his barrel chest again and gave her another hug.

"Thank you." She blinked as though trying to hold back tears.

Chuck's approval meant a lot to Celeste; Grant could see it on her face. Just as he could see the older man's affection for her written all over his smiling face. Why couldn't her father have been this accepting and encouraging of her dreams?

Grant cleared his throat, and Celeste pulled away from Chuck. She took Grant's hand again.

"Chuck, I'd like you to meet my... good friend, Grant Foster."

"*The* Grant Foster?" Chuck's eyes widened.

"Shh!" She slapped Chuck's arm as pink tinged her cheeks.

Grant stared first at Celeste then Chuck. Why did Chuck say his name like he knew more about him than Grant wanted any stranger to know?

Chuck's gaze dropped to Celeste and Grant's clasped hands then returned to Grant's face. The older man's eyes narrowed, and an expression that looked like a combination of a warning and a challenge filled his face. He held his right hand out.

Grant took the older man's hand in a confident grip, but the firmness of Chuck's grip surprised him. He tightened his own hold while maintaining eye contact with Chuck.

"Actually, what Celeste meant to say was I'm her boyfriend."

"No kidding." Chuck's voice lost its joviality. He continued to stare Grant down for another long moment before releasing his hand.

Grant had expected to feel this kind of judgment from Owen Hightower. He hadn't expected to get the third degree and an if-you-hurt-my-daughter-I'll-kill-you kind of warning in a single look from a total stranger.

He flexed his fingers, biting back a smile when Chuck did the same.

"Don't you dare hurt my girl, you hear." Chuck slapped Grant on the shoulder before giving him a big grin.

"Wouldn't dream of it, sir." He gave the other man a curt nod.

Chuck nodded then grabbed some menus and turned away. Before Grant knew it, they were seated at a semi-private booth in the back.

Chuck laid the menus on the table. "You like the menu your girl here designed for me a few years ago?"

Your girl.

Grant liked the sound of that. He gave the menu an appraising look. "She's talented, isn't she?"

"She's the best!" Chuck patted Celeste's shoulder. "I'll send Amy your way."

Grant slumped back in his seat and exhaled. He pointed a finger at Celeste. "That was so not funny. I can't believe you did that to me."

"Did what?" She bit back a smile.

"You could have told me you were on best terms with the manager."

"The owner," she corrected.

"The owner? Of course, Chuck is a nickname for Charlie." He shook his head, still reeling from the confrontation. "You know, I expected that kind of stare down when we went to lunch with your father. I was not expecting it from the owner of a bar and grill."

She laughed. "Sorry, even though I'd hoped to see Chuck tonight, I didn't expect him to be manning the hostess' station."

"So, how do you know Chuck so well?"

"Amy started busing tables here when she was fifteen. Charlie took her under his wing, and this became her second home. Then when I moved in with Amy at age eighteen, I hung out here a lot, and he took me in too. He became the father neither of us had in our lives."

"I can see he cares a great deal about you. He makes your real father seem cold and heartless."

"Right. I didn't realize how caring and supportive other dads could be until I left home."

"Celeste!" A pretty, very pregnant, blond waitress deposited two glasses of ice water on the table before bending over to hug Celeste. "I haven't seen you in forever. I've missed our Saturday lunches these past couple weeks. How are the stories coming?"

"Good. I've got eight of them finished, and I plan to write at least four more." Celeste waved a hand toward Grant. "Amy, I'd like you to meet my... boyfriend, Grant Foster." Her lips turned up as she said boyfriend, and he couldn't hide a smile of his own.

He liked the idea of being Celeste's boyfriend.

"Grant, this is my best friend since fifth grade, Amy Lawson."

Finally, I get to meet Amy!

"Finally, I get to meet Grant!" Amy gave him an appraising look as they shook hands, but she talked to Celeste out the side of her mouth. "He's so much better looking in person than that picture you showed me on 3D's website. And your boyfriend-girlfriend now, huh? Congratulations to both of you."

Celeste's cheeks turned rosy. "Aim, don't you have other customers to take care of?"

Amy clapped a hand over her mouth. "I'm sorry I embarrassed you, C. You know I love you, right?" Amy turned to Grant. "I have a habit of speaking thoughts that shouldn't be spoken out loud." She took their drink orders then backed away from the table. "Have a look at the menu. Chuck said order anything you want. Your dinner is on the house."

Grant stared at Celeste after Amy walked away. She glanced everywhere except at him. He grinned as he kept his gaze on her face.

"What?" she finally said.

"Two things." He held up his fingers. "First, if I don't pay for dinner, do I still get a goodnight kiss?"

The corners of her mouth quirked up. "You promised me dinner and you're delivering. I don't think it matters who pays for it."

"Good." Because he had every intention of kissing her again before the night was over. "Now, second question: why did Chuck say, 'The Grant Foster' when you introduced me? And why have you shown Amy my profile on 3D's website?"

She picked up her water glass and guzzled half of its contents. Judging by the rosiness in her cheeks, the icy liquid didn't accomplish what she'd hoped it would.

His gaze never wavered from hers, letting her know he expected an answer.

She cleared her throat. "I may have talked about you to Amy while I was here at Charlie's."

"May have?" He continued to stare her down.

"Okay, I talked about you... a few times. Amy wanted to know what you looked like, so I showed her your picture from the website."

His smile grew. "So, why did you talk about me? And how many is a few times?"

She lowered her eyes and fiddled with the corner of her menu. "I've had a crush on you for a while now," she mumbled.

A lightness filled his chest, and warmth rushed through his body. "What was that? I didn't hear you very well. It sounded like you said you had a crush on me."

Celeste shrugged, fighting a smile. "Sorry, I don't repeat myself."

He laughed and took her hand across the table. "How long exactly have you had a crush on me?"

"Four years," she mumbled. "Ever since we worked on that General Electric project together."

She'd been attracted to him for four years? Grant didn't know why, but the knowledge pleased him.

"Hmm..." He leaned in and pressed his lips to her knuckles. "That's about the time I noticed the raven-haired beauty from the Graphic Arts Department. She had the biggest brown eyes I had ever seen, and I wanted to get lost in them."

She pulled her hand away, laughing. "Stop it, you did not."

He sat back in his seat, but his eyes never left her face. "I noticed you, Celeste, but I was dating someone at the time. And then when that relationship ended, I didn't feel like I could act on my attraction for you, because we worked together. And you know how I feel about inter-office relationships."

"It's a good thing I don't work at 3D anymore then, isn't it?" She gave him a smile that lit up her eyes and exposed her dimples.

Grant's chest expanded with warmth. He loved her smile, her big brown eyes, the feel of her hand in his. He loved Celeste.

The realization both thrilled and terrified him. This was only their first date. How long did he need to wait before he told her? He didn't want to scare her away when she'd just barely become his girlfriend.

"A very good thing." He sat back in his seat and gave her a lazy smile. One that hopefully hid the emotions ricocheting through him.

"What happened to the girlfriend you had back then?"

His smile faded. He didn't want to talk about Laney. "She didn't feel as strongly about me as I did her, and she wasn't there for me when I needed her most. I was getting ready to propose to her last year when I got custody of Reagan and Josh. And she made it clear right away she wasn't ready to get married, let alone be a mother."

Her rejection had hurt terribly at the time and raising Reagan and Josh this past year by himself had been the hardest thing he'd ever done, but he was grateful now that Laney had dumped him, because he never would have gotten to know Celeste like this if Laney had stuck around.

She reached out and squeezed his hand again. "I'm sorry, Grant. That must have been painful."

He gripped her hand tighter, preventing her from pulling away. "I know this thing between us is still relatively new, C, and I'll try not to rush you, but I want you to know I'm all in."

She smiled, whether at his use of her friends' nickname for her or because of the words he'd said, he wasn't sure. "So am I, G."

Grant laughed at her nickname for him. "You know my life is complicated. So I hope you understand that I have no interest in getting involved in a relationship that doesn't eventually lead to marriage."

Celeste's eyes widened, and she sucked in a sharp breath.

"I'm sorry, I don't want to scare you away, but I need to be honest with you."

"You're not scaring me away, and yes, it feels like this is moving fast, but it also feels right." She took his other hand, and those empty places inside of him flooded with warmth. "I promise I will always be there for you, Grant. I never thought I'd become a mother to teenagers at twenty-five, but I love Reagan and Josh. I'm more than willing to take you all as a package deal."

"Don't you two look cozy?" Amy set their sodas on the table. "Do you lovebirds know what you want?"

Grant's face burned. It was probably as red as the menus they hadn't opened yet. He squeezed Celeste's hand before releasing it. "I think Celeste should order for us since she knows what's good."

Celeste gave Amy a nod, and the pregnant waitress gathered up the menus. "Two number eights it is."

He looked back at Celeste. "What's a number eight? Please tell me I will not regret trusting you." He hadn't meant for his comment to sound like he referred to a lot more than food choices. But opening himself up and trusting someone with his heart wasn't easy.

"You won't, I promise." Her gaze pinned him as though she read his thoughts.

The conversation took a lighter turn as they waited for their food. They talked about how Celeste had frequented Charlie's while she was in college and how Chuck took pity on the poor, starving college student.

When Amy arrived with their good ol' southern barbecue sampler platters, Grant quizzed her, gaining snippets of information about Celeste. He found out that she not only danced along to the eighties music she blasted when she cleaned, she sang too. And she often stayed in her pajamas all day on Saturdays when she got caught up in her stories.

Grant filed away each piece of information he learned about Celeste, letting it shape what he knew about the woman across from him. He couldn't wait to learn more.

They talked about all kinds of things with few pauses as they downed their barbecue platters, which were amazing. Following dinner, she pulled him over to the bar side of Charlie's where they ate dessert and listened to Amy's boyfriend's band play.

He put his arm around Celeste and leaned close to be heard over the music. "They're pretty good. I like their sound."

She scowled. "Yeah, but look at the way he keeps looking at that redhead at the bar. I bet he goes and talks to her when the band takes a break."

They didn't have to wait long for the lead singer, Lance Hayes, to announce a break. And sure enough, Lance headed straight to the redhead.

"I take it there's trouble in Amy's paradise?" Grant asked, feeling sorry for the pregnant waitress.

Celeste sighed. "I tried to warn her Lance was a player, but he swept her off her feet by showering her with the attention she'd always craved. Now, I think she doesn't want to admit she was wrong about him, because she's afraid she'll end up alone again."

"Being pregnant, I imagine she feels like she needs to stay with him for the baby's sake."

"Yeah, she's kind of an I-made-my-bed-now-I-have-to-lie-in-it kind of person. Which makes me sad, because she is such an amazing person, and I know somewhere out there is a man who will love Amy and treat her like a queen, instead of dropping crumbs of affection to keep her hanging on. Sometimes, I hate her mother for the way she treated Amy. She grew up thinking she wasn't lovable."

The band started up again, and he pulled Celeste to her feet. "Come on, I don't think I care to listen to any more of their music. I'd rather have you read your stories to me."

He saw the trepidation on her face again and knew it wasn't easy for her to share her stories that were so personal with him. So he planned on giving her plenty of words of affirmation as well as kisses.

CHAPTER 15

"*A*dmit it. Our working together was distracting." Celeste's voice on the phone warmed Grant.

"I admit I've been extremely productive these past three weeks since you quit, but it's not the same without you there. I miss you."

"Yeah, I'm sure you miss the questions at lunchtime and me doing my eyebrow thing every time you get bossy."

"I miss a lot more than that." He dropped his voice, letting it take on a seductive quality. "I miss the way your smile lights up the room, and your dimples that play peek-a-boo with me." He checked over his shoulder to make sure he was alone in the family room. "I've missed you in the evenings too. I'm so glad tomorrow's Friday."

"You don't have to miss me in the evenings, you know that. I'm more than willing to come over there so you can stay at home to make sure Reagan and Josh get their homework done and to bed on time."

"I know, and I appreciate that. But we've already established what a distraction you are."

Having Celeste here every night would establish a pattern that Grant feared he'd become too accustomed to. Things had moved so fast between them, he felt like he needed to slow them down a little.

He wanted to make sure they weren't rushing into something neither of them was ready for.

He'd told Celeste he was all in, and he'd meant it, but a little part of him feared it was all too good to be true. She was a temptation, the likes of which he'd never experienced. And he'd been tempted plenty in his life.

Besides, he didn't want Reagan and Josh to feel like he ignored them because Celeste was here. When she was around, it was so easy to get lost in her big brown eyes. But on the weekends, his siblings spent more time hanging out with their friends, so he didn't feel so guilty about spending so much time with Celeste.

It was nice when he could go to her apartment where he could steal a kiss or two or three. Here, both of his siblings had already caught him and Celeste kissing more than once.

"Grant?" Josh stepped in front of him, his expression telling Grant this wasn't the first time he'd called his name.

"Excuse me a minute, C." Grant held the phone against his chest. "What is it, Josh?"

"Can I hang out with Brad after school tomorrow?"

"Did you get your English homework caught up?"

"I finished the last essay, and I promise I'll remember to turn it in tomorrow."

Ever since Grant had figured out Josh's love language was words of affirmation and focused on complimenting him, the kid had been trying a little harder in school. He still struggled in some subjects, but Grant could tell he was trying. Of course, Grant was mindful of speaking the other love languages too. He still struggled with physical touch with his siblings, though.

Reagan would likely ask to hang out with Shelby tomorrow, which meant Grant could spend the evening alone with Celeste. A spark lit in him, warming him from the inside out. He was so in love with her he didn't know which way was up most of the time. Judging by her sighs every time they said their goodbyes, he was certain the feeling was mutual.

Maybe I should plan something special this weekend and tell her I'm in love with her.

"Sure, you can hang out with Brad."

"Okay, I'll walk home from school with him then," Josh said as he headed back upstairs.

Grant returned to his call with Celeste, trying to keep the conversation casual because when they got flirty, it drove him crazy.

Nearly an hour later, he said goodbye so he could make sure the kids were getting ready for bed. As he ended the call, he spotted an email notification at the top of his screen. Normally, he ignored emails after work, but since he was being considered for a vice president position, he didn't dare ignore something that might be important.

He opened his email. At the top of his inbox sat a message from the high school. *What now?*

He tapped the email.

Your student, Reagan Foster, missed one or more classes today.

Grant double-checked the date.

Reagan missed school today? *But that's impossible. I dropped her off this morning.*

Things had been pretty good between him and Reagan lately. He'd finally made some headway on speaking her love language—acts of service. The first time he offered to do the dishes so she could study for her history test, Reagan had looked at him like he'd sprouted a second head, but she'd acted truly appreciative when he'd agreed to mop the kitchen floor last week so she could accept the impromptu invitation from Victoria to go to a movie.

Like Josh, Grant had also continued to use all the love languages with Reagan, and it had made a difference in their relationship. Coming down on her for missing school would likely undo all his hard work, but he couldn't afford to overlook this. If Reagan was going to break the rules, she needed to suffer the consequences.

Grant climbed the stairs two at a time. He ducked his head into Josh's room to tell him it was time to get ready for bed before continuing down the hall to Reagan's room.

He knocked on the closed door and waited for it to open. He'd made the mistake once of opening the door before getting an invitation to enter only to catch her dressing. He'd never make that mistake again, no matter how upset he was.

The door opened. "I know, I know. I'm getting ready for bed, and yes, my homework is all done."

"Are you sure about that?" He folded his arms across his chest and leaned against the door frame. "I mean you probably have assignments you aren't even aware of, seeing as how you missed more than one class period today."

The color drained from Reagan's face, and she gave him a stiff smile. A smile he recognized as fake. It was the same one she always adopted when she got defensive and was about to blow her top.

"What do you mean? I went to school today."

"Don't play games with me, Reagan. I don't for one second believe multiple teachers accidentally marked you absent on the same day." He prided himself on keeping his voice even.

"Fine." The word came out as s huff. "Shelby and I took the city bus to the mall during lunch because we were just having some dumb mindfulness assembly all afternoon."

A three-hour assembly on mindfulness? Grant didn't blame her for ditching. He'd done it himself occasionally when he was a Junior and Senior in high school, but he never hung out at the mall with friends. He used it as an opportunity to clock extra hours at the grocery store where he stocked shelves.

If Reagan thought skipping school was acceptable in ninth grade, what rules would she break when she was a Junior or Senior? Even though she'd been obeying her curfew lately, Grant hadn't forgotten about that boy she'd met up with at the mall a couple of months ago. The one who brought her home late after taking her to a party with alcohol. The one she'd kissed before getting out of his car.

"So, if there was an assembly, why were you marked absent in your classes?"

She dropped her gaze. "Josie said they canceled the assembly last minute because the presenter was sick or something. So they ended up holding classes."

"You know the punishment for skipping school, Rae." He held out his hand and looked pointedly at her cell phone laying on her bed. He could have leaned over and grabbed it but making her hand it over felt like a more appropriate punishment.

"Come on. It's not like I knew they were going to cancel the assembly."

"You should never have skipped school in the first place, assembly or not. You broke the rules, now you have to suffer the consequences."

Reagan's eyes turned hard in a flash, and Grant fought the urge to take a step back. A storm brewed behind those eyes. One that had Grant bracing himself.

Reagan growled as she snatched her phone off the bed. "I hate your stupid rules. Josh and I never agreed to them, yet you force us to follow them like some sort of dictator." Her eyes narrowed as she clung to her phone. "I saw that book on your nightstand last week when I went to go find the nail clippers. I know what you're trying to do. You're being nice to me and Josh by giving us gifts and stuff, making us think you care about us so we don't complain when you impose all of your stupid rules. You're trying to butter us up so you can better control us."

Grant's defenses rose. He hadn't wanted them—especially Reagan —to see the book, because he knew she'd think he had ulterior motives for trying to show them he cared. But accusing him of trying to control them was taking things too far.

"I'm not trying to control you, Rae, and I do care about you. The book is helping me learn how to show it."

"If you cared about me, you wouldn't take my phone away." She was practically shouting now. "How are my friends supposed to get a hold of me? If they text me and I don't respond, they'll think I don't like them. Then they'll hate me and won't want anything to do with me."

He bit his tongue to keep from telling her she was being dramatic and overreacting. Celeste had explained to him that friends were everything to a teenage girl, and that Reagan's friends' opinion meant more to her than his did, but in times like this he felt she was being ridiculous.

"Listen," he kept his voice low, controlled. "It's bedtime anyway, which means you're done texting for the night, and you'll see your friends at school in the morning. You can explain to them you lost your phone privileges for a week or two."

"A week or two? I only missed three class periods."

Grant was losing his patience. He needed to put an end to this now before he extended her grounding to three weeks out of spite. That wouldn't go over well. He reached out and plucked the cell phone from her hand.

"You skip school, you lose your phone privileges. End of discussion." He turned and walked away.

"Argh. My friends are going to think I'm such a loser, and it's all your fault." She slammed the door, barely missing his backside. "I hate you!" The closed door did nothing to soften the words she screamed on the other side.

Grant's heart sank. Things had been going so well, but that was all gone now.

We're back to square one.

He wanted to call Celeste again, to discuss Reagan's behavior, but if she ended up defending Reagan in any way, he didn't think he could handle that right now. He and Reagan both needed time to cool off.

CHAPTER 16

*C*eleste groaned when her ringing phone broke her concentration. She stretched, causing her shoulder and neck muscles to protest.

"Oh, I've been bent over my stories too long." She would need to invest in a better desk than her coffee table if she was going to be a serious author.

She picked up her phone, surprised to see Amy's smiling face.

Celeste pressed talk. "You better get off your phone while you're at work or Chuck will fire you." They both knew he'd never do it. Amy was one of his best servers.

"Chuck is sending me home."

"What? Why?"

"Actually, he told me to go to the hospital and forget about packing a bag."

Alarm bells went off inside Celeste's head. "Hospital? Bag? What's going on?"

It couldn't be the baby already. Amy wasn't due for another two weeks.

"Chuck is positive I'm in labor, but I'm not sure I am."

162

"Are you having contractions?" Celeste tried to remember all the things the birthing coach was supposed to know.

"My stomach keeps tightening, and it's uncomfortable, but it's my back that's killing me."

"Does your stomach tightening feel the same as the Braxton Hicks you've been having the past couple of weeks, or does it tighten all over, specifically on the top?" She pressed a hand to her chest as she struggled to catch her breath.

"Give me a second, I'm having another contraction—if that's what it is." A long pause filled the phone. "Yeah, it's tight on the top."

Celeste slipped on her shoes and grabbed her purse. "That definitely sounds like a contraction. How frequent are they? And how long have they been going on?"

"I've been having pains in my back most of the day. That was the second one since leaving the restaurant, and I'm almost home."

"That means they are four to five minutes apart. Chuck's right, you should go to the hospital."

"Well, I'm home now, so come help me pack a bag. Then you can drive me to the hospital."

"I'm walking out the door right now. Be there in a few minutes." That had been Celeste's biggest requirement with this apartment. It needed to be close to Amy.

She paused halfway out the door, then dashed back inside for her camera. Her photography skills weren't superb, but she could document the birth of Amy's first child. It would give her something to focus on besides being a birthing coach, which scared her to death.

CELESTE TUCKED each item Amy tossed her way into the overnight bag.

"So where is Lance?" She tried to keep her voice conversational because she knew it was a sore spot with Amy that Lance was gone so much lately.

Amy might not be so upset if she'd seen any of the money Lance had made the past couple of months, but like the loser Celeste knew he was, Lance wasn't helping with rent or any of the expenses.

"The club Lance's band has been playing at in Seattle wanted to see how the weekend crowds reacted to them. So he stayed up there this weekend."

He probably thought nothing of leaving Chuck high and dry. Lance was that kind of person.

"Did you call him and tell him you're in labor?"

"Yes, but he didn't answer. I left a message, but I'm not holding my breath waiting for him to get back to me." Amy had often complained that Lance ignored her when he was out of town. Her bitterness was clear in her tone. "He never returns my calls or texts. When I asked him why, he said it's because he's always busy. Who's he kidding? His band only plays for two or three hours a day. What's he so busy doing the rest of the time?"

Celeste bit her tongue. She had a pretty good idea of what Lance was doing, and he wasn't doing it alone, nor was he doing it with his fellow musicians. Her heart hurt for her friend, who was the sweetest person. She deserved a man who worshiped the ground she walked on instead of a man who expected her to worship him.

Amy rubbed her low back, and Celeste noted the time on the clock. This was the second contraction since they'd started packing. She needed to get her friend to the hospital.

"I'm sure Lance wishes he could be here," Celeste said.

He could be here if he wanted. Celeste doubted Amy would end up delivering within the next three hours. But if Amy was right, and Lance never checked his messages from her when he was away, it could be days before he found out Amy had given birth to his daughter.

Even if Lance got Amy's message, Celeste doubted he'd attempt to get here. He never made Amy a priority. He only loved himself. Amy deserved better.

Celeste went back to packing the bag, but when Amy stopped handing her stuff, she looked at her friend.

Amy sat on the end of the bed, shoulders slumped, sniffling.

Celeste sat beside her and put her arm around her friend's shoulders. "Hey, what's wrong?"

"I don't want to do this alone."

"You're not doing this alone. You've got me, remember?"

Amy leaned into her and sniffled. "Thank you, C. But I wasn't referring to just the delivery. I don't know if I can count on Lance to help. You know what I mean?"

Celeste did know, and her heart hurt for Amy. She squeezed Amy's shoulders. "I'm here for you, Aim. You don't have to do any of this alone. I'll babysit any time you need me, and I'll come sleep over so I can help with the middle of the night feedings. I'll be right there with you through it all."

"You don't know how much that means to me." Amy swiped at her tears. "I swore years ago that I'd never be a single mother like my mom. But here I am."

"Having a baby out of wedlock does not mean you'll be the kind of mother your mom was. You love this baby already. I can see it in your eyes every time you feel the baby move. You are already ten times the mother your mom was. And you are going to rock motherhood, with or without Lance."

"You think so?"

"I know so."

Amy let out a soft moan and started rubbing her back again.

"Come on." Celeste stood, pulling Amy up with her. "We better get you to the hospital. I promise to be by your side through thick and thin, but I cannot deliver this baby."

Forty-five minutes later, Celeste waited while the nurse checked Amy. They had already strapped a band around Amy's stomach that monitored the contractions and the baby's heart rate.

The nurse stepped away and pulled off her glove. "Almost four and a half centimeters." She looked at the printout from the baby monitor. "And judging by the strength of that contraction, your labor is here to stay, Congratulations! You are having a baby. Today, hopefully."

Amy turned wide eyes on Celeste. Her expression mirrored Celeste's emotions: equal parts excitement and trepidation.

As the nurse set about putting an I.V. in Amy's arm, Celeste sent Grant a text: *Something has come up. Amy needs my help. I won't be able to come over tonight.*

They had only been planning on fixing dinner together and watching a movie, but Celeste had been looking forward to it all week. She had planned on telling him how much she loved him this weekend. She'd sensed lately that Grant had been trying to put the brakes on, since their relationship had grown serious so quickly.

She didn't know if it was because he didn't want to rush her or because he was afraid to open himself up to love again after being hurt by Laney, but she was almost certain he felt as strongly as she did. She needed to convince him it was okay to love again.

She had shied away from relationships herself over the years because she hadn't wanted to let someone in who might hurt her like her father had. But Grant had been hurt too. If they could trust each other, they could help each other heal. He was exactly what she needed, and she liked thinking she was what he needed too.

I suppose it can wait until tomorrow.

Her feelings weren't going to change overnight.

She turned off her phone and dropped it into her purse. Amy deserved Celeste's undivided attention.

CHAPTER 17

*G*rant walked through the door, dropped his computer bag, and stretched. *What a week.*

The Armstrong project was progressing nicely, but he missed working with Celeste. He was more than ready to start the weekend and spend some time with her. His spirits had totally plummeted, though, when he received a text from her as he left work saying something had come up with Amy, and she wouldn't make it over tonight.

He'd wanted to talk to her about his fight with Reagan last night. He'd wondered all day if he should have handled things differently. He thought he'd kept his calm pretty well last night, but Reagan's icy glare and stony silence this morning said she wouldn't forgive him anytime soon.

No matter how hard he tried to use all the love languages with her, he doubted they'd have any effect for a long, long time.

The quiet permeating the house settled over him, and every muscle in his body tensed. *Something's wrong.*

The house was never this quiet on Friday afternoons. When Grant wasn't home, Josh played his video games at full volume, and Reagan

—trying to drown out Josh's games—blasted her music through the house. But there were no video games or music today. Only silence.

Grant hurried up the stairs. Both Reagan's and Josh's rooms were empty. His chest tightened, and he pulled out his cell phone and typed: *Where are you guys?*

He paced the upstairs hallway as he waited for a response. When none came, he went downstairs and paced from the kitchen through the dining room and on to the family room and back. He checked out the front window each time he stepped into the family room.

Why do I give the kids a cell phone if they aren't going to answ—

His phone pinged.

Josh: *I'm at Brad's. Remember, you told me I could go home with him after school?*

That's right. Grant remembered agreeing to that while he was on the phone with Celeste last night.

Grant: *Where's Reagan?*

Josh: *Don't know. You took her cell phone away, remember? She's not going to see this.*

Grant swore out loud. And because the kids weren't around to hear it, he swore again.

He located Shelby's mom's number and pressed call. "Martha, is Reagan at your house?"

"No, she's not."

"She's not?" The vice around his chest tightened.

"Shelby asked if Reagan could come over today, but she had a dentist appointment after school, so I said Reagan could come over later. She was waiting for you to get home so she could call and see if Reagan could hang out since Reagan got her phone tak—."

"She's not here, Martha." The words came out tight, strangled.

"Does Josh know where she is?"

"No, he went home with a friend. And I can't get a hold of Reagan because she lost her phone privileges."

"Well, where could she be?"

"I have no idea." He plunged his free hand into his hair. "Can I talk to Shelby, please?"

"Sure, hang on a minute." Rustling filled the phone, followed by Martha calling Shelby's name. Before Shelby came on the phone, he heard Martha say that Reagan was missing—that word tightened his throat—and if Shelby knew anything, she needed to tell Grant the truth.

"Hello?" The concern in Shelby's voice did nothing to dispel Grant's concern.

"Shelby, did you talk to Reagan after school today?"

"No, but I told her after lunch I would call her after my dentist appointment."

"So you didn't see her leaving school, either walking or... with someone?"

"She was talking to Jace when my mom picked me up."

"Jace!" A chill swept over Grant. Wasn't that the senior boy Reagan had met up with at the mall? "Do you know where he lives?"

"No." Rustling came over the line, suggesting movement on the other end. Shelby continued in a quiet voice. "We met up with them one time at the mall, and he took us for a ride in his car. We hung out at his friend's house, not his."

"Do you know where his friend lives?"

"No, it was dark that night, and I didn't pay attention to where we were going."

He let out a low growl. Didn't these girls realize how dangerous that was? No wonder it sounded like Shelby had moved to another room. Her mom probably had no idea that she and Reagan had met up with boys at the mall.

"Um... Mr. Foster? You have Reagan's cell phone. Why don't you just text Jace?"

"Good thinking. Thanks, Shelby."

Grant couldn't end the call fast enough. He raced to his bedroom to get Reagan's cell phone out of his dresser. He pushed the button to turn it on.

Nothing. The phone was dead.

Swearing, he hurried to the charger near his bed and plugged it in. Because he couldn't stand to sit and do nothing, he pulled his phone back out and texted Celeste: *I know you said something come up. But I really need to talk to you. Call me ASAP, please.*

Then he stood and paced his room. He'd felt strange moving into the master bedroom, the room his dad had shared with Catherine. But the only other room in the house was a small office that wasn't big enough to be considered a bedroom. Now, as he paced, it hit him that this room wasn't really all that large. It only took six steps to get from the door to the window.

Grant plopped back on the bed and powered up Reagan's phone. She'd been asking for a new phone because this one was so slow. He hadn't even considered it. Kids these days didn't need all the newest and greatest gadgets. They only needed to text and make phone calls. Not all the other stuff they wasted their time with.

But Reagan was right. This phone was slow. It took an eternity to boot up. Of course, it didn't help that the battery was so low.

The home screen came to life. Finally.

Careful not to lift the phone higher than the cord allowed, he found the name Jace in Reagan's contacts and tapped on the phone icon.

Five rings later, a recorded message came on. "Looks like you missed me. Leave a message."

Grant cleared his throat. "This is Reagan Foster's older brother—and guardian," he added, in case the kid thought he could ignore the message. "Reagan didn't make it home from school today. Do you know where she is? Please call me." He rattled off his cell phone number. "Or you can call Reagan's number."

He ended the call and went straight to Reagan's messages. Several unread messages in bold sat at the top of the list. Grant quickly scanned through them. Some were friends whose name he recognized. Others appeared to be classmates asking about homework assignments. But none of them gave any clue to where Reagan could be.

He scrolled until Jace's name popped up. He tapped the text box and sent a message similar to his phone message in case he was one of those kids that never answered the phone but couldn't bear to ignore a text message.

He continued to scroll through the thread of texts between Reagan and Jace, hoping for a quick response. The most recent text from Jace was almost two weeks ago, when he invited Reagan to come hang out with him and his buddies at a party. Thankfully, Reagan had the sense to decline.

Grant scrolled further through the messages, finding nothing more than mindless exchanges of *what are you doing?* And *nothing, how about you?* Mingled with talk about favorite movies and music and least favorite classes and teachers.

Relief washed over him when he didn't find any inappropriate messages, nor evidence that Jace had been grooming Reagan so he could take advantage of her.

Grant didn't dare walk away from the phone, but he couldn't sit here and do nothing. He raced downstairs, intently listening for the ring of Reagan's phone. He grabbed the portable charger from his work bag and darted back upstairs. With his cell phone in his pocket and Reagan's attached to the portable charger in his hand, he headed to Mrs. Simmons' house. The woman always sat in her front room watching the neighborhood.

He tapped his fingers against his pant leg as he waited for the elderly woman to open her door.

"Well hello, Grant. I haven't seen you in forever. Spoken to you, I mean, of course I see you coming and going every day. But nobody comes to visit me anymore." The older woman's wrinkled pout was quite comical, but Grant couldn't smile today.

"Mrs. Simmons, did you see Reagan come home from school this afternoon?"

"Come on in, and I'll make you some tea. I'll tell you all about who I saw come and go today." She backed up and waved Grant in.

Any other day he would have taken pity on the lonely, old lady and sat down with her while she gossiped about the neighbors. Not that he cared for the gossip at all. Especially since she probably had a few opinions about Celeste's visits to Grant's house last Saturday and Sunday. Visits that lasted all day.

He checked his phone. He couldn't believe Celeste hadn't responded to his text yet. And neither had Jace.

"I'm sorry, I can't stay today. I just need to know if you saw Reagan come home from school."

She pressed a red fingernail to her lips and contemplated for a long moment before shaking her head. "No, I never saw her. I saw Josh and that Thompson kid pass by but no Reagan. I assumed she went home with that nice girl Shelby. Those two are inseparable, aren't they?"

He gave an absent nod. If Reagan didn't come home, where on earth is she?

"Thank you, Mrs. Simmons." Grant walked away on the woman while she rambled on about the mailman and how wonderful she thought it was that the young new mother took her baby for a walk every day, now that the weather was warming up.

The pit that had opened in his stomach grew to epic proportions. *Where is she?*

After returning to his house, he again checked both phones and resisted the urge to throw them across the room when both screens showed no missed calls or new notifications.

He found the number for the junior high and called it. He was disappointed but not surprised when his call wasn't answered. School had let out almost three hours ago. Three hours was a long time if someone had taken Reagan, intent on foul play.

Afraid that line of thinking might make him physically ill, he forced those thoughts from his mind. *But where could she be?*

Grabbing his keys, he headed to his car. He couldn't sit around here any longer. He drove straight to the school to prove to himself there wasn't some sort of extra-curricular activity going on that Reagan had neglected to tell him about. The school parking lot was mostly empty, but Grant pounded on the locked front doors until a janitor opened it. When Grant showed him and a second janitor a picture of Reagan on his cell phone, they denied seeing her at the school this afternoon.

Fear and helplessness had swamped him by the time he got back into his car. Again, he checked both phones, cursing when they showed nothing new. He called Martha again.

"Grant," Martha's breathless voice answered after the second ring. "Have you found Reagan?"

"No." The word sounded tortured. "Shelby suggested I contact the boy she saw Reagan talking to after school, but he's not answering his phone or texts. I don't know where else to look. I checked with my neighbor, who said she never saw Reagan come home from school. I double-checked the school to make sure there wasn't a volleyball game or something, but it's locked. I don't know where else to look."

"You'll get through this. I'm sure Reagan is fine." Martha's voice lacked conviction, and the vice that had been tightening around his chest since he arrived home almost an hour ago clamped tight. Like an air-tight lid sealing shut. "She's just being really inconsiderate of you right now, but I'm sure she's fine. I'm going to have Shelby check with all of their mutual friends and see if any of them have seen her."

"Thank you, and will you ask Mason if he knows this Jace kid? Evidently, Reagan met him when she and Shelby went to a football game with Mason last fall."

"Yes, I'll see if he knows anything. Don't you worry; we'll find her."

He bit back the hysterical laughter that clawed at his throat. *Don't worry?*

How was he supposed to do that? Reagan was his sister, his responsibility. She drove him crazy at times, but he loved her. He'd never forgive himself if something happened to her.

"Martha, what am I supposed to do while you're checking with her friends?"

"I hate to say it, but maybe you should go to the police."

～

CELESTE HELD her breath as the nurse once again checked Amy's progress.

They had been here for five hours already. At three hours in, Amy had given in and requested an epidural. But her progress had slowed down after she got the pain medicine, so they'd started administering Pitocin to keep her dilating.

The nurse stepped back and pulled her glove off. "Eight centimeters. Those last two centimeters could go quickly, but since this is your first baby, it'll probably be a couple of hours still."

A couple hours? Celeste was exhausted, and they still had the hardest part to go.

They'd wandered the halls for the first couple of hours until Amy decided she couldn't do it anymore. Once her friend had gotten the epidural, Celeste's responsibilities had shifted to fetching crushed ice and unplugging all of Amy's cords and wheeling the I.V. to the bathroom for her. Thanks to the fluids the I.V. was pumping into her, the bathroom trips were frequent.

They had enjoyed watching a romantic comedy on the television until Amy broke down in tears. Then Celeste's duties had shifted to holding Amy's hand and consoling her while she cried.

"What's wrong?" Celeste rubbed Amy's back.

"I just want that, you know."

"What?"

"A happily ever after with a once in a lifetime love."

Celeste hugged her friend. She knew it was mostly the hormones talking, but she wanted that for Amy too. She wanted her to find what she'd found with Grant.

He'd been so supportive of her desire to pursue her dreams. He'd devoted more time searching children's book publishers than she had. He'd also critiqued her work to help her get the words and artwork just right. Celeste's eyebrow hadn't risen once because he'd done it in the kindest way possible. Of course, it helped that he was always touching, massaging, or holding her. It was impossible to get upset with someone who made her feel so amazing.

She had even gone to church with him twice now and enjoyed it. It helped to strengthen the relationship building between them. She hoped he wasn't mad at her for canceling their plans tonight. She couldn't wait to send him a picture of Kallie—that was the name Amy had chosen for her baby. She was going to be the most beautiful baby ever. Celeste was sure of it.

CHAPTER 18

Grant lowered his phone after attempting to call Celeste for the third time. He really needed a shoulder to cry on. He swiped at the tear that crept out as the helplessness he'd experienced all afternoon overwhelmed him.

He'd sent her a message while he was at the police station, telling her Reagan was missing. He'd expected her to call him back right away. Even if she was too busy—doing whatever it was she was helping Amy with—to take a phone call, surely, she'd check her messages at some point.

But she hadn't called or texted, and Grant was losing his grip. He felt ignored all over again but this time by the woman he loved.

The police had practically ignored him, too. They had taken Reagan's description and his information then sent him home to wait. So he wouldn't miss his sister if she came home.

An officer had come by to get more information, but his questioning had turned into an interrogation about Grant's relationship with his younger sister, making Grant sound like some sort of abusive pedophile. Not only that, it made him feel like the worst father figure ever for taking away Reagan's phone privileges.

Like he needed help with that.

Then the questioning had turned to *"Is it possible she ran away and doesn't want to be found?"*

"No way," he'd assured the officer.

Grant didn't disagree that Reagan hated him at times, but they had been doing so much better lately, until last night's fight. He couldn't for one second believe Reagan would run away, leaving Josh behind. The two of them fought plenty, but they'd been especially close since their parents died. He often heard them late at night in one or the other's room talking.

Josh.

Grant was relieved Josh was apparently having a good enough time at Brad's that he hadn't given anymore thought to Grant's initial text this afternoon. But what was he going to tell the kid if they couldn't find Reagan?

Pain shot through Grant's chest—sharp and icy—at the thought of Reagan never coming home again. Already, he missed the way she rolled her eyes at everything he said and her laughter when Grant's OCD tendencies got a little out of hand. He even missed the music she blasted through the kitchen when she mopped. She took three times longer to complete the task than necessary because she was too busy dancing.

His phone vibrated in his hand, and his heart leapt into his throat. He looked at his screen, hoping to see Jace's number—he'd left a dozen calls and texts for the kid, each one becoming a little more threatening.

But it wasn't Jace. Martha's name filled his screen.

"Hello." Grant couldn't help the spark of hope that raced through him.

"Have you heard from Reagan?"

Those words dashed the spark faster than a fire hose against a candle.

"No, please tell me one of Reagan's and Shelby's friends knows something."

"Victoria said she saw Reagan get into the car with that Jace kid, but nobody knows where he lives. Mason doesn't actually know him all that well."

"Can you give me Victoria's number and address? I need to pass it along to the police." He grabbed a random piece of paper and a pen.

Martha gave him the information he needed then said, "They're going to find her. Don't give up hope."

"Thank you, Martha. I needed that."

He ended the call and pulled out the card Officer Pickins had given him. When the other man answered, Grant gave him the new information.

"This helps," said the officer. "I'll contact this Victoria girl to get more information about this Jace kid and a description of his car, then I'll put out a BOLO. I'll also put in for a warrant to ping his cell phone."

Finally, some progress. The candle lit in Grant's chest again.

"But you still need to consider that she may not want to be found."

And the flame was doused again.

The call ended, and Grant shook his head. *No.* Deep down, he knew Reagan would come home if she could.

Gruesome images filled his mind as he considered all the horrendous things that might prevent her from calling him or coming home.

He sat at the dining table and dropped his head into his hands. The pressure built behind his eyes. Giving in to the tears wouldn't do him any good, except give him an even bigger headache. He should probably eat something, but the thought of trying to stomach anything made him nauseous. He couldn't eat when Reagan was out there going through who knows what.

His phone buzzed on the table beside him, and once again, hope filled his chest. *Please let it be Reagan or Jace.*

He'd even love to get a text from Celeste right now.

But the name on his phone was the last one he wanted to see tonight. *Josh.*

A lump clogged Grant's throat as he opened the text, making it impossible to breathe.

Josh: *Can I sleep over at Brad's tonight? His mom is okay with it if you are.*

Grant's throat relaxed, and he let out a deep breath. He should tell Josh what was going on, but he couldn't bring himself to cause the kid the same pain that was killing him right now.

He chickened out.

Grant: *Yes, but don't stay up all night.*

Josh: *Awesome, thanks.*

Grant dropped his phone on the table then lowered his head to his folded arms. This was going to kill Josh, and he'd never forgive Grant for keeping it from him.

I'll never forgive myself.

Grant remembered Celeste's motto. *Failure isn't an option.*

In his drive to be successful, he'd always agreed with that, but he'd failed in the worst way possible. He'd failed Reagan, Josh, and his dad and Catherine. And Celeste had failed him when he needed her most.

Hopelessness and desperation settled over him like a thick, oppressive fog. He hated sitting here doing nothing. He hated that he'd let everyone he loved down. He hated that all he wanted to do was bawl like a baby.

Because no one was there to see him, and there was nothing else he could do, that's exactly what he did. And amid his tears, he prayed. Like he'd never prayed before. Pouring his heart out to God to bring Reagan safely home.

CELESTE WIPED AMY'S BROW, then scooped ice chips into her mouth. Her poor friend was exhausted. It was almost midnight, and Amy had been pushing for over an hour. But the baby's head simply wasn't moving past a certain point.

"You're doing fantastic, Amy," said Dr. Brooks. "On this next contraction, I don't want you to push. In fact, I'm going to push on the baby's head. I think you still have some amniotic fluid trapped in there. It's preventing all your hard work from pushing the baby out."

Celeste waited anxiously for the next contraction to see if the seasoned doctor was right. She watched the monitor that showed the contractions along with the doctor. As soon as the needle began to rise, her gaze shifted back to Dr. Brooks.

"Bingo." Dr. Brooks smiled up at Amy. "Nurse, we need some more towels here. I think that's going to make a big difference. Shouldn't be much longer now."

Celeste grew increasingly anxious as Amy continued pushing. The *not much longer now* stretched into another half an hour.

"There's the head." Dr. Brooks finally said. "One more good push and you'll be able to meet this little beauty."

Celeste's heart lodged in her throat, and she held her breath until the baby's cries split the air. The next few minutes passed in a blur as the doctor put the tiny red screaming baby on Amy's tummy and let Celeste help cut the cord. Then Kallie was swaddled in a receiving blanket and laid in Amy's arms.

Celeste wiped the tears from her eyes as she grabbed her camera. This was a night she would never forget. As she snapped photo after photo, she imagined herself in Amy's place, holding her newborn in her arms.

It was all too easy to picture a tiny baby boy with Grant's prominent brow and blue-gray eyes.

CHAPTER 19

Grant's head popped up when a phone started ringing on the table in front of him. He must have dozed off but why at the table? And why did his head feel like it was full of cement?

Confused, he glanced at the clock on the stove. Twelve thirty.

He looked at the ringing phone in the dim light. *Reagan's phone.*

It all came racing back to him. The fear, heartache, and helplessness.

Heart racing, he picked up the phone, not daring to hope it was Reagan. *Unknown number* covered the screen. He pressed talk.

"Hello?"

"Oh, thank goodness," came Reagan's breathless voice. "Grant, can you come get me—"

Her voice broke, and he lunged to his feet. "Where are you? Are you hurt?"

He grabbed his keys and bolted for the door.

"I'm so sorry. I didn't mean to disobey you," she sobbed. "I didn't realize what would happen, and I know you're probably so mad at me." Another sob. "And you have every right to be, but will you please come get me? I just want to go home." Reagan cried in earnest now.

"Calm down, Princess. I'm on my way, but I need you to tell me exactly where you are." He paused at the entrance to their subdivision, not knowing whether to turn left or right.

Grant listened to her talking to someone on her end. He gasped when he heard them mention Elk Creek campground and highway six that led to Tillamook State Forest. She was at least forty minutes away. He turned right and punched the gas. His tires squealed against the pavement.

They talked back and forth for several seconds hashing out a place to meet, finally agreeing on a McDonald's near the mouth of the canyon.

"Now tell me, are you hurt? Do you need an ambulance?"

From the way she was conversing, he didn't think she'd been injured. *Thank goodness.*

"No, I'm fine. I just want to come home—"

Her voice broke again, and the vice that had stayed clamped around his heart all night cinched a little tighter. *What on earth had she been through for the past nine hours?*

"Carrie's phone is about to die, so I need to go. Hurry, please."

"I will!"

The line went dead, and his heart took up residence in his throat. What if something happened to her before he got there? He put a call through to Officer Pickins to let him know Reagan had contacted him and her location. The detective made Grant promise to keep him apprised of the situation before he ended the call.

Thirty minutes later, Grant brought his car to a screeching halt in front of McDonald's. His eyes searching the parking lot for Reagan. *Please don't let this be some sick joke.*

As soon as Grant got out of his car, Reagan climbed out of a silver Ford Focus. The car drove away, leaving Reagan standing there alone, a look of trepidation on her face.

He worried that jerk Jace was getting away, but he couldn't pull his mind away from the fact that Reagan stood in front of him in one piece.

His gaze roamed over her as he closed the distance between them, searching for signs of physical injury or worse. Streetlights illuminated the tear steaks on her face, and the dam he'd hastily erected to hide his emotions burst.

"I'm so sor—"

Grant pulled her into his arms, cutting off her words.

"Please tell me you're okay. That he didn't hurt you."

"I'm okay."

He didn't miss the fact that she only responded to the first part of his request.

He loosened his hold enough to look into her eyes. "I'm so mad at you right now, but I'm so da— dang glad to see you. Alive."

"I know, and I'm so sorry. I swear I never meant for this to happen. I totally deserve whatever punishment you want to give me, but..." Her bottom lip trembled. "Thank you for coming for me."

Fresh tears spilled from her eyes, and Grant pulled her back into his arms, crushing her against his chest. The fermented scent of alcohol hit him, but he was determined not to be mad about that right now. They would deal with that later.

"I'll always come for you, Rae." Emotion clogged his throat.

The massive ball of knots that had consumed him for the past six hours slowly unraveled. Gratitude swept over him, weakening his knees, and he clung to Reagan as much for his sake as for hers.

"Grant?"

"What?" The word came out harsher than he'd intended.

"I can't breathe." At least that's what he thought her muffled voice said against his chest.

He released her and tried to laugh, but his emotions still ran too high, and the air stuck in his throat. Realizing she was trembling, he led her to his car with an arm around her shoulders. He started the engine and turned the heat on to take off the chill that had seeped into them both.

"Okay, start at the beginning, and tell me if I need to call the police to follow that Jace jerk." He pointed in the direction the silver Ford had gone, although it was long gone by now.

"That wasn't Jace. That was some college girls who gave me a ride down from the campground."

"Campground? Talk quick girl. My heart can't take any more stress tonight."

Grant alternately clenched his teeth and held the steering wheel in a death grip as Reagan talked about how one poor decision led to the nightmare she'd suffered tonight.

"Jace caught me after school before I started walking home. He offered to buy me a soda then drive me home." She shrugged. "I agreed because I didn't see any harm in it. But he didn't take me home after we got our drinks. He drove us to Liam's house. He and Aiden were starting a movie. Jake talked me into staying, promising to take me home as soon as it was over. I knew you wouldn't be home for over two hours, so I agreed." Her voice dropped, and her gaze fell to her hands in her lap. "I wished I hadn't, because he was kind of handsy and really made me uncomfortable. I was so glad when the movie was finally over."

Reagan tugged at her sleeves as she talked. "As soon as the movie ended, though, the guys started talking about some party. A bonfire. I told Jace he needed to take me home, but he kept driving the opposite direction. We drove forever, up into the mountains."

"When we got there, he started k-kissing me in the car. I mean really kissing me. I kept telling him to knock it off and take me home, but he wouldn't listen. I tried to get out of the car, but he caught my arm a-and..."

Reagan twisted her hands together, and Grant's stomach turned sour in the wake of the agitation rolling off her. *I think I'm going to be sick.* The odor of alcohol coming from Reagan didn't help.

It's a good thing he hadn't been able to eat anything tonight. Swallowing the bile that rose in his throat, he reached over and gently squeezed her arm. "What did he do, Rae? You can tell me. I won't be mad at you. I want to help you, honey."

Tears again filled her eyes. "He promised he'd take me home if I..."

"You can tell me." He kept his voice as even as possible despite the acid burning his throat.

Reagan raised her chin. "He said he'd take me home if I had sex with him." The words came out in a rush, as though she feared she wouldn't be able to get them out if she didn't do it quickly.

Grant squeezed his eyes shut, trying to block out the image of some jerk forcing himself on his sister. She must have been terrified.

"I didn't," she said, surprising him.

"What?"

"I didn't have sex with him. I swear I'm telling the truth. I just wanted you to know because you look like you're going to either punch something or be sick."

"Maybe both," he said in a tight voice.

"Just so you know, I gave Jace a bloody nose when he tried to force himself on me."

Relief shot through him so powerfully he thought he might faint. Good thing he hadn't started driving yet.

"I spent most of the night avoiding him, especially because he kept drinking. I asked several people if I could borrow their cell phone to call you, but there was no service up there. I kept waiting for someone to leave, but more and more people just kept coming, and they all brought alcohol with them. I swear I didn't drink any, but some guy spilled half of his beer on my jacket. The smell made me nauseous, but it was too cold to take it off."

"I'm glad you're okay, princess." He leaned over and gave her an awkward side hug, pressing his cheek to her hair.

"That's what Dad used to call me."

"I know."

Reagan's stomach growled, and she pressed a hand to her abdomen. "Do you think we can get something to eat? All I've had since school got out was a soda, a handful of chips, and a couple of Oreos."

Now that the danger to Reagan was over and the knots in his stomach had relaxed, his stomach protested too. He looked out the window up at the golden arches. Not his favorite place to eat, but it was way too late, and he was too hungry to be picky. He'd probably have an ulcer after tonight anyway. What harm could a greasy hamburger and fries do?

"Give me a minute, I need to call the police and let them know you're okay. And that there are a bunch of inebriated underage kids in the mountains that'll probably try to drive home at some point."

The contrite look that settled on Reagan's face pleased Grant. Hopefully, she wouldn't make this mistake again.

He dropped her cell phone in her lap. "Let Martha and Shelby know you're okay."

After a trip through the drive-thru, they started the drive home. Even though he was exhausted and couldn't wait to get home and go to bed, Grant drove much slower than he had on the way here so he and Reagan could iron out some rules.

The first rule they both agreed on was to not tell Josh anything about tonight.

CHAPTER 20

$\mathcal{C}$eleste rolled over and stretched as the mid-morning sun hit her in the eyes. Normally, she enjoyed waking up with the sun but not after getting to bed at three a.m.

Amy had given birth at eleven fifty-eight p.m., but Celeste had stuck around to offer encouragement while she attempted to nurse for the first time. Then Celeste had gone with the nurses when they took Kallie for her first bath. She'd waited until they'd settled Amy in her room, and Kallie was back with her mommy, before finally heading home. She'd been so exhausted; she'd fallen straight into bed.

Celeste wanted to rollover and go back to sleep, but she knew it would never happen. She couldn't wait to get back to the hospital to hold Kallie. She should probably call Lance and let him know he was a father. She glanced at the clock. Ten thirty. Lance wouldn't be out of bed for at least two more hours.

I'll just send him a picture. Too bad she couldn't be a fly on the wall when he opened it. Would he be remorseful that he missed his daughter's birth? Or would he even care? She had a feeling it would be the latter.

Maybe I'll send Grant a picture too.

She dug her camera and phone out of her purse. The phone was dead, of course. She plugged it in to charge and plopped down on the couch to go through the pictures she'd taken.

Ten minutes later, too impatient to wait for her phone to charge fully, she turned it on. Her brows raised at the repetitive chime of multiple notifications. Her screen showed two missed calls and two texts from Grant. A twinge of guilt hit her for not calling him last night. Canceling a date via text was a lame move.

Her eyes focused on the most recent text message: Reagan is missing!

Heart in her throat, Celeste leapt to her feet. Within a matter of seconds, she'd slipped shoes on and grabbed her keys and purse and darted out the door. She tried calling Grant as she drove, but her call went straight to voicemail.

"Grant, I'm so sorry I missed your calls last night. Please call me back. Tell me what I can do to help."

She only ran one red light and broke the speed limit by a little as she raced to Grant's house. Thank goodness she hadn't passed any cops. Her breaths came in short bursts as she pulled into Grant's driveway. He must be worried sick. And Poor Reagan. What had happened to her?

Celeste rang the doorbell, then, too impatient to wait for an answer, she knocked as well. She bounced on her toes while she waited for the door to open. When it didn't, she rang again. And knocked again. Long and loud.

Finally, the door opened and there stood Grant, hair mussed, face covered in stubble.

She would think him incredibly handsome if it wasn't for the dark shadows around his red-rimmed eyes. She stepped through the doorway and hugged him.

"I'm so sorry I missed your calls and messages. My phone was off. Have they found Reagan yet?"

Grant pushed her away and stepped back. "She's fine and home safe." His voice was deep and gravelly. "No thanks to you."

She reeled back as though he'd struck her. "I'm so sorry I wasn't there for you, Grant. Amy needed me—"

"I needed you! But you're just like everyone else I've ever cared about. You're only there for people when it's convenient for you." Grant's voice was hard as stone, and a sharp pain pierced her chest. "You weren't there when I needed you most, Celeste. You're just like my dad."

A cold shock passed over her as her eyebrow raised. Grant had never looked and sounded more like her dad than he did in that moment. He'd basically called her a failure, as a friend and a girl-friend. And it stung!

She knew he was hurting, but so was she now. Her pain quickly turned to anger.

"Yeah, and you're every bit as overbearing and condescending as my father, expecting everyone to obey your every command and bend to your will."

"At least I don't leave my friends to face their worst nightmare all alone."

"No, because you don't have any friends."

She'd taken it too far, but man, he infuriated her. Eyes burning with tears that refused to be held back, she raced away from his front door as quickly as she'd come.

GRANT SLAMMED the door and turned to find Reagan at the bottom of the stairs.

"Who was at the door, and why did you slam it on them?"

"No one."

How dare Celeste call him overbearing and condescending? *I am nothing like her dad.*

"It sounded like Celeste. Why were you shouting at her?"

He let out a long sigh, his heart heavy. "You wouldn't understand."

"It's all my fault, isn't it?" Tears filled Reagan's eyes. "You're still upset about last night, and Celeste was probably worried too."

Was she? Celeste had hugged him and said she was sorry, but she hadn't even suffered a tiny portion of the hell he'd gone through last night, worrying about where Reagan was and what she was going through.

She couldn't possibly understand. Especially when she didn't care enough about him to answer his calls or read his texts.

And that's what hurt the most. It wasn't only that she wasn't there when he needed her. It was that she didn't care about him as much as he did her. It was Laney all over again.

"I'm so sorry, Grant. I promise I won't ever do anything so stupid again." Reagan wrapped her arms around herself.

Grant pulled her into his arms. "It's not all your fault, Princess. Yes, what you did was dumb, and yes, it scared me to death. But it's not your fault Celeste—"

He bit back a comment about Celeste that was demeaning and probably not true. Even though he didn't feel like he could trust the woman anymore, especially with his heart, that didn't mean he should destroy Reagan's trust in her. The two of them had become close over the past six weeks, and it had been good for Reagan.

"Celeste and I have our own problems. I guess we aren't as suited to be together as I thought."

Reagan stepped back and scowled at him. "What do you mean? You guys are perfect for each other. She helps you let loose and have fun, and you are so supportive and encouraging of her."

"Did she tell you that?" The weight settling in his chest made it feel like he might have just made the biggest mistake of his life.

"She didn't have to. I saw the way you helped her a couple weeks ago to get her stories submitted. She did say that's one thing she loved about you. That you believed in her."

Love? Did Celeste really love him, like he loved her?

No. If she loved me, she would have answered my calls and not left me to deal with Reagan's disappearance all alone.

Grant raised his chin and squared his shoulders. "Well, maybe we were wrong about each other." Without giving Reagan a chance to argue, he turned and climbed the stairs. "I'm going to take a shower, and then we'll fix a big breakfast together."

And I will not think about how much I enjoy cooking with Celeste.

~

CELESTE HELD little Kallie against her chest and wandered Amy's hospital room. She wasn't pacing, not really. She simply couldn't sit still. Because every time she did, she thought about her fight with Grant that morning. And she got angry all over again.

How dare he tell her she was never there when someone needed her?

Yes, she felt terrible about not being there for him when he was going through something unimaginable, but she would have been if she could.

"What's wrong?" Amy's voice pulled Celeste from her musings.

"Nothing. Why do you think something is wrong?"

"Because you're practically pacing, and even though you're wearing make-up, you look worse than I feel. And you said you'd be back here by noon, but it's two o'clock."

Amy was right.

Celeste had been so angry at Grant that she hadn't wanted to come see Amy until she'd settled down. So, she'd gone home to take a shower and eat something. As soon as the hot water hit her, the tears that had been a trickle all the way home from Grant's house turned into geysers, and she'd cried long and hard.

It hurt that he'd been so judgmental of her and thought she'd deliberately ignored him when he was going through something so horrible. And it hurt that their blossoming relationship that had felt so perfect was suddenly over.

She'd also canceled the lunch date she was supposed to have with her father today. She had finally written him a letter—it was just easier—a couple of weeks ago, agreeing to meet him for lunch on the first Saturday of each month. There was no way she could face him today, though. Not after her fight with Grant.

Celeste dropped into a chair and hugged Amy's precious little baby close.

"Grant and I had a fight this morning."

"I'm so sorry, C. What happened?"

"Apparently, Reagan never came home from school yesterday." Celeste's throat grew tight as she thought about how horrendous the ordeal must have been for Grant. "He ended up at the police station because he couldn't find her."

Amy gasped and pressed a hand to her chest, her gaze resting on Kallie. "How awful!"

Celeste stood and handed Amy her baby. It was obvious her mother's heart needed her baby close after hearing such news.

Amy gathered Kallie close and pressed her lips to the soft curly blond hair. "Did they find her? Is she okay?"

"He said she was home and safe, no thanks to me." Celeste's voice hardened.

"What? Why would he say that?"

She didn't want to tell Amy why Grant was so upset with her, because she knew Amy would feel guilty.

"Wait, you said she didn't come home yesterday? So, he probably tried to call and text you last night... but you were with me." Remorse filled Amy's face. "That's why he was mad at you, isn't it? I'm so sorry, C."

"It's not your fault. Yes, he was upset with me because I ignored his calls and texts. But I didn't even know since I turned my phone off when the nurses admitted you."

"Did you tell him you were with me and why?"

"He knew I was with you."

"But you didn't tell him why?"

"I texted him before I met you at your apartment that something had come up. But I was so nervous and excited when the nurse said you were having a baby that I didn't think to text him again and explain where I was."

"And you didn't tell him this morning that you were holding your best friend's hand while she gave birth because her loser boyfriend couldn't be bothered to answer his phone?" The note of self-recrimination in Amy's voice surprised Celeste. This was the first time Amy sounded like she regretted ever getting involved with Lance. She often complained about the musician, but this was the first time she sounded like she truly regretted her choices.

"He didn't give me a chance." Celeste picked at her fingernails. "I guess I don't blame him, though. I wasn't there when he needed me, and I can't imagine what he went through last night." Her voice dropped as tears threatened again.

It broke her heart to think of how distraught Grant must have been. She hated that he'd had to go through that all alone. And knowing how abandoned he felt by his father after his mom died, it was natural for him to feel like Celeste had abandoned him too. But it hurt that he would assume that of her. She'd trusted him with her heart, and he'd turned out as critical and quick to judge as her father.

"You would have been there for him if you hadn't been with me. Here, give me his number, and I'll call and explain."

"You will do no such thing."

"He needs to understand why you weren't there for him. You and I both know you would have been there if you could have. *He* needs to know that."

He should know me well enough to know that. I shouldn't have to beg for his acceptance and love. She'd done that for too many years to count with her father, and it had changed nothing.

"I don't owe him an explanation. If he truly thinks I ignored his calls on purpose, then he doesn't trust me, and I'm better off without him."

"But you're in love with him, C. I'm afraid you'll regret this forever if you don't fight for him."

Amy was right. Celeste would regret this, but she refused to beg for acceptance and love.

CHAPTER 21

*R*eagan's phone dinged, and Grant looked up from the ground beef he was browning to add to the spaghetti sauce. He didn't even try to hide his curiosity.

Math homework forgotten, Reagan dropped her pencil and picked up her phone. She smiled when she read the text, then her fingers flew across the screen as she typed a response. Several seconds later, her phone pinged again.

She continued to text back and forth several times, smiling each time a response came.

Reagan had been very penitent the past few days. She'd done nothing that could be considered breaking the rules. In fact, she acted a little too much like him, lately.

She'd texted back and forth most of Saturday afternoon with someone even though most of her friends stopped by to visit her. She wore the same sad smile now that she'd worn Saturday afternoon.

It must be the same person. *So help me if it's that Jace kid...*

Reagan hadn't wanted to press charges against Jace, so Grant had dropped it. Especially since she'd gotten into the car with him willingly each time, he doubted the police would take her claim seriously.

Grant and Reagan had tried to keep things under wraps, but it

194

blew up in their faces Saturday afternoon when Josh stormed into the family room asking why Brad was asking if Reagan had really been kidnapped?

Grant should have known the rumors would fly and Josh would eventually hear them. He sat back and let Reagan do the explaining. But that hadn't made Josh any less angry with Grant for not telling him his sister had been missing.

Josh had acted sullen the rest of the day, but he'd perked up on Sunday, and Grant assumed he was forgiven.

Reagan's phone pinged *again*.

Grant couldn't stand it anymore. If she was texting some boy, he was going to blow a gasket and ground her forever. He'd gone easy this time because he felt like she'd learned her lesson the hard way. But he wouldn't stand around and let her repeat her mistake with some other boy. And he definitely wouldn't let her hide a relationship right under his nose.

He cleared his throat. "Who keeps texting you, Rae?"

Good. That sounds less accusatory than who are you texting?

Reagan's smile died, and she dropped the phone to her lap. "No one."

"Come on, we agreed, remember? No secrets. No hiding things from me." He worked hard to keep his voice even. Casual.

"I'm not hiding anything from you. I'm just... not sure you really want to know."

"Of course I want to know. I wouldn't have asked if I didn't." His patience was wearing thin.

"Okay, I'll tell you. But please promise me you won't get mad."

The only reason he would get mad was if it was a boy.

"I promise I won't get mad." The words probably didn't sound very convincing since they came out through clenched teeth.

"Fine. Celeste texted me on Saturday."

Her name hit him like a bucket of cold water, sending a jolt clear through him, settling with a sharp pain in his chest.

Grant took a deep breath and took his time stirring the ground beef before responding. "Oh, what did she want?"

"She was worried about me and wanted to make sure I was okay."

Of course, she was worried enough about Reagan to pick up her phone, but she couldn't do the same for me?

Grant had tried all weekend to put his fight with Celeste out of his mind, but the void her sudden departure from his life created was every bit as immense as the pain he'd felt Friday as he worried about Reagan.

"She's still texting you even though you've told her you were fine?" He couldn't keep the jealousy from his voice.

Reagan's chin raised with an air of defiance. "Just because you had a fight with her doesn't mean I can't be friends with her."

"No, you're right."

It wasn't fair of him to expect Reagan to give up her friendship with Celeste because she'd hurt him. Celeste had been good for Reagan. He wouldn't take that away from his sister, no matter how much it stung that she reached out to Reagan and not to him.

And it hurt. A lot.

Trying to pretend his heart wasn't breaking, he forced an air of nonchalance. "So, what's new with her?"

"Um... nothing." Reagan avoided eye contact by picking at her nail polish, which was a clear sign she was hiding something.

Her phone pinged again, and Grant stifled the urge to snatch it out of her hand. He wanted to read Celeste's words. Wanted to feel close to her.

Reagan gave him a hesitant look before tapping her screen.

The sound of a tiny baby crying came from Reagan's phone, and confusion filled him. *Whose baby is that?*

Celeste's voice came over the sound of the cry. "Isn't her sad little face the cutest thing you've ever seen?"

Grant's heart stalled at the sound of Celeste's voice. He dropped the spatula and turned the stove down. He stepped closer to the counter where Reagan sat, the urge to take the phone from her hand stronger than ever.

"Whose..." his voice squeaked. Clearing his throat, he tried again. "Whose baby was that?"

Reagan looked up, indecision on her face. "Celeste's friend Amy had her baby."

"Oh? When?" His chest tightened as he waited for the answer.

"Last Friday," Reagan blurted out.

Last Friday?

Celeste texted him last Friday saying something had come up with Amy. He dropped onto the bar stool beside Reagan. The hurtful things he'd said about her not being there for him tumbled around inside his head.

"The baby was born at 11:58 p.m. after more than eight hours of labor," Reagan said.

Each word struck him like a giant hailstone, pelting him in the face.

"She didn't want me to tell you, you know?"

"Then why did you?" His voice was low, quiet.

"Because I think you were a jerk to her, and you should apologize."

Grant's defenses rose. "She ignored my calls and texts when you... when I needed her."

"Because she was busy holding her friend's hand while she gave birth." Reagan rolled her eyes at him as if she couldn't believe she needed to spell it out for him. "Evidently, Amy's boyfriend was out of town and wouldn't come home for the birth. Amy didn't have anyone else. Only Celeste."

Grant braced his elbows on the counter and dropped his head into his hands. He'd hurled such hurtful words at Celeste, whose love language was words of affirmation.

"When she came over Saturday to see if I was okay, she tried to tell you where she was, but you didn't give her a chance to explain. You just said—"

"I know what I said, Rae." Grant held up his hand. "And you're right... I was a jerk. I was hurting, and I took it out on her."

Reagan grunted. "Glad we got that straight." She folded her arms and narrowed her gaze at him. "So, what are you going to do about it?"

"I don't know." A simple *I'm sorry* wasn't an adequate apology for the way he'd acted. For the things he'd said to Celeste.

He waved a hand toward the stove. "Finish up dinner, please. Let Josh know when it's ready. I'm not hungry anymore."

~

SHARON LOOKED up from her computer. "Mr. Davenport will see you now, Grant."

"Thank you." He stood and buttoned his suit coat. This meeting was the routine, weekly progress report he'd had with Mr. Davenport since they started the Armstrong project. But Grant was just as anxious today as he was on his first visit to the CEO's office over two months ago. Ever since his fight with Celeste a few days ago, he'd had trouble eating and sleeping, and working had been darn near impossible.

"Grant, come in." Mr. Davenport clasped his hand and pulled him through the door in his usual charismatic manner.

They jumped straight into how the Armstrong project was progressing. It took all of Grant's focus, but he must have said something right, because the older man repeatedly smiled and nodded.

"I have to admit," Mr. Davenport said when Grant finished, "I was disappointed when Miss Hightower resigned. I worried the Armstrong project would fall apart. She assured me you were more than competent to coach your team, and she was right."

The mere mention of Celeste caused a sharp ache to fill Grant's chest. He still hadn't found the courage to call or visit her. He considered writing her a letter like her father had. But that felt like such a cop out, especially after she'd accused him of being as bad as her dad.

Knowing Celeste needed words of affirmation, and that she dreamed of being an author of children's books, he'd written her a story about a young boy who struggled to find the lost piece of his identity—like Peter Pan trying to catch his shadow. Then he met a girl who completed him so fully he forgot a piece of him had ever been missing. Until he lost the girl. Then she'd taken the most important part of him. His heart.

It was cheesy, but he'd poured over it for two days. And walking up to Celeste and presenting her with a few pages of story felt so inadequate.

"We're headed into the play-offs now, son." Mr. Davenport's voice pulled Grant back to the present. "I need to know your head is in the game."

"It is sir."

"Are you sure? Because I got the impression that there was more than a professional relationship between you and Miss Hightower. And I worry—despite you proving you're capable of coaching your team through the playoffs—that not having her as your assistant coach might mess with your head."

"Excuse me?"

"Come on, Grant, I saw the way you looked at each other when you made your presentation to Armstrong."

Grant tugged at his collar as heat crept up his neck. Had his admiration of Celeste and his attraction to her been that obvious? And how had she looked at him?

"Each of you looked at the other person like they'd made the winning shot in a championship basketball game."

Did this man ever think in anything other than sports analogies?

"I assure you, sir, we kept our relationship strictly professional at work." *Mostly.*

"That's good to hear, but she doesn't work here anymore."

"No, she doesn't," Grant said cautiously. Had the boss heard that he and Celeste had been in a relationship, but Grant had blown it already? "I'm not sure I understand what you're getting at."

"I'm saying the best players are the ones that are as happy off the field as they are on the field."

Perspiration pricked Grant's brow as confusion flooded over him. *Am I the coach or am I a player on the team?*

It almost sounded like Mr. Davenport was encouraging him to

pursue a relationship with Celeste. What would he say if Grant told him he'd already struck out?

Great. Now I'm thinking in sports terms again.

Grant suddenly missed the comfortable relationship he had with Mr. Hardman, who had been like a father to him over the past ten years. His former boss had returned from his cruise, but Grant rarely saw him now that his sole focus was the Armstrong campaign. He'd love to sit down with the older man and talk out some of his problems.

"So, are you going to ensure you have Celeste, uh, Miss Hightower in your corner, cheering you on?"

Mr. Davenport's blunt manner surprised Grant. *Who knew the big boss, who was such a sports fanatic, was also a matchmaker?*

Grant cleared his throat. "I uh... did. Um... Celeste and I have dated pretty seriously the past few weeks."

"That's good. What's that saying? Behind every great man is an even greater woman."

Grant wasn't sure that was the way he'd heard the quote, but he liked Mr. Davenport's interpretation. He wanted Celeste back in his corner, and Mr. Davenport was right: Grant would be a much better coach and team player if he wasn't distracted by how badly he'd screwed things up with her.

"I fouled out though, sir," he blurted.

Mr. Davenport's brows rose. He circled his desk to sit in the chair beside Grant, body angled toward him "What do you mean?"

Without going into too much detail about Reagan's disappearance, Grant told his boss Celeste hadn't been there for him when he'd gone through something extremely difficult and how critical he'd been toward her. He left out how badly her accusations that he was like her father cut him, because he understood how hurt she must have felt when he hurled his insults at her. It hadn't helped that they were both exhausted from their late night.

"I realize now that I was wrong, and I know I need to make amends, but saying 'I'm sorry' feels so inadequate."

Mr. Davenport pinched his lips. "The ball is firmly in your court.

What happens in your relationship with Celeste depends entirely on you. You need to make some sort of grand gesture. Women love that sort of thing. So, What's your game plan?"

"Plan?" Grant's voice squeaked. He cleared his throat. "I... uh wrote her a story... but without some illustrations it's just a bunch of words."

"So, get your team to help you illustrate it."

"I couldn't do that, sir. This is personal."

"Grant." Mr. Davenport paused and waited for Grant to meet his gaze. "In a few short months, you'll be made Vice President of Marketing. With the office comes privileges. I'm sure you remember helping design that billboard a few years ago for my anniversary."

Grant nodded. He'd thought it inappropriate for the boss to ask his employees to do something for his personal gain. He would never feel right about asking his teammates to help him design and illustrate a book for his girlfriend.

Of course, she wouldn't be his girlfriend again, if he didn't do something soon to win her back.

Mr. Davenport must have seen the indecision on Grant's face, because he leaned forward. "Look at it this way, son. You can hire another company to provide illustrations, cover, and binding for your book, or you can trust the company you work for to handle it."

The man had a point.

Grant wouldn't feel right about asking them to do it on company time though, but he'd hate to encroach on their personal time too.

Mr. Davenport stood, as though the decision had been made. "Do what you need to do to make sure your home life is happy, and your head is in the game as we head into the playoffs."

Grant left Mr. Davenport's office in a cloud of indecision. By the time he'd ridden the elevator down to the second floor, he decided the boss was right. He needed to do whatever it took to get Celeste back, and if that meant asking for help from his coworkers, so be it.

He'd give them a gift card or something to make it worth their while.

CHAPTER 22

"*I* think I found a daycare for Kallie finally." Amy's voice came through Celeste's speaker phone.

"That's good, but don't you still have like five weeks of maternity leave?"

"Yeah, but I might have to go back—at least part time—when she's four weeks old. Otherwise, I won't be able to pay rent next month.

"I thought Lance was making good money with this gig in Seattle." Celeste knew it was a sore spot with Amy, but she hated that Lance did little to help financially. At least when Celeste shared the apartment with Amy, she never had to worry about Celeste coming up with her share of the rent.

"He gave me enough money to cover this month's rent, but..." Amy's voice went quiet, and Celeste heard Kallie's little squawks and mews on the other end of the phone.

She couldn't wait for her daily dose of loving on that precious little doll. She'd made it her daily reward for being productive during the day. It had been the one thing that kept her from sinking into a deep depression after the fight with Grant last week. Despite all the baby snuggles, though, Celeste's heart was as raw as ever.

"So have you heard from Grant?" Amy changed the subject.

What was that saying? Misery loves company.

Amy's relationship with Lance was on the rocks, and Celeste's relationship with Grant... well, it had crashed and burned.

"No." The word came out clipped.

"I thought you said his sister told him why you didn't answer his calls that night."

"She did." Celeste didn't have the heart to be mad at Reagan for telling Grant. Asking her to keep it to herself put Reagan in a tricky situation with her brother, especially since Grant had a rule about not keeping secrets.

"But he hasn't called or anything?" Amy's voice was full of the disappointment Celeste felt so acutely.

"Nope."

It had been a whole week since he'd found out the truth, and Celeste still hadn't heard from him. *It's not like I expect him to come crawling on his hands and knees begging me to take him back.* But she'd hoped he'd reach out to her with an apology.

She considered apologizing to him for telling him he was as bad as her father, but her pride got in the way. *What if nothing changes, and he still feels I let him down?* Each day she didn't hear from him, while she dragged her feet, made her think maybe he was more like her father than she thought.

Even her father had apologized. *After seven years.*

The prospect of spending even one more day away from Grant was painful enough, Celeste would never survive seven years.

"I'm sorry, C. Why do men have to be such idiots?"

"Or maybe we're the idiots for falling in love with them."

"Maybe."

Celeste clicked on her email icon to distract herself. She'd gotten in the habit of checking it often since she sent out her submissions. And of course, she couldn't help but hope to find Grant's name there. She wanted to hear from him in person, not email. But at this point, she'd take anything she could get.

In her inbox sat an email from Sleeping Bear Press.

Celeste's heart leapt to her throat, and her hand froze on the mouse.

"Uh... Aim, I need to get back to work. I'll see you this afternoon."

Celeste ended the call then stared at her computer screen. The rejection letters had slowly trickled in from the dozens of queries Grant had helped her send out to agents and editors weeks ago. She'd taken them in stride, knowing some of the most successful authors got hundreds of rejection letters before they ever got an acceptance. With each rejection though, her dream of becoming a children's author slipped a little further away, and she wondered if she'd made a mistake quitting her job.

But this one... if it was a rejection, would be harder to accept than the others because Celeste really wanted her books published by Sleeping Bear Press. In all the research she and Grant had done on children's book publishers, this one had stood out to her, and she wanted to see that publisher's name on her books.

Not sure she could handle a rejection from her dream publisher right now, she closed her laptop and went to the sink for a drink of water. The cool liquid felt good on her suddenly dry throat, but it didn't calm her nerves.

She paced her apartment for five long minutes, wishing she could call Grant. Warmth filled her as she remembered how he'd distracted her when she'd been nervous about opening her father's letter. Pain caused by all she'd lost chased away the warmth, and Celeste blocked out thoughts of Grant.

She leaned against the counter and stared at her laptop from across the room. *I'll never find out what it says if I don't open it.* She nodded, trying to encourage herself. *It won't open itself.*

With deliberate strides, she crossed the room and pulled her computer onto her lap. She opened it to find her email had refreshed. On top of the email from Sleeping Bear Press sat a message from Penny Halstrom at Hi-Lo Publishing.

She was almost certain that one would be positive. *It's best to get the possible rejection over first.*

Celeste took a deep breath and braced herself before opening the Sleeping Bear Press email.

Dear Celeste,

Thank you for your submission of Rachel's Big Mistake. We've read it and reviewed your series proposal. We loved Rachel's Big Mistake and the idea of the Rachel and Her Daddy series of children's books. We are excited to extend an offer of publication for your series of stories, for which in-house illustrations will be provided.

In house? Did that mean they didn't like her illustrations?

The excitement that had risen in Celeste as she read suddenly evaporated, leaving her deflated. *They want my stories, but not my art?*

Both Amy and Grant loved her art. Reagan and Josh had even told her it was good. Celeste loved the artwork she'd done in that book. It was as much a part of her as the story was. Her artwork had helped win multi-million-dollar contracts. Sure, her story art was a different style, but still…

She blinked away the tears as she looked out the window. Why did she have to work so hard to convince herself she wasn't a failure because of a stupid acceptance letter that wasn't really an acceptance at all?

Because you don't have anyone else to tell you you're not a failure.

All Celeste needed to do was call Amy, and she'd have a cheerleader. But Amy wasn't the one she wanted cheering her on. She wanted Grant.

Swiping away the lone tear that fell on her cheek, she took a deep breath and opened the email from Hi-Lo Publishing.

The words were similar to those from Sleeping Bear Press but with a more personal touch. She knew Penny after all. Celeste's pulse picked up as she read the offer listed in the email. She'd never dreamed she could get that kind of advance for a children's book series.

The email closed with a line that to Celeste sounded less like a form letter and more like a note from a good friend. *I'm so excited to work with you on your own stories. You are such a talented artist and writer (who knew), and I'd feel honored to have you on our team.*

Celeste read over the letter again, making sure she'd read it right and making sure it didn't say she couldn't do her own artwork for her stories. She'd always enjoyed working with Hi-Lo as an illustrator, and the thought of doing so as an author made her blood pump a little faster.

"I'm going to be a published author!" Her squeal sounded strange to her ears in the quiet of her apartment, but she didn't care.

Since she couldn't share this with Grant, she decided she wanted to share this with her father. She texted him to see if he was free for an impromptu lunch. While she waited for his response, she called Amy back.

Looks like I'm not doing much writing and drawing today.

CELESTE LOOKED at the clock when her doorbell rang. Eleven thirty on a Wednesday morning.

Who's at my door at this time of the day?

Setting her computer aside, she stood and stretched.

She doubted it was Amy, since she always visited her in the afternoons, and they had already talked on the phone this morning.

She opened her door to find a young, familiar-looking man holding a bouquet of roses in a pretty crystal cut vase.

"Celeste Hightower?"

"Yes?"

"These are for you." He thrust the flowers toward her.

She took them, and he turned and walked away before she could figure out where she knew him from. Her heart rate kicked up a notch as she set the vase on her kitchen counter. She pulled the card from the flowers.

I was such an idiot. I'm so sorry. G—

A heaviness filled her chest as disappointment flooded over her. The flowers were a sweet gesture, but it would have meant so much more if Grant had delivered them in person. But he was at work, so of course he couldn't be bothered to deliver them himself.

She was debating sending him a text to say thank you when the doorbell rang again.

This time, a young woman, who also looked familiar, stood there holding the largest box of chocolates Celeste had ever seen with a small card taped to it.

"Hi, Miss Hightower." She said the words like she knew Celeste.

"Hi?" Like the young man, Celeste couldn't figure out where she knew the young woman from.

She held the box out to Celeste. "This is for you. Enjoy!"

"Thank You."

Celeste returned to the kitchen after closing the door. Again, her heart sped up. She pulled the card off the box and opened it.

You are the best thing that has ever happened to me. I don't deserve your forgiveness, but please... forgive me. G—

She had to give him an "A" for effort, but she still wished he'd shown up on her doorstep himself and said the words he'd written in his notes.

Her doorbell rang a third time, and her lips curved up in a smile. *Maybe it's him this time.*

Her smile faded when she opened the door to find yet another young, familiar-looking man standing there with a small package wrapped in brown paper. This time, however, she realized where she knew him from. He worked in the mailroom at 3D Media. All the delivery people did. Had Grant really used 3D employees to carry out his apology. Wasn't there some sort of rule against using employees for personal gain?

Her smile returned. *Grant broke the rules for me.*

"Miss Hightower, this is for you." The messenger—she thought his name was Eric—held out the small flat package.

Celeste took the gift and closed the door. She sat on the sofa to open it. There was no card, so she tore the brown paper off. Her breath caught in her throat when she saw the beautiful cover of the book titled *My Heart* written by Grant Foster.

Tears soon filled her eyes as she opened the book and read a story about a little boy who searched everywhere for the missing part of him himself. It was so well written, her heart ached for the little boy's loss.

Her tears turned to a smile as she read about the little girl who patiently helped the little boy look for his missing part—in the pantry, under a rock, up in a tree. Then one day, the boy realized he was no longer missing a piece of himself, because he felt whole when he was with her.

Then the little girl's family moved, and Celeste's heart broke again for the little boy as she studied the image of him standing alone, a heart-shaped hole in his chest.

It was the sweetest story she'd ever read, but the ending was horrible. It wasn't lost on her that Grant was the boy in the story and Celeste was supposed to be the little girl. But she didn't want their story to end like that.

Our story needs a happy ending.

She grabbed her gel pens—they would color best on the single blank glossy page inside the back cover—and started sketching. She tried to mimic the artistic style of the rest of the book.

The doorbell rang, and her heart leapt to her throat again. *It's Grant this time.* She knew it, and as anxious as she was to see him, she wished he'd given her a few more minutes to finish her sketch.

She opened the door to find Grant standing there with a takeout bag from Leonardo's. She could practically smell the garlic in the Chicken Carbonara, and her stomach growled in anticipation.

In addition to a contrite look, he wore a blue polo shirt and jeans. He'd never looked so handsome, and Celeste found it difficult to breathe.

Silence stretched between them as he no doubt waited for a response to his gifts, and Celeste struggled to catch her breath.

"Of course, I forgive you, and I'm so sorry for saying you were as bad as my dad. I didn't mean it." She stepped closer to him. "But I do mean this: I love you, Grant Foster. Thank you for the flowers, chocolates, and the sweet story."

She flung herself at him.

He wrapped his arms around her, and she felt his muscles relax as a lengthy sigh escaped him. He held her close, the takeout bag pressed against her back, for the longest time.

"I love you too, Celeste. I never should have said those hurtful things to you. You are the most amazing friend. I know I don't deserve to call you my friend, but I want you to be my best friend and so much more."

Finally, his hold relaxed, and disappointment filled Celeste. She looked into his blue-gray eyes and smiled.

"You might have to share the best friend title with Amy, but I definitely like the sound of *so much more*." She pulled him into her apartment and closed the door.

Grant set the bag down on the closest flat surface—an armchair—and pulled her into his arms again. His lips settled on hers, and the knot that had occupied her stomach for the last two weeks melted. She'd found the missing part of herself. The part that made her whole.

She tightened her arms around his neck and deepened the kiss.

He groaned as his mouth moved with hers.

Celeste was glad to have her father back in her life, and if Amy ever left Portland, Celeste would miss her like crazy, but this... This was one relationship she could never live without.

They separated after several long moments, both a little breathless.

"I brought Leonardo's. I was hoping you'd join me for lunch, followed by a walk through the park. Then we can do whatever else you'd like to do, as long as we do it together."

"Don't you have to get back to work?" Although he didn't look like he was dressed for work.

He shrugged. "I took the day off."

"Grant Foster lied and called in sick?" Celeste laughed. She wasn't sure she recognized the man standing in front of her, but she sure liked this version of Grant.

"I didn't say I was sick. I simply took some personal time off. Besides, even if I had said I was sick, it would have been true. I've been heartsick for the last ten days thinking I'd screwed up so badly you'd never forgive me."

"I forgive you, Grant. I can't believe you not only took the day off work for me, but you used employees from the mail room as your messengers."

His cheeks colored. "I got permission from their supervisor for them to take an extra-long lunch break and offered to buy them lunch."

Celeste laughed. *The man was full of surprises.* She slipped her hand into his and led him to the couch.

"Thank you for the story. I loved it. You are a talented writer."

"I needed some help from the graphic design department to illustrate it. That's why it took me so long to get around to apologizing. I've been hounding them to get it finished."

"You had the graphics design department do a personal job for you?" This man really was full of surprises.

"Mr. Davenport insisted I get whatever help I needed to get you back in my corner so I can get my head in the game before the championships close in."

Her brow wrinkled. She wasn't sure what he meant, but she wasn't surprised to hear Mr. Davenport's name linked to the sports analogy. She was shocked, however, that he'd insisted Grant get her back in his corner.

"Mr. Davenport knows about us?"

"I think he was playing matchmaker when he paired us together for the Armstrong project."

"Really?" Celeste never would have guessed it of the shrewd businessman.

He wrapped his other hand around their clasped fingers. "I came over here prepared to beg you to forgive me, on my knees if necessary." He slid off the couch and onto one knee. "Since that wasn't necessary, I'm begging you to never leave me. Please promise me you'll be my best friend, my partner, and eventually my wife."

He held up a finger when she leaned forward. "This isn't a marriage proposal, but only because I don't have a ring yet. I'd marry you tomorrow though, if you were willing." Then his face fell. "Although, I suppose we should wait until the Armstrong campaign launches before we get married, because there is no way I can keep my head in the game if I'm thinking about a honeymoon—"

Celeste pressed a finger to his lips to shut him up. "I promise to be your best friend, partner, and eventually your wife, G. I want to marry you, but I don't want to rush this. I want to experience all the fun and joy of getting to know all sides of the man I love."

He slid back onto the sofa and pulled her into his arms again for another lengthy kiss.

When they finally parted, she shooed him to the kitchen to dish up and reheat their food while she pulled his book onto her lap. She was still drawing on the last page when he brought their food over.

"What are you doing?"

She hid the page from his view. "I'm finishing our story."

She set the book aside, and while they ate, she told him about the contract Sleeping Bear Publishing had offered her.

"They don't want to use your illustrations? That's ridiculous. Your artwork is amazing."

That's what she needed to hear after she opened the email from Sleeping Bear. Not because she wanted his praise, but she needed to know Grant still believed in her.

"Thank you. I decided I couldn't do it though. My illustrations are as much a part of my stories as the words themselves. I went back and looked at the books on their website, and as much as I liked their artwork, I realized they all looked the same. I don't want my books to blend in with all the others. They'd lose their uniqueness, you know."

"You need to hold out for a publisher who appreciates your illustrations. They are amazing works of art."

Celeste laughed. "Okay, that's laying it on a little thick, especially since I've already forgiven you, but thank you." Warmth filled her as she smiled. She'd waited three long days to share her exciting news with the man she loved. "Well, as it turns out, I didn't need to hold out for very long. On the same day, I got an offer from Hi-Lo Publishing. They loved my stories *and* my illustrations."

"That's amazing, C!" He hugged her close. "I knew you could do it."

He let out a long, low whistle when she told him how much they offered her for the series. He grinned then, making him look like the little boy in his book. "I'm going to marry a famous children's author. I'm so proud of you, Celeste."

It meant a lot to her to have her father tell her he was proud of her earlier this week when she told him about the offer she'd received. But Grant's unfailing faith in her meant the world to her. If her books didn't sell, and she ended up falling flat on her face, as far as she was concerned, she'd succeeded in the area that mattered most.

She'd won in love.

They finished their food, then Grant pulled her legs across his lap while she finished her drawing in the back of his book. They talked about the progress of the Armstrong project and how adorable Amy's baby was. Which led to talk of them eventually having children together.

Happiness filled Celeste's chest as desire curled in her stomach. She didn't want to rush this relationship with Grant, but the idea of carrying his child filled her with so much joy she could hardly contain it.

Finally, she turned the book so he could see the last page.

He stared at the image of a mature version of the girl handing the boy—now a man—her own heart with one hand as she held his heart close to her chest with the other.

She'd been careful to color the hearts different colors so there would be no mistaking the intent of the picture. Below the picture she wrote the words: My heart is yours to keep, forever and always.

His eyes glistened as he smiled and touched the page. "It's perfect."

GRANT PEERED at his hair in the mirror. He'd run his hands through it so many times today it practically stood on end. Dampening his fingers, he smoothed out the waves. Too bad he couldn't smooth out the ripples of anxiety radiating through his core as easily.

He dampened a paper towel and wiped at a speck on his lapel.

Today was the biggest, most important day of his life, and he didn't want anything to go wrong. He'd expected to feel a huge relief when they launched the Armstrong campaign. And he had, until Mr. Davenport decided they needed to celebrate the launch with a small party.

It wasn't the party that had him feeling like he might throw up, though. It wasn't even the fact that Mr. Davenport planned to announce that Grant would be made the new Vice President of Marketing at the end of the year. No, it was the fact that the CEO informed him last night that he'd invited Celeste to come to the wrap-up celebration.

Grant patted his pocket for the millionth time today. The bulky ring box pressed against his palm. He'd bought the engagement ring—with Amy's help—almost three weeks ago, but he'd been waiting for the right time to propose. He was pretty sure Celeste would say yes, but he feared he was rushing her.

Becoming a mother to two moody teenagers was not something he wanted to push on her. It seemed appropriate to propose here at 3D where it all started, but now he was second-guessing his idea of proposing in front of an audience like he'd originally planned.

He gave his appearance a final glance and headed to the door. "I can do th—"

Grant wasn't sure if the "oomph" came from him or the raven haired, brown-eyed beauty with the most kissable lips he'd ever seen, but he was certain his smile was as big as hers.

"Talk about deja-vu." Her soft voice sounded as breathless as he felt.

"Fancy meeting you here," he murmured as he slid his hands around her waist.

"Do you want me to dump my purse on the floor, or would you like to do that?"

He chuckled. "Nah, I'd rather kiss you." And that's exactly what he did.

Until Celeste pulled away, that is. "Mmm... as much as I enjoy that, don't we have somewhere to be?"

"You're right, come on." He took her hand and tried to tug her toward the elevator, but she resisted.

"Wait, I need to pee first."

Grant burst into laughter. "Yep, talk about deja-vu."

She grinned, causing her dimples to wink at him before disappearing into the bathroom.

He slipped his hand into hers when she came out and led her to the conference room on the third floor. It was bigger than the one on the second floor, so they'd decided to have the party there.

For the next hour, she stayed by his side, and the ring burned a hole in his pocket. But he couldn't get himself to drop to one knee in front of everyone who had been involved in the Armstrong campaign and propose. Knowing Celeste hated the limelight, he didn't want to make a scene.

He'd planned to do it after Mr. Davenport made the VP announcement, but he was bombarded by congratulations and well wishes, and the opportunity slipped away from him. Despite his planning and preparation, this didn't feel like the right time or place.

Finally as the crowd in the third-floor conference room thinned, inspiration struck.

He took Celeste's hand and pulled her out the door. "Come with me."

"Where are we going?"

"You'll see."

The smile that took over her face a few minutes later when he led her into the second-floor conference room made him catch his breath.

He led her to the chair she'd always sat in when they worked together, then he took the seat beside her. "I miss working with you here in this room. And I miss asking you questions at this table."

Grant didn't think her smile could get any bigger, but he was wrong.

"Good, because I have a question for you too?"

"You do?" His eyebrows rose. "What is it?"

"Oh no you don't. You have to ask your question first."

"Very well." He pulled the ring box from his pocket as he slid off his chair. Dropping to one knee, he opened the box and took her left hand in his. He caressed her knuckles. "Celeste Hightower, I love you with all my heart and soul. Will you please be my wife and my partner for the rest of my life? Will you help me finish raising Reagan and Josh? And more importantly, will you be the mother of my children?"

Celeste's lips quirked. "That was three questions."

"They were follow-up questions. You know, in case the first one wasn't clear enough."

She pulled her hand from his and cupped his face. "The first one was plenty clear." Then she leaned down and kissed him.

He pulled her against his body, loving the feel of her lips on his. All the empty places inside of him had long ago filled up, and he now had a reserve. One that let him know without a doubt that Celeste loved him and would always be there for him.

It was several long moments before they broke apart. Breathless, he asked, "Does that mean yes?"

"That means yes—emphatically, wholly, and completely. Yes, yes, yes." She grinned. "You know, in case my first answer wasn't clear enough. I'm so in love with you, Grant Foster."

He slipped the ring on her finger then pulled her to her feet and into his arms again. They shared another passionate kiss.

When they finally broke apart, he led her toward the door. "We should celebrate. Let's go get Reagan and Josh and go to a nice restaurant."

"Not so fast." She tugged on his hand. "I haven't asked my question yet."

"Ask away."

A mischievous gleam filled her eyes. "Why did you take so long to propose?"

"Amy told you I bought the ring weeks ago, didn't she?"

Celeste nodded. "She's horrible at keeping secrets."

He mulled over his answer for a moment then pulled her into his arms again. "I was afraid my life was too complicated to foist upon you, but I've come to realize that it'll always be complicated if you aren't a part of it."

She smiled. "Hmm... good thing I like complicated."

∽

If you enjoyed It's Complicated, please consider leaving a review on Amazon.

∽

Continue reading for a sneak peak of Amy's story.

RESCUED

CHAPTER 1

a my needed help.

She approached the modest brick home, hoping the light coming through the window meant Celeste was still awake. It was late, but Celeste was her oldest and dearest friend, and Amy desperately needed to talk to someone.

Thank goodness Celeste is a night owl.

Crickets chirped from somewhere deep inside the dappled willow trees forming a privacy hedge between Amy's friends and the neighbors. The scent of freshly mowed grass hung in the air.

A cat screeched somewhere down the street, and a shiver raced through Amy despite the pleasant August night. She chalked her reaction up to the disturbing events from earlier.

How did my life fall apart in a matter of hours?

Fighting the urge to give in to the tears that had been threatening for the past hour, she knocked on Celeste's door. Amy was not a crier. She'd learned at a young age crying solved nothing.

The porch light came on, blinding Amy, and the door opened a crack. She couldn't fault Celeste's caution. This Portland neighborhood was much nicer than the one Amy lived in, but it still left something to be desired. Especially at midnight.

"Amy? What's wrong? What are you doing here?" Celeste had cause for concern since she tended Amy's daughter, Kallie, through the night. Celeste had come to Amy's rescue six months ago when her new boss, Dennis, moved her to the night shift.

Celeste swung the door wide, and Amy walked in, pressing a hand to her stomach to quell the churning happening there.

What am I going to do?

Amy kicked off her shoes and made herself comfortable on the overstuffed couch in the family room. She hugged a throw pillow to her chest and chewed on her bottom lip. Pages with colorful sketches in various stages of completion for Celeste's next children's book littered the coffee table.

Celeste sat at the other end of the couch, cradling her hands around her seven-month baby bump. "Okay, spill. I can tell by the way you're gnawing on your lip something bad has happened."

Trust Celeste to perceive in a matter of seconds how messed up Amy's life was.

"I left work early tonight—"

"Why?"

Amy let out a heavy sigh. "Because I quit."

"What? Why?" Celeste's left eyebrow shot up.

"Dennis gave me an ultimatum." A shiver of disgust swept over Amy as she recalled how he'd backed her into a corner of the storage room.

Celeste scowled. "What kind of ultimatum?"

"If I want my job as day manager back, I have to make it worth his while." Amy didn't even attempt to hide the disgust in her voice.

"Worth his while? As in…?"

"Sleep with him." Amy filled in the blank.

"That louse! Isn't he married?"

Amy winced at Celeste's volume as she nodded. She glanced at the door to the master bedroom where Celeste's husband, Grant, slept.

"Doesn't he realize you're in a...relationship with Lance?"

Celeste's hesitation before saying *relationship* reminded Amy, her friend didn't have a high opinion of Amy's boyfriend and Kallie's father. If Celeste knew what Amy walked in on less than an hour ago her hesitation would have been much longer.

The knot in Amy's stomach tightened, and a crawling sensation pricked her skin.

Someone should have reminded Lance *he* was in a relationship. Not only did he have a sexy voice—a perfect mix of mellow and gravelly—he was gorgeous too. So, it never surprised her when girls showered him with attention. Problem was Lance never discouraged it.

"Dennis knows I was with Lance." Before Celeste could pick up on Amy's use of the past tense, she hurried on. "He said it didn't matter. He doesn't want a relationship. He..." Bile rose in her throat as she made air quotes with her fingers. "Just wanted some workplace perks."

Celeste gasped. "What a scumbag!"

The bedroom door to Amy's right flew open, and Grant darted out wearing boxers, hands balled into fists. "What's wrong?"

Celeste sprang to her feet and pushed her wide-eyed husband back into the bedroom. "Nothing. Sorry, honey. I'm talking to Amy."

"Oh." His mumbled acknowledgment proof Celeste often got excited when Amy was around.

Celeste often got excitable, period. With her, it was all or nothing. She never did anything halfway. Amy wished she was more outgoing, like her friend.

No time like the present.

She needed to get far away from Lance and Dennis.

After a few muffled words and the unmistakable smack of a kiss, Celeste returned to the family room. A grin split her face. "He'll be so embarrassed if he remembers this tomorrow."

Amy's face heated. She'd seen plenty of her mother's boyfriends wander around the apartment in their boxers when she was young, but Grant was her best friend's attractive husband. A few months ago, she accidentally told him, "You make me hot." When what she meant to say was, "You make me mad." A slip he wouldn't let her live down. Every time Grant got within five feet of Amy, he asked, "Am I making you hot?"

Amy grinned. "Even if he doesn't remember flashing me, I'll never let *him* live it down."

"You shouldn't." Celeste's smile faded. "Seriously though, A, what're you going to do without a job?"

"There's more," Amy whispered.

"More what?" Celeste leaned forward, brow furrowed.

"I went home early after quitting my job. Figured I'd get Kallie in the morning like I usually do." A dull pounding resonated in Amy's head.

I should have eaten something tonight.

But she'd been too busy trying to avoid her lecherous boss. She sucked in a deep breath and forced herself to tell her friend the worst part of the night. "Lance wasn't alone when I got home."

"Did he take the band home for an after-party again?" Celeste rolled her eyes. "When will he realize his weekend gig at Charlie's Bar and Grill isn't the same as being on tour?"

"He wasn't with the band." Amy squeezed her eyes shut and took a slow steadying breath to fight the nausea that arose with the memory of Lance in her bed with a long-legged brunette. The same one that had ogled him all night at the bar.

She'd already spent fifteen minutes dry-heaving at the realization that while she'd been working nights, Lance had had plenty of opportunities to entertain other women in her bed.

"Oh." Celeste put a hand on Amy's knee. "I'm so sorry." The absence of Celeste's usual animation told Amy her friend was not surprised.

Amy planted her elbows on her knees. She rubbed her temples with trembling fingers. Apparently, she wasn't the only one who suspected Lance was cheating on her again. Or was it still?

He'd made such a fool of her for who knows how long. That's why she'd planned on leaving him.

Lance had never made her any promises. He'd made no commitment to her, except to act like he was doing her a favor by moving in with her. He'd sucked her in with his good looks and charm, and she'd let him walk all over her, knowing he'd never commit.

I'm such an idiot.

"If I had the money I'd been saving, Kallie and I would be okay for a while, but..."

Celeste let out a low growl. "Lance had no right to blow your hard-earned money on another guitar."

Amy had only told Celeste about the money, because her friend insisted on knowing how she'd gotten the black eye last week. She hadn't told her she'd been saving the money so she could leave Lance and make a fresh start somewhere.

She didn't want to admit Lance didn't love her anymore.

Am I really that hard to love?

Amy mustered the determination she'd experienced as she packed her bags before walking out on Lance. "I'm leaving, C."

"Darn right, you're leaving that loser. It's about time."

"No, I'm leaving Portland."

"What?" Celeste shrieked.

Amy shushed her, casting a glance at the bedroom door.

Celeste lowered her voice. "You and Kallie can stay here as long as you need. You don't have to leave Portland."

Warmth flooded Amy's chest. Celeste and Grant didn't have much room, so the invitation meant a lot to her. With Grant's younger siblings living with them and a baby of their own on the way, they didn't need Amy and Kallie underfoot.

"That means the world to me, C, but that isn't necessary." Amy squared her shoulders and raised her chin. "I have to leave. If I stay here, I'll end up letting Lance talk me into coming back." As disgusted as she was with Lance, her resolve always weakened when he turned on the charm. It made her sick to realize how easily he'd played her.

"Over my dead body. I'll make Grant go beat up Lance tomorrow and threaten him if he ever comes near you."

Her best friend since fifth grade would do anything for her, and Grant, who was hopelessly in love with his wife, would do whatever she asked. But the last thing Amy wanted was Celeste coming to her rescue, again.

No, I need to do this by myself.

"It's just as well I quit my job," Amy said, getting to her feet. "This way I can leave without any ties. Without regrets."

Except she had regrets. The last three years were full of them.

"That doesn't mean you have to leave the city." Celeste stood too.

Amy opened the door to the partially finished nursery where her daughter slept and studied Kallie's peaceful, angelic face. *When did my baby get so big?*

Kallie was the best thing that ever happened to Amy. She'd taught Amy what it meant to love, wholly and unconditionally. Amy could never regret or resent that like her mother had resented her.

My mother.

"I turned out like my mother," Amy said in a strained whisper.

"No, you are nothing like her. You're ten times the woman she was."

Oh, how she wanted to believe Celeste, but Amy's actions betrayed her. "I'm taking my child out of bed in the middle of the night to leave an abusive, cheating boyfriend—exactly like my mother did on more than one occasion."

Celeste's gaze dropped to the floor.

Amy lifted Kallie from the crib and cradled the toddler in her arms, drawing comfort from the powerful surge of love that flow through her. She buried her nose in Kallie's soft curls and inhaled her daughter's clean, innocent scent. It wouldn't stay that way. Life had a way of stealing innocence.

Not if I can help it.

She'd protect Kallie as long as she could. Starting by getting as far away from Lance as possible.

"Where will you go?" Celeste followed her to the front door.

Fear and uncertainty tightened Amy's chest. "I don't know, but my next job won't be in a bar. And I swear, I'm done with men."

"Come on, Amy, just because Lance was a jerk, doesn't mean all men are."

After the day she'd had, Amy couldn't disagree more, but she didn't want to argue with her best friend.

Celeste had been as jaded as Amy, but she'd found happiness a year ago with Grant, and ever since, she'd been an advocate for love. That's partly why Celeste had never liked Lance—he was self-centered and not at all concerned about Amy's happiness.

As Lance's true colors had shown themselves, Amy had been too proud to leave because it meant she'd turned out like her mother.

"I'll call you tomorrow and let you know where I end up."

"You better." Celeste's voice grew husky. "Drive safe and take care of my sweet Kallie."

"I will." Amy blinked back tears and gave her friend a one-armed hug before leaving.

"Amy, wait. I know you need time to heal from this but promise me you won't lock your heart too tightly. Who knows, you might find love when you least expect it."

Celeste had almost lost out on love because of stubbornness, but this wasn't a promise Amy could make. She wouldn't give her heart to a man unless she was sure he was committed to her. Since she couldn't see that ever happening, she said the only thing she could.

"Bye, C. Love you."

~

Get Amy's story,
Rescued
Finding Providence Book 1,
Free on Kindle Unlimited, or from Amazon.

~

If you enjoyed It's Complicated, please consider leaving a review on Amazon.

ACKNOWLEDGMENTS

THANK YOU to my critique group for your invaluable feedback. Special thanks to my beta readers Michelle, Emily, Mariella, Padma, and Mary. You caught the things that I was too close to the story to see.

Thank you to Aaron and Megan Walker for proofreading this book. And thank you to Kelli Ann Morgan at Inspire Creative Service for the awesome cover. Thank you Tia for the chapter heading art.

And most of all, thank you to my amazing husband for your support and the many gentle nudges you've given me along the way.

ABOUT THE AUTHOR

JILL HAS always been an avid reader, and romance has always been her favorite genre. If she's not writing or folding laundry her head is usually in a book.

When her father told her, "I've got a story I want you to write," she didn't think she'd ever actually do it.

But after twenty years of being a stay-at-home mom with seven children, the idea of writing and publishing a book sounded less terrifying than entering the workforce again. Boy, was she wrong!

Keep in touch with Jill Burrell
www.jillburrell.com